Painkiller

Out of the Box, Book 8

Robert J. Crane

Painkiller
Out of the Box #8
Robert J. Crane
Copyright © 2016 Revelen Press
All Rights Reserved.

1st Edition

This book is a work of fiction. Names, characters, places and incidents are products of the author's imagination or are used fictitiously. Any resemblance to actual events or locales or persons, living or dead, is entirely coincidental.

1

Chicago, Illinois

The alley was dark, a slick of melted snow and recent rain coating the asphalt surface. The liquid caught the glare of the lone light hanging above, the only bulb in the long, narrow alley that hadn't burned out. It gave the ground a sheen like a sun was burning somewhere overhead beyond a layer of clouds, but this was a lie; the night was dark, but State Street's brilliant beams seeping in from the entrance to the alley cast a little illumination.

Dumpsters lined both sides of the alley, and the stink of rotting food hung in the cold night. Both the scent of the garbage and the chill air seeped into the waiting man's nasal passages. He was crouched behind one of the dumpsters, just listening, the sounds of State Street in the early morning filtering into the alley. Noise from an occasional passing car or drunken pedestrian weaving up the slick sidewalk made its way to his ears over the sound of the heating units running above his head, their ticks and clicks fighting to be heard over the electrical hum as they pushed heat into the brick buildings on either side of the alley.

He'd been waiting for a while; the ache of crouching had long ago settled on his muscles. His thighs hurt, his knees hurt, his ankles positively moaned their displeasure. This wasn't his gig, this sitting and waiting. This wasn't his life. He preferred

1

booze, cigarettes, and well-heated, smoke-filled casino rooms. Dark alleys in the middle of the night? Not really his thing. Aching joints? Well, that was mostly in his mind, but still not his thing. He massaged his thigh carefully, as though it would help, then he stiffened when he heard the sound he'd been waiting for.

The scuff of a shoe against the wet pavement heralded someone's approach. Consistent footfalls followed, the steady clop of heel-to-toe walking in dress shoes. He'd seen the shoes before, when he'd decided to wait here, in the damned cold, for their wearer. They were nice. The guy wearing them? Well, he was dressed to match—trousers that covered his long, skinny legs, a brown-toned tweed jacket, and a tie that had been positioned to hide the top button of his thin-striped dress shirt that had been left undone. It looked like a high-end brand, bought at Macy's or Nordstrom or even a designer suit maker on the Magnificent Mile. The whole look of this guy was like that: top-shelf stuff. He was exceptionally well dressed for a professor.

The Professor—that was how the waiting man thought of him—approached steadily. There was no caution in those footsteps. This was a man who had taken this path many times, was familiar with it. What was that old saying about familiarity breeding contempt? This guy had the familiarity and he had the contempt too; no thought for crossing down a dark alley in the middle of the night with ten good dumpsters on either side that anyone could be hiding behind.

Not too bright, Professor, the waiting man thought. *Not too bright at all.*

The footfalls echoed ever closer then passed the waiting man. The Professor ambled by with his hands thrust into his jacket pockets against the cold. It wasn't quite warm enough to be out for long without gloves, Chicago's bitter winter still clinging on to life and refusing to let go for its rival, spring, to come forth. The cold didn't seem to bother the Professor too much, though. He made his way toward State Street at a steady clip, but slower than he probably could have.

The waiting man took a quiet breath, trying to keep it low so the Professor wouldn't hear him. This was the moment. The waiting man let his breath out in a slow exhalation, and it misted in front of him. It was time. He stood up.

The Professor must have sensed him. Either his ears perceived the sound of the waiting man unfolding himself behind the dumpster, or he caught a hint of the motion of air coming from behind him, or maybe he saw the shadow fall across the gleaming pavement as the waiting man blocked the lone bulb illuminating the alley. Maybe subconsciously he caught all three. Whatever the case, the Professor had started to turn when the waiting man fell upon him.

The man caught the Professor with a solid cuff to the back of the jaw as he was turning to look behind him. Bones broke, force was transferred in a way the Professor had probably never felt it before. It was a hard punch, aided by momentum from the two long steps the waiting man had taken before he'd reached his quarry. He'd covered the ground quickly, with metahuman speed, and clipped the Professor before the man had even had a chance to turn all the way around.

The Professor took the hit hard, his head snapping sideways, vertebrae in his neck breaking with the force of impact. His jaw looked funny, slack and hanging at an odd angle for the second before the force of the blow carried him away. He flew sideways and hit the alley wall, slumping limply already, his head smashing into the brick and cracking it, leaving a smear of blood that sprayed from the point of impact.

The Professor dropped awkwardly, his body like a ragdoll thrown against the brick wall of the alley. The waiting man looked in either direction out of habit to be sure he hadn't been seen. He knew he hadn't been. He took a few steps over to the Professor. The light had already gone out of the man's eyes. He was good and dead.

The waiting man thought about repositioning him, ran

3

through a series of scenarios in his mind about what he could do to delay the inevitable discovery—sit him upright, hide him behind a dumpster—but ultimately, none of that mattered. The body would be found in a few hours, and taken to the morgue, and have the usual battery of tests performed on it. From there, it would be handed over to the Chicago Police Department, and they'd beat the pavement, scour for witnesses who didn't exist, and try to find forensic evidence that would point to one answer—this man had been killed with a punch that no ordinary human being could have managed. From there, the investigation would be handed off to a very different investigator.

The waiting man took one more minute to look over his handiwork. He hadn't done this sort of thing in a while. A trickle of blood, begun before his heart had fully stopped pumping, ran down the Professor's cheek from a laceration above his hairline. The waiting man clenched his fist experimentally and checked his knuckles. They were a little scuffed from the impact, but they weren't bloody. That surprised him a little. But then, the hit had been so fast, and the Professor had been knocked away into the wall before he could really bleed.

The waiting man sniffed in the night, white mist coming out of his nose and lips like clouds heading for the heavens. He'd lingered too long already, even though it had been only a few seconds since the deed. He sighed once more, watched the cold air cloud the night as it left his body, and gave one last glance at the man he'd killed.

"It's better this way," he murmured, and turned up his collar as he strode off onto State Street, shuffling off toward the L train. By the time he got there, he'd already almost forgotten what he'd done.

2.

Sienna Nealon
Eden Prairie, Minnesota

"Aren't you Sienna Nealon?" the lady asked me, her face telling me she already knew the answer before she'd even asked the question. She was dark-haired, probably mid-thirties, and was wearing a full-length coat in spite of the fact that the bar we were standing in was plenty warm. It was also lit with blue and pink neon, and those colors gave the lady's face a funny cast. She was tanned, which was unusual for Minnesota in late winter. Most of us don't tend to tan in the middle of winter. Something about the low winter sun, I guess, or the fact that almost no one is crazy enough to go outside and expose their face to the elements on days when the average temperature hovers well below freezing.

"Yeah," I said, standing next to the bar waiting for the bartender to deliver my order. The place was pretty big, but it wasn't too crowded. It was a weekday night, after all, and most people don't get their drink on during the week for some strange reason. Okay, well, truth be told, I didn't usually get my drink on during the week, either, but seeing how I was less than a week away from being unemployed, it didn't seem to matter. "That's me."

My tanned admirer smiled for just a second then reached into her long coat and started to pull something out. I was watching her carefully in case she pulled out a shotgun or something, but when her hand re-emerged—slowly and smartly, I might add—she had a long, thin envelope clutched in her fingers. She extended it to me. "Sienna Nealon ... you've just been served."

"Gee, thanks, but I ordered a round of beers," I said, looking at the envelope skeptically. This wasn't the first time I'd had a process server drop legal papers on me, but it had been a little while. "I don't think I can drink that."

"This is notification of a cease and desist order issued by the Federal Aviation Administration," she went on, smiling slightly at my wit. "In light of your termination from government service—"

"Hey, I quit, okay?" I got a little huffy with her. "They didn't fire me, dammit."

She shrugged. "I don't really care. This is just a job."

"Uh huh," I said, gently taking the envelope from her. "What does the FAA want with me?"

"They want you to stop flying."

"The hell you say." I took a look at the envelope as if I could read that on the outside. It was blank, though, just a manila envelope that looked pink and blue in the neon light. "Why?"

"Apparently you're a hazard to navigation," she said with another shrug. I could tell she wanted to get out of there.

"I've never hit a plane ... that I didn't mean to," I amended quickly after starting out with indignant outrage. "Is there like ... a hearing or something?"

"Nope," she said, starting to edge away from me. "Just a cease and desist order. No flying. Unaided, I mean. You can still get on a plane. Probably."

"Thanks," I said, looking at the envelope in my hand like it contained dog poop. So the FAA wanted me to stop flying now that I was leaving government service? What a bunch of assholes.

"You're welcome," she said, and gave me a salutatory wave

as she beat a hasty path toward the door. She needn't have bothered; I don't kill messengers. Usually.

"Hey," the bartender said, slapping a round of beers down on a tray that rattled on the bar in front of me. "You need some help schlepping these back to your table?"

I looked around the bar. There was one waitress to cover about ten occupied tables, hence my need to place my own drink order. "I got it," I said, sliding the tray off the counter and balancing it on the tips of my fingers, the cease and desist order between my fingers and the plastic tray. With metahuman dexterity and strength to help, carrying a round of beers on a tray was the easiest thing in the world. Way easier than resisting the temptation to smack people for asking stupid questions. Yeah, carrying drinks was easy compared to that. Maybe I could be a waitress.

Wait, me in customer service? That would end in tears. And flames.

I made my way back up a couple steps to the second tier of the bar. Loud music played over speakers, and a glance at all the empty tables around my little party told me that privacy was pretty much a guarantee. Not even a meta could eavesdrop on us in this place, not with the music turned up like it was and the massive gap between us and the other patrons.

I put the tray down on the table as I stepped back to my empty chair. There were five people waiting for me, chatting amiably among themselves. "I just got served by the FAA," I said, lifting up the envelope. "Apparently they don't want me to fly anymore."

"Well, you are a hazard to navigation," Augustus Coleman said, the beer in front of him still half-full. He was a youthful, energetic young black man, nodding along with my pronouncement like it made utmost sense to him. He was also underage, but no one at the bar needed to know that. "Remember that time you smashed up that plane?"

"On purpose, because it was full of fleeing Russian terrorists," I said, glaring at him. "Remember that time I saved

7

that other plane full of innocent civilians from crashing by flying a pilot out to them? Or the time I saved Chicago by stopping a massive meteor from crashing into Lake Michigan and unleashing a tidal wave?"

He frowned. "You did? I don't think I heard about those."

"I'm such an unsung hero," I muttered, slumping back into my seat. It was not comfortable.

"I've heard you sing," my brother Reed said, barely disguising his grin as he took a jab at me. His hair was back to roughly neck-length, still quite a bit shorter than he usually wore it. "It's better this way." He swiped the beer I'd just bought him off the tray and took a sip, hiding his grin behind the massive glass mug.

Doctor Isabella Perugini smacked him on the arm from where she sat next to him. "Be nice to your sister," she said in a thick, Italian accent. "She is almost unemployed. It is a difficult time."

"Uh, we're all almost unemployed," Ariadne Fraser said, looking glum behind a mug of her own. She, too, swiped a fresh beer off the tray, her red hair catching pink neon, her eyes slightly dulled from several previous rounds.

"You'll get a job," I said, waving her off. "I hear finance is a hot sector right now, and Minneapolis has a booming job market."

"Whereas face-punching is something of a limited-growth industry," Reed said, smirking. "The government tends to want to keep the monopoly on that, see, so if you do it without their blessing you're operating outside the law and thus subject to being put away like the criminals that we've been locking up forever without a trial—"

"Oh, God, you are so sanctimonious," Kat Forrest burbled, slurring her words. "I mean, I love you, Reed," she said, looking right at him, clearly in the "I love you guys" phase of drunk that produced the greatest honesty, "but seriously … just … you know, dial it back, man. It's really off-putting. I think it probably costs you a lot of friendships."

Reed stared back at her, mouth open slightly. "Uh ... okay."

"Thank you," Kat said sincerely, reaching across the table and patting him on the hand. Dr. Perugini watched her with both suspicion and irritation. "You're such a good guy. If you just ... like, lay off doing that one thing, I think you'll be like ... golden and stuff. People will love you. Because you're a lovable guy." She sniffed and looked around. "Really, you all are—" she said, starting to prove my point about how drunk she was.

"So," I said, cutting her off before she got sappy ... er, "Augustus ... what are you going to do?"

"Well, my semester is paid for," Augustus said, shrugging, "so I'm going to see it through, of course. I'm just trying to figure out if I want to transfer to DC after that and keep working for the man, you know."

"I don't know if you can call Andrew Phillips 'The Man,'" I said, staring into my amber mug. "Maybe 'The *Ass* Man'."

"We set aside the money so your entire college career is paid for," Ariadne said, looking at him seriously. "I suspect it'll be okay, that it'll survive whoever takes over my job, because it was well hidden, and it's set up to auto-draft to your account. If I could have pulled off just transferring it all immediately, I would have, but the penalties would be stiff, heading toward criminal, if I'd gotten caught, whereas the slow trickle is easily attributable to governmental incompetence—"

"And these are the people who want a monopoly on the use of force," Reed said, shaking his head.

"You said you would stop," Kat moaned her eyes rolled. "And ... also, another thing," she slurred, and turned to look right at me, "Why did I follow you up here so I could work for like two months before we all quit? I left Hollywood behind, you know—"

"I thought you start filming on the new season of your show next month?" Augustus asked, frowning.

Kat either didn't hear him or ignored him. Probably the

former. "Whyyyyyy?" She put her hands in the air like she was asking the heavens.

I stared her down. "Because you were sick of soulless, materialistic wandering and wanted to serve a higher purpose than just showing your sculpted ass on television and trying to contrive 'storylines' to mine pointless drama out of your life for the sake of entertaining people." I paused.

She stared at me through cloudy, drunken eyes then broke into a lazy smile. "You really think my ass is sculpted? Everyone else always calls it 'bony,' but I've been working on it and—"

"I propose a toast," Reed said, cutting her off, raising his mug.

"—I was thinking about maybe getting ass implants, but—"

"Kat," I said, trying to stifle her. I looked at Reed.

Reed's eyes were glimmering, thick with the emotion of the moment. "In honor of our last week working together in glorious cause … to us, the line between the metahuman world and humanity. May whoever follows us do as much or more good as we did."

I frowned. "Well, that's awfully chipper."

He gave me a cool grin. "Would you prefer they do oh-so-much worse? Chaos and destruction in the streets and all that?"

I thought about it for a second. "Honestly … yes. I want to see the agency fall apart without me so that they know how badly they screwed up by wanting me out. I want President Gerry Harmon to be calling every day for the next year apologizing and telling me he'll move the agency back to Minnesota or do whatever I want as long as I'll come back and do my job again. Yes, I want chaos in the streets and cataclysms in the sky and the world to fall apart without me." I pursed my lips. "I mean, I don't really want any of that, not really, but … on a very basic, emotional level … yes, I want that. I want to be needed, to feel like all these years I put into carrying this thing on my back weren't a waste."

"You've done a lot of good," Kat said, a hint of regret on her face behind those flushed cheeks.

"You've saved the world," Augustus said, lifting his own mug. "Ain't nobody can take that away from you."

"It is true," Dr. Perugini said, nodding. "No one may ever really know it, or thank you for it, or care that you're gone, but—"

Reed cut in over her with a fake laugh. "Honey … maybe try and help instead?"

She gave him daggers. "I am helping."

"So what are you going to do, Sienna?" Ariadne asked me, looking forlornly over her mug. Her new one was already half empty and she wasn't really much of a beer drinker.

I stopped with my mug halfway to my mouth. "I'm …"

"Excuse me?" came a polite voice from behind me. I turned to see a middle-aged Asian man looking down at me, a polite expression of reserve upon his face that tended toward a faint smile. "You're Sienna Nealon, correct?"

"Oh, for crying out—" I put down my beer. "Who are you with? The EPA, right? You want me to cease and desist with setting things on fire?"

He raised an eyebrow. "My name is Jonathan Chang. I'm a lawyer with the firm of Rothman, Curtis and Chang, here in Minneapolis."

"Oh, really?" I picked up my mug again and held it at the ready, staring at Mr. Chang with a wary eye. "Who's suing me this time?"

His faint smile twitched at the corners of his mouth. "You misunderstand my purpose." He reached into his coat and pulled out envelope, this one white and long, a letter envelope that looked thick. "I'm not here about anyone suing you." He placed the envelope on the table next to me as I watched him carefully. "I have a job offer for you."

3.

I gave Jonathan Chang, esquire, attorney at law, blah blah blah, a wary, cocked eye. "You want to hire me? Because my registration with the Minnesota bar is sadly nonexistent."

"Who do you work for again?" Reed asked, voice cloudy with booze and suspicion. "Wolfram and Hart?"

"No," Mr. Chang said coolly, still with that faint smile, "my firm is named Rothman, Curtis and Chang. But I'm not making the offer on our own behalf. I've been contracted by an employer who would like to hire you."

"As what?" I asked, looking right at him. "A security guard? Muscle? An assassin?"

"Hardly," Mr. Chang said, looking very slightly affronted. "We only deal with legal and aboveboard entities."

"So says every lawyer, I'm sure," Augustus said, looking extremely amused, "even the ones that deal with murderers and rapists."

"We don't work in the realm of criminal law," Mr. Chang said.

"So you defend big, dirty corporations in lawsuits?" Reed asked, suspicion far outpacing the booze.

"Sometimes," Mr. Chang said, "and sometimes we defend big, clean corporations against some idiot who wants to sue them because they shoved the staple remover the company manufactured into their own eye and think someone else should pay for their stupidity."

"Eye for an eye," Reed said. "That'd fix it."

"Yes, and then no one would make staple removers," Mr. Chang said, and shifted his attention away from Reed. "And while I'm sure that a world without staple removers would be a better world for all, clearly … that has little to do with why I'm here."

"What's the job?" I asked, frowning. I kept my face carefully neutral.

"A Non-Governmental Organization is forming," Mr. Chang said, "backed by someone with considerable resources and focused on assisting with metahuman threats that the United States Government is unable or unwilling to address."

"So wait," Augustus asked, his brown furrowing, "what would she be doing?"

"In her current capacity with the government," Mr. Chang said, utterly calm, "Ms. Nealon presently assists state and local jurisdictions because they're unable to handle metahuman threats. After her exit for—the agency, I think you call it—the U.S. government will be tasked with replacing her, and thus assisting these state and local jurisdictions will fall to this new FBI-led task force, should the state and local governments desire the help. However, they may be finding their assistance somewhat lacking, since the only metahuman available to assist them now will be—"

"Guy Friday," I said. "Which, I mean, he can probably handle some of the stuff we dealt with, but … he's a blunt instrument. Like, really blunt. Like, his head is a hammer and everything else in the world is a nail—"

"As you say," Mr. Chang nodded, "the U.S. government approach will be somewhat one-dimensional for the foreseeable future, leaving state and local jurisdictions without anyone to turn to in a time of crisis. For example, if the recent incident in Los Angeles had been left to Mr. Friday, as you call him—"

"He would have played skee-ball at Santa Monica pier while the Elysium neighborhood went kablooey," Kat gurgled, unable to hold her head up straight. "And I would have died horribly, too."

"Furthermore," Mr. Chang said, "if the events of last January, the robbery at the Federal Reserve, had been left to Mr. Friday—"

"We'd be off the gold standard permanently," Reed said. "But maybe they'd finally audit the—"

"Reed, shut it," I said, focusing on Mr. Chang. "So what does this … Non-Governmental Organization do, then? Butt in whenever they see something like this happening?"

"It will make our resources available under the aegis of the state jurisdiction, if the local authorities want the help," Mr. Chang said, "and most of them will, because you have a reputation—"

"For lighting tires and starting fires," Augustus said, raising his glass to me before taking a drink.

"For raising ires and burning shires," Kat burbled senselessly.

"I think that's more Saruman's territory," Reed said, his brow furrowed in thought. "Or Sharkey, if you prefer—"

"So you want to hire me," I said, spelling it back to Mr. Chang, "to do … basically my job right now, but without the federal government on my back?" He nodded, and I narrowed my eyes in practiced skepticism. "Who would I answer to?"

"The state authority on each job would be your employer," Mr. Chang said, "but the NGO—the organization—would be run by you."

"That doesn't make any sense," Ariadne said, frowning. "You said the money comes from somewhere. Who's bankrolling this and why?"

"A concerned citizen of the world," Mr. Chang said, inclining his head to look at Ariadne. He was wearing a suit under his fancy, fancy coat, and it didn't look cheap either. "Someone worried about where things will go without Ms. Nealon at the helm."

"Who is this concerned citizen?" Reed asked.

"Your benefactor would prefer to remain anonymous," Mr. Chang said with a sniff.

"Oh, that'll end well," Reed said, slumping back in his seat. "This guy could be a megalomaniac wanting to use Sienna for world domination, for all we know—"

"Ms. Nealon will be in charge of this new organization," Mr. Chang said. "Fully, completely. She can choose her own team—"

"Oooh," Kat said, raising her hand in the air and waving it drunkenly. "Pick me!"

"—and I can assure you," Mr. Chang said with a gleam in his eyes, "the salary pool will be considerably better than government scale. In addition, there is funding for research and development, a medical unit ..." He looked at Ariadne. "Someone will, of course, need to manage the budget of this entity."

"I told you finance was a hot sector right now," I said to Ariadne.

"You also said there wasn't much market for your skill set," she said without looking at me.

"You'll be able piece together your very own version of your old agency," Mr. Chang said, "without the government breathing down your necks."

"That is so very, very generous of some random stranger who's concerned about the world," Reed said, by now fully suspicious. "This guy is willing to throw away millions and millions of dollars to let Sienna run a meta fantasy camp. That's damned decent. But what does he get out of it?"

"Your benefactor gets a sense of self-satisfaction," Mr. Chang said, "knowing that the world is a better place with Ms. Nealon delivering aid to those who need it. In addition, there are some tasks you'll be able to decline involvement in that you otherwise might have been forced to take while in government service, and also some things you'll be able to investigate or consult on that you might not have been able to. Opportunities abound in the metahuman world."

"Meaning we could hire ourselves out to be security guards if we wanted to," Reed said, a cloud over his face.

"If you wanted to," Mr. Chang said. "But you could also extend your talents into other arenas if you wished. Private investigation, for instance—"

"I'll to need to switch to drinking whiskey if I'm going to become Jessica Jones," I said, lifting my beer glass.

"You can do whatever you wish," Mr. Chang said, nodding at me. "However you feel you would best serve the world at large, whether holding out until the world-ending sort of events require your attention, or getting involved in human missing persons cases is your … area of interest. This opportunity is flexible, and you will be able to set your own course."

I stared at Mr. Chang, almost not daring to look away. I took a breath, the smell of my beer wafting up at me. "Tempting," I said. "Very tempting."

"You cannot be serious," Reed said, looking at me with stark disbelief.

"So would there be college paid for in this deal?" Augustus asked seriously.

"I'm sure something could be worked out," Mr. Chang said with a smile.

"Could I structure filming on my new season around this job?" Kat asked, her eyes half-open.

"That would be entirely dependent on Ms. Nealon, as head of the organization," Mr. Chang said, "but I don't see a conflict there."

Kat turned to me. "Could I—"

"You can do whatever the hell you want with those cameras as long as they don't land on me even once," I said, brushing her off. "Could we—" My phone buzzed, hard, in my pocket. "Dammit."

"The sky is the limit," Mr. Chang said as I pulled out my phone.

"Not according to the FAA," I muttered, thrusting the

envelope at him as I answered the phone. "House of Style," I said into the phone.

Andrew Phillips was at the other end. I could tell it was him by the disappointed sound of the breathing. "Where are you?"

"At a whorehouse," I said.

"What?"

"Yeah, I took a job with the Secret Service," I said. "They have the weirdest initiation rituals, but hey, who am I to argue as the new gal, right?"

"You are not working for the Secret Service," Phillips breathed into the phone, his annoyance rising.

"You never supported my dreams," I said, letting my voice faux-break. "Why didn't you believe in me?"

"Probably because of your frequenting of whorehouses," he grunted. "We've got a murder victim in Chicago."

"Chicago has quite a few murder victims as I understand it," I replied. "What makes this one special?"

"That is cold," Reed said, frowning his disapproval from across the table.

"It's winter," I threw back at him, "and I'm me."

"Who was that?" Phillips asked.

"Just a sweet little gigolo with a heart of gold, clearly," I said. "Why are you calling me about a body in Chicago? What's the Sienna of this?"

"The—what?"

I rolled my eyes. "What does this have to do with me?" Duh.

"Oh, yeah, that's obvious," Augustus said. The sarcasm was strong with this one.

"The guy was killed with one punch to the side of the head," Phillips said.

"Brock Lesnar could do that," I said.

"He was thrown ten feet by the impact, into a brick wall—"

"Seriously, have you checked with Brock Lesnar for an alibi? He's a really big guy. I mean, I'd say Floyd Mayweather, but you said this vic was a guy—"

"—fractured skull even before the impact—"

"—I mean, big. Big, big, big. And have you seen Lesnar fight? I wouldn't want to tangle with him, and I'm *me*—"

"—Chicago PD says it's a metahuman incident," Phillips said tightly, his annoyance and loathing draping themselves over every syllable. I could tell he was just barely controlling himself. "Are you going to do your job or are you already mentally out the door?"

"Fine," I said, sighing. "But will you at least get the FAA to lift this stupid cease and desist order so I can fly down to Chicago without having to take a commuter flight?"

"No," Phillips said. "It's not my department first of all, and second of all … just no. I'm not doing it. It's less than an hour flight to Chicago. I already had my secretary book you and Reed on the last one of the night. Get to the airport."

"Your secretary?" I asked, arching an eyebrow. "How is Guy Friday?"

"Busy," Phillips said, and then he paused. "Also, he's not my secretary and this is not really his … area of expertise."

"You're gonna miss me when I'm gone," I said, smirking. I was sure he could hear the smirk over the phone.

"No, I'm not," he said, certain. "Get your clothes on and get to the airport."

"Clothes on?" I asked, frowning. "What the hell are you talking about?"

"You said you were at a whorehouse."

I laughed. "I'm at a bar, with the team, celebrating our imminent emancipation from your dictatorial rule, but it's nice to know I can still pull one over on you with nothing but repeated assurances." I hung up on him. "Reed, we're going to Chicago."

"We are?" He looked at me funny. "Really?"

"Yeah," I said, glancing at Mr. Chang, who was reading over the paperwork in the envelope I'd handed him. "You're a lawyer. What do you make of that?"

"I'm employed by your benefactor as your legal counsel," he said, and he nodded once. "I'll work on it. It's not exactly a settled area of case law, though. Try and obey the order until I can see if I can get it reversed."

"All righty," I said, and stood. Reed took another drink, leaned over and kissed his sweetie, and then mirrored my movement. "Off we go."

"One last hurrah," Reed said, then he glanced at Mr. Chang suspiciously. "I hope."

"Why would you hope this is it?" Augustus asked with a frown of his own. "You got big plans after this week? I mean, you could hire yourself out to birthday parties as a human wind tunnel experience, but other than that—"

"It's all right," Dr. Perugini said, reaching up to pat Reed on the face. "I can find a job easily."

"You really are going to be a gigolo," Kat said with a giggle, "just like Sienna said." She slapped the table and the wood made a cracking sound. "Hahahahaha!"

"Once more unto the breach?" I asked him, trying to draw his sour gaze away from Kat.

He nodded. "Once more," he said as a woman threaded her way through the platforms over to him and tapped him on the shoulder. Blame it on the alcohol, because it took me a second to realize it was the same woman who'd served me the FAA order.

"Are you Reed Treston?" she asked sweetly.

"No—" I started to say.

"Yeah," he said, puffing up with pride. "I am."

"You've been served," she said, slapping another envelope against his chest.

"What?" He blinked, taking the envelope and staring at it. "But I—I barely even fly!"

"And now you won't at all," she said, walking away. "Have a good night."

"I think the ship has already kind of sailed off the edge of the world on that one," I said, motioning to Reed. "Come on, we have to get to the airport before our flight."

"But it's the Windy City," Reed protested, looking completely crestfallen. "The updrafts between the buildings, the wind off the lake—I was practically born to fly there!"

"Consider my offer, Ms. Nealon," Mr. Chang said as I started to walk away. "We'll talk soon."

I nodded at him, threading my arm through poor Reed's and dragging him away, his face still fallen like someone had stolen his best toy. "Sounds good," I said to Chang. Turning my attention to Reed, I said, "Come on, bro. One last adventure on the government dime."

"Why do they hate me?" he asked, sounding all broken and pathetic.

"According to Kat, it's because—"

"Oh, shush," he said, switching to sullen as we followed the rail toward the bar's exit. He stopped me about ten feet from the door, taking hold of my elbow and pulling me gently around to look me in the eye. "Why are we doing this? We're government employees leaving service at the end of the week. We don't have to do anything. They can't fire us, and even if by some miracle or act of Congress they could … who cares at this point?"

I opened my mouth to answer with snark, but sincerity fell out instead. "Because this is what we do," I said.

He blinked like I'd slapped him across the face. "Okay, then," he said after a moment.

"Okay," I repeated, and off we went to Chicago.

4.

I found myself standing in a back alley in Chicago in the early hours of the morning, next to an overripe dumpster that even the cold couldn't contain the stink of. Fortunately for me, the smell of the murder victim was being contained by the cold, and was not yet overripe in spite of having his life's blood splattered across the brick all the way to the mouth of the alley. I surveyed the scene from within the police tape barrier that fenced me in, casting wary glances as the CPD investigators milling around out on State Street as I looked up at the enormous buildings I could see in either direction.

"Well, it's certainly looking like Chicago is my sort of town, isn't it?" I muttered to Reed, who stood with his arms folded next to me, apparently undeterred by the nearest dumpster's wafting aroma of rot or the sight of the murder victim's shattered jaw and the strange tilt of his neck.

"I'd follow up on that," Reed said, nodding at the photographers and video cameras lurking behind the police tape, "but we'd probably get sued for copyright violation or something." He nodded at the body. "You think anyone's going to come along and explain anything to us, or are we supposed to just start poking around the corpse ourselves for clues?"

"I've always been met by the local cops at these things," I said, folding my own arms in front of me to ward off the cold. It was better than lighting my skin on fire, probably. "They don't typically love surrendering to federal involvement, but what choice do they have?"

"Apparently a new, privatized option now," Reed said sourly.

I glanced at him. "You're really cynical about this whole thing, aren't you?"

He grimaced. "A powerful, invisible ally sitting in the shadows and offering you everything you've ever wanted—essentially the same job, but without the government strings? I'm sorry, no." He shook his head. "We had that once, remember, with the Directorate? Once the genie came out of the bottle on the meta secret and the world found out about us, working in the shadows went right out the window. This is either a fantasy daydream or your backer's got ulterior motives, and either way … yeah, I'm suspicious about it." He gave me a careful look, lips pursed. "And I'm trying to figure out why you're not."

"I haven't had much chance to think about it yet," I said, brushing him off as I nodded to the corpse in front of us. "You know, soberly, with lots of time for reflection and consideration."

He rubbed his forehead, and I could tell he was feeling the "soberly" part of it. "Yeah. I'm kinda glad no one's said anything to us yet. I feel like I need a little more time to regain my wits."

I knew what he meant; the flight certainly hadn't helped. We'd breezed through security with our federal agent IDs and gotten on the small commuter plane just before it pulled back from the gate. We hadn't even had time to stop off to grab a suitcase or a change of clothes.

Or a toothbrush, which, I reflected as I breathed into my hand and felt like I'd been punched in the face by my own dragon breath, was a more pressing need.

"Sienna Nealon?" I turned to see an older guy standing at the mouth of the alley, a traditional trench coat with the collar turned up and a wrinkled white shirt and khaki pants beneath.

His badge hung on his belt, which was old and showed plenty of wear at its current notch, like he'd had it for years. The cop had a file in his hand, and he sauntered over to us. "I'm Detective Maclean."

"Nice to meet you, Detective," I said with a nod, keeping my fingers firmly anchored inside my coat since I'd forgotten my gloves. Not because I minded him brushing my skin, but because it was chilly. "This is my brother—partner—Reed."

He frowned. "Uhh … nice to meetcha." He had an accent that I would describe as Chicago by way of cop. "You taken a look at the scene yet?"

"I've seen that this man is dead," I said with a nod at the body. "Also, that this dumpster stinks, and that this night is dark. Everything else, you can feel free to explain to me."

Detective Maclean pursed his lips with an utter lack of amusement. "Fine," he said, and I knew it wasn't. "Victim is one Dr. Carlton Jacobs, a professor at a nearby college—"

"Which one?" Reed asked, barely stifling a yawn as he spoke.

"Northern Illinois Technical University," Maclean said, looking down at the file to read it off. "It's up Lakeshore drive a little. Medical school, science and tech research—looks like it's only been around a few years now."

"Uh huh," I said, "what was the victim a doctor of?"

"Philosophy for all I care," Detective Maclean said, holding off exasperation by a thin effort. "Will you just let me finish my bit and then ask?" He gave me a steady gaze until I nodded almost imperceptibly. "All right. Vic is age 45, he's a professor at NITU, lives in a condo up on the Gold Coast—"

"What's—" I started to ask, drawing an irritable look from Detective Maclean.

"It's a neighborhood north of here on the lake, lots of condos and mansions and whatnot, really ritzy," Reed said, and I turned to look at him. "I used to come down here a lot on assignment when I worked for Alpha."

"If I may?" Maclean asked. "Dr. Jacobs's wallet was left on

23

his person, along with a roll of cash in his front pocket in the amount of $4,000—"

"Whoa," I said, my eyebrows lurching up. "I guess robbery wasn't the motive."

"We have no idea where he came from," Maclean said icily, "and no idea where he was going, other than to State Street." He flipped the folder closed. "Death, as you may have guessed, was probably the result of traumatic brain injury, either from the initial impact or when his head hit the wall. Either way, no sign of a weapon used. Preliminary forensics says the impact sight on the jaw shows hints of knuckles being the weapon, and so …" He extended the folder toward me. "Looks like it's one of yours."

"Thanks," I said and stepped up to take the folder from him. I opened it and skimmed; he'd done a pretty good job of summarizing what they had so far. "Does the professor have a car registered to him?"

Maclean shrugged. "I can check if you want. Central's pretty backed up, though, so it might take a while."

I sighed. "I miss J.J. already."

"Never thought you'd say that," Reed chuckled.

J.J. was my own personal tech geek. Well, maybe not my personal one, but he'd worked for our agency and had been instrumental in solving more cases than I could count. I looked around, hoping for an obvious surveillance camera. There wasn't one. If there had been, J.J. could have cracked it in like two seconds and just given us our murderer on a silver platter. "Any chance you've got some uniforms digging up surveillance footage from the area?" I asked Detective Maclean.

"Yeah, they're canvassing, too," Maclean said with a frown. "Probably be a few days on that, though."

"So …" I said, glancing down the file as I reached the end, "robbery's not the motive, probably—"

"Probably?" Reed looked at me like I was an idiot. "There's like four grand on the guy, plus his wallet."

"That doesn't mean something else wasn't taken," I said, staring at the folder, "or that the murderer wasn't interrupted or scared off before he could do his thieving."

"Fair point," Reed said with the air of a man who didn't quite let go of his skepticism. "But unlikely."

"Agreed," I said, closing the folder. "We'll need to go to his place of work, and his home." I looked around the alley, trying to reconstruct the event in my head. I wasn't Sherlock, so it didn't happen easily. I tried to imagine him flying, hitting the wall, and cast my eyes over the damp asphalt. "He probably got clocked somewhere over there," I motioned to a few blood spots that had fallen in the alley, and I started over there, careful where I stepped so as not to disturb potential evidence.

"Yeah," Reed said, following along behind me, matching his steps to mine. "That's a solid hit. You're talking a high on the scale meta to hit like that."

"Scale?" Detective Maclean said, staying right where he was by the corpse.

"There's a scale of powers," I answered idly as I threaded over to the place of attack. "Low-grade metas don't hit much harder than a normal person. High scale, though …" I waved at the body next to him. "Like a car doing ninety. They're also correspondingly faster, more dexterous, agile …"

"Uh huh," Maclean said, now with his arms folded in front of him. "When I was a beat cop, probably twenty-five years ago, I saw this guy pick another guy up with one hand and throw him ten feet. You think that was a meta?"

"Probably," I said, stooping to look at the blood spatter at my feet. I sniffed, catching a whiff of something that was neither a dumpster nor our corpse. I looked up at Reed, whose nose was twitching. "You getting this?"

He frowned, wrinkling his nose as his nostrils flared. "Is that … cigarettes?"

"Yeah," I said, following my nose to the origin point of the scent, "and rosemary, I think." The smell lingered faintly behind a dumpster maybe ten feet from the place where

Professor Dr. Carlton Jacobs had met his fateful sucker punch.

"Rosemary?" Detective Maclean called to us from where he stood near the mouth of the alley. "From what?"

"Either the perp's dinner or some sort of herbal remedy, maybe?" I asked, shrugging. "Not sure, it's pretty faint and masked by the scent of smoked cigarettes." I looked around but didn't see any discarded butts. "I don't think he smoked any here, he's just trailing the aroma." I sniffed and caught it lingering under the cold.

"I don't smell anything," Maclean said, sniffing. He made a face like he'd gotten a brain freeze headache from huffing the Chicago air.

"You wouldn't," I said, taking another whiff. Definitely rosemary. Weird.

"Where should we go first?" Reed asked.

"His college is closed at this hour, I'm assuming." I stood up, looking back down the alley to catch Maclean's nod. "To his place, I guess, so we can pore over the details of Professor Jacobs's life, see if we might be able to find a motive for the killer." I made my way carefully back to the body. "Because it looks to me like whoever did this … they waited for a while, either for him or someone else."

"Premeditation," Maclean said, nodding.

"They didn't throw a love tap, that's for sure," I said, "and if he was the target, and they waited for him … it means they knew he was coming. And hopefully we'll be able to find some idea of why he was here in this alley in the middle of the night," I stared down at Professor Jacobs's blank face, the blood wreathing his head like a crown of red, "and where exactly he was going when he got murdered."

5.

I stepped out of the cab after about a five-minute ride onto a road overlooking Lake Shore Drive, which I had already realized was probably one of the swankier addresses for Chicago. Lake Michigan was glittering black, lights sparkling along its surface just across the street and over the freeway-like version of Lake Shore Drive that was separated from the residential one I was standing on by a waist-high barrier with fencing. Occasional cars were zooming past over there, while I stood on a much more placid residential drive, in front of a decidedly upscale apartment building.

It was either an old and refurbished brick building, or it was a new building constructed to look old; either way, I could tell a lot of money had gone into it. A cop car was parked out front as Reed and I breezed our way in wordlessly to where a doorman waited behind a desk, talking to a couple of uniformed CPD officers.

I flashed my badge at the guys waiting and Reed followed my lead. "Evening, gents," I said. "I need to take a look at Professor Jacobs's apartment."

"Sure thing," the doorman behind the desk leapt to his feet. He was a little darker-skinned, bald like he shaved his head, probably just south of forty. "I already got the spare key for the officers here." He nodded at the cops.

"Breckinridge," one of them, a fair-haired guy with a flat expression said, reaching out to shake my hand. I took it and he pumped firmly but not obnoxiously. He nodded at his partner. "This is Tanner." Tanner was not, in fact, tan. He was the whitest dude I've ever laid eyes on, and he wore a completely implacable look that would not have been out of place on Andrew Phillips's face.

"You guys take a look upstairs yet?" Reed asked politely.

Breckinridge seemed eager to please. "Not yet. We just came and delivered the news, rustled up the keys so the detective assigned could do the honors. We'll bat cleanup once you get done, though, bag any evidence, get stuff sent off to the lab if we get any idea of clues." He held up his hands, all excited. He already had blue latex gloves on.

"All right, then," I said and nodded toward the doorman. "You gonna take us up?"

He looked torn for a second. "I'm supposed to watch the door ..."

"Not a problem," I said, quickly snatching the keys out of his hand. "You keep an eye on that door in case a flood of burglars and junkies comes wandering through randomly right at this very moment." I headed for the elevator. "I can probably find my way up. I'll just keep knocking on doors at random until I find the right one."

The doorman shot me a pained expression. "Twelfth floor. Number fifteen."

"Awww," I said, feigning disappointment. "It would have so fun to do it my way." I headed for the elevators, Reed and Breckinridge trailing behind me. I glanced back and saw Tanner hanging by the front desk, watching me go with a healthy dose of suspicion. I brought that out in people.

I waited until the reflective steel elevator doors slid shut on the three of us before I spoke. "Breckinridge, your partner seems like a shithead."

"Oh, he's not that bad," Breckinridge said, shaking his head. "He's just stiff."

"Yeah, well," I said, "after four hours, you're supposed to call the hotline for that problem."

Breckinridge frowned at me as the elevator carried us up pretty quickly. Understanding dawned over his face and he snapped his fingers as he pointed at me. "Ohhh! Oh! Got it. Good one."

Reed just stood there shaking his head, face buried in one of his hands. "No. Just … no."

"What?" I asked.

Reed pulled his hand out of his face to reveal an indulgent smile. "Breckinridge … you want to wait at the door while we scope out the apartment, please?"

"Sure," Breckinridge said, eager beaver that he was, as the elevator dinged and the doors slid open to reveal a pristine, well-lit white hallway. "I'll be right outside if you need anything." He followed us dutifully down the hall until we reached 1215.

I fiddled with the keys until I found the right one. There were a lot of them on the ring, but fortunately they were each labeled, thus preventing me from losing patience and kicking down the door. I unlocked it and listened, hoping my job would be made easy by finding the murderer sleeping in the victim's bed or something. I stuck my head in the door and waited. No such luck; it sounded quiet in there.

"Okay, in we go," I said, popping in the front door and flipping the light switch. I found myself in a small entryway, and suddenly wondering if Professor Jacobs was married. If so, this was about to be awkward. This is why I normally left this stuff up to local PD and just made my entrance after they'd done the scut work.

The entry had a coat closet framed with a dark mahogany sliding door. I slid it open and looked to see a few coats hanging within. No women's coats, though. All the shoes below were men's, and there were only a half dozen pairs of varying kinds from dress to tennis shoes to snow boots, which probably ruled out a male domestic partner as well. I was also relieved to see no children's shoes of any kind.

"I think we're on our own, here," I said, stepping through

the entry into a well-furnished living room area. There was a rug in the middle of the room that was squared to look like tile, each in a subtle different shade of grey moving across the spectrum to beige and brown. It was a little weird, but it kind of worked with the grey-scale sofa and two white leather chairs that stood with their backs to me. A coffee table anchored the middle of the room, cluttered with paperwork and further convincing me that Professor Jacobs lived alone.

I took it all in, sniffing for the smell of cigarette smoke and finding instead some kind of faint vanilla scent mingled with one of the prominent brands of men's deodorant.

Reed stepped up next to me, still shaking his head.

"What?" I asked him.

"Still stuck on your erection joke back there," he said, looking at me with faint disappointment. "I haven't been this embarrassed since I had that party for the last Packer/Viking game, when you asked me which team was which."

"Don't be ridiculous," I said, stepping around the wall at the far end of the living room to find myself in a kitchen separated by a long counter from another livingroom-esque space, this one coupled with a glass kitchen table sitting just on the other side of the counter. Beyond the brown leather couch in this room was a view of Lake Michigan on one side and to my right a commanding view back down the lakeshore toward downtown. "I know we're the Vikings."

"Uh huh," Reed said. "What are the team colors?"

I looked out the windows, taking in the view. This place was expensive. "Uh … red and … green?"

"Not even close," Reed said. "That's the colors for the North Pole Santas."

I blinked. "There are no North Pole Santas in the NFL."

"I bet you don't know that for a fact," he said, breaking off from me to go rummage through the kitchen. He pulled on a pair of leather gloves as he did so, opening the drawers and giving each a quick glance before shutting them again.

I found myself drawn to the view. This was a corner

apartment with a stunning view of both the lake and the city. "Reed?" I asked, looking at the Hancock tower glinting like a black obelisk in the distance, "what do you figure a place like this runs per month?"

"A lot," he said, opening drawers and closing them again. "Twenty, thirty grand a month, maybe?"

"Does that strike you as a lot for a college professor?" I asked, turning my back on the view.

"Four grand of cash rolled up in his pocket strikes me as a lot for a college professor," Reed said, glancing up from his search to look at me. "Twenty or thirty K for rent on a monthly basis seems absurd."

"We should get his bank records," I said, wishing I could call J.J. and get them right now. "Something funny's going on there."

"Might be easier to get his payroll info from the college when they open," Reed said idly, picking through a drawer. "Hmm. Receipts here."

"Anything interesting?" I asked, making my way past Professor Jacobs's pretty damned luxurious furniture in order to take a look for myself.

"Guy shops at the Whole Foods down on the Mag Mile," Reed said, pulling a half dozen receipts out and laying them on the spotless counter, which was a hell of a contrast to the strewn mess he'd left in the living room. "Not exactly budget grocery shopping."

"So maybe he's loaded outside of his job," I said, glancing toward the bedroom door to my left. It was cracked open, the view of Lake Michigan sparkling visible through the door. "He could come from money."

"Could be," Reed said. "Everything we're picking up here so far is about money, which is weird considering this doesn't look like a robbery."

"Maybe," I said, heading for the bedroom door. "It's just strange to kill someone in an alley and not take the four grand they've got in their pocket."

"Well, what are the options if it wasn't for money?" Reed asked as I pushed open the bedroom door to step inside. "Personal grudge?"

"Yeah," I said, looking over the bedroom. "Friend, co-worker, family member, lover, the usual suspects."

"Maybe someone killed him so they could buy his apartment," Reed called after me.

"Maybe," I said, not ruling anything out. I flipped the light switch and the lamp at the bedside snapped on, glaring against the reflective windows and giving me a dark, mirrored reflection of myself alone in the empty bedroom. "It could be anything at this point."

I wandered through the room, riffling through drawers in the dresser and finding clothes. I was no fashionista, clearly, but this guy's closet was pretty top shelf stuff, name brands that I recognized even in my limited capacity. "You were living quite the high life, Mr. Jacobs," I said quietly as I ran my fingers over one of five Brooks Brothers suits.

"Find anything?" Reed called from the main room.

"More money spent than any number of third world countries have in their entire budget," I said at a normal volume, which was all I needed in order for Reed to hear me. I looked between two of the suits and found something in the back of the closet that was hidden back there. I pushed the clothing aside, the hangars making a rattling noise as they slid along the metal bar, revealing a black metal safe at the back of the closet. "Hello," I said.

"Did you find something?" Reed asked from the doorway. I nodded and he came wandering over and looked in. "Hmmm. How do we get into this bad boy?"

"With greatest ease," I said, looking it over.

Reed gave me a blank stare. "It's a safe."

I smiled. "It's a safe that's pre-meta."

Safe tech had taken a leap in both cost and quality in the last four years since metahumans had been announced to the world. Mostly it was stupid, in my opinion, since the majority of metas in the world couldn't have cracked an old-school home safe if they had a gun to their head. What were they going to do? Push their flesh and blood fingers into the centimeter wide crack of the door and try and rip it open? Only a Wolfe-type could do that without tearing their fingers apart, and the only Wolfe left in the world was a prisoner in my head.

Sure, there were other ways, but the truth was that the newer, anti-meta safes did nothing to keep us serious metas out. Once again, panic had ruled the day and cost people tons of money to little purpose. It's not like most metas had embraced careers in safecracking anyway.

"This should be good," Reed said, folding his arms in front of him as I squatted down to look at the safe door at face level. "Hey, we found another employable skill for you if this works—you could be a bank robber."

I grunted as I stretched my fingers out. The mechanism was one of those classic spin dials rather than one of the newer electronic ones. The safe looked kinda old, actually, but definitely solid, with thick steel around the edges. "Good to know I've got options," I said as I lit up my index finger like a blowtorch, a stream of fire extending an inch from it, blue and hot enough that I could feel it on my face. I applied it to the front side of the safe, intending to slice about three-quarters of the way through.

"So," Reed said as I started to cut into the metal with my makeshift blowtorch, "what are you going to do? I mean really. If you don't take this job you just got offered?"

"Why wouldn't I take this job I just got offered?" I asked, sparks flying from the blackened metal, hot, liquid steel sloughing down to the carpet. I extended my other hand and sapped the heat from the metal as it fell, causing it to turn solid before it hit the carpet and caused a fire. It made no noise as it dropped in tiny ovoid pieces onto the soft pile carpeting.

"Because you'd be crazy to take it," Reed said, and he sounded certain. "You don't know who you'd be working for."

"And you assume the devil I know—Gerry Harmon,

President of the United States and ginormous tool—is better than a devil I don't?"

"Why work for a devil at all?" Reed asked, sounding like he was fighting disbelief. "You'd be better off working as a guard at the Federal Reserve."

"I'd be bored working as a guard," I grunted, about half the face of the safe cut off. "I'd feel like I was wasting my life and my talents."

"Well, you could potentially live a long time, so wasting a fraction of your life doesn't seem that unwise to me," Reed said, "especially since it could potentially be lucrative. You could play meta security consultant to half the major corporations in the world, rack up a bank account that would see you through your entire long life without working another day in it—"

"I still could do that," I said, peeling back the front layer of the safe as I went, working the malleable, heated steel like I was folding paper. "It sounds like this job offer would allow all that and more."

"Which is why you should be cautious," Reed said. "Haven't you ever heard that old saying about fearing the Greeks when they bring gifts?"

"Sounds kinda racist against the Greeks," I muttered. "Also, there's no Trojan horse here ..." I paused. "Wait. Is that where the 'Gift horse in the mouth' thing comes from, too?"

"I don't know," Reed said, suddenly impatient. "I don't care. The point is—"

"It's all suddenly so clear," I said, finishing ripping the front of the safe open, "because if they'd looked in the mouth of the Trojan horse, they would have seen all the Greek guys hiding inside—"

"I think you've lost the plot, as the Brits say," Reed interrupted, sounding a little huffy.

"Where do you think 'lost the plot' comes from?" I asked. "Like, people, chasing after a nefarious scheme and trying to uncover—"

"Unghhhh," Reed said, low, at a growl, "why are you doing this?"

"Because I need to get into this safe, duh—"

"You're pushing off this job offer question like it's no big deal," Reed said, almost as hot as the safe panel I had just sheared off, "like it's a perfectly normal thing to come waltzing through your door, when in fact it's weird. It's abnormal. It's bizarre. It's—"

"It's a traaaaaaaaaap?" I asked, setting the sheared front panel of the safe, the heat all drawn off it, aside.

Reed looked right at me, and I could tell he was unamused. "You don't seem concerned that it might be."

"Probably because I haven't given it much thought yet," I said, turning back to the safe. I'd stripped away all but a few centimeters of the steel at the front in order to protect the contents from being flambéed by my fire finger. "I've been kinda busy for the last few hours since the offer was made. Also, I haven't exactly been inundated with job opportunities, and the news of my leaving government service broke like … weeks ago."

"You can't just jump onto the first thing you see," Reed said. "If they're offering this now, it'll still be there a month from now. You need consider carefully. You need to think it through."

"Yeah, yeah," I said, and I called Wolfe forward in my mind to harden my hand. "All due consideration, of course. When have I ever acted hastily?" I shot him a dipshit grin and slammed my hand through the front of the safe, bursting through the remaining steel up to my wrist. I then pulled, ripping the remainder of the door off with one good yank.

"When have you not?" Reed muttered. We both knew I could hear him and chose to ignore his commentary.

"Well, well," I said, looking at the neatly stacked bills within the safe. It was all cash, piled from bottom to top of the approximately three-foot by two-foot steel encasement. I let it fall out in a puddle at my knees, eyeing it as it slid, looking for anything hidden within.

"If whoever killed this guy knew him, like really knew him, they'd have to know he was swimming in money."

"Not necessarily," Reed said. "Lots of people live a lavish lifestyle on credit. He could be up to his eyeballs in debt for all we know. He could poorer than us."

I frowned. "He lives in a palatial apartment and has—" I looked down and did a quick estimation of the money at my feet, "—at least a million in cash, shops at high end stores, and has a wardrobe that would instantly turn you from 'Meh' to 'YEH!' in any gold-digger's eyes—"

"What? I am already so 'YEH!'—"

"How is he poorer than government employees who haven't even been on the pay scale for more than a few years?" I finished.

"Ugh," Reed said, rubbing his face. "Look … there's a difference between income and wealth, okay? You can make a lot of money, but if you spend it all and more so you can live the high life, you're actually poor, okay? If you're making a million a year but owe ten million to creditors and have nothing in assets to your name, you're poor. Period. If you're in that situation, the guy working at the corner store who has two grand in his 401k is actually, measurably wealthier than you. You just look better from the outside."

I blinked, thinking that over. "But … the guy working at the corner store doesn't live in this swank pad."

He frowned. "You've become the Kat of finance. Stop being so damned superficial."

"Hey!" I said, feeling insulted just by the comparison and responding like one of my captive souls. "This guy's got money. Clearly. At least some." I gestured to the pile on the floor.

"You're right. CPD will dig into the bank records to confirm it, but …" Reed let a heavy sigh. "We've got a murder victim that appears not to have been robbed in spite of being fully loaded."

"Yep," I said, coming to my feet, a pile of cash discarded at my feet. "Which means so far … we've got nada."

6.

When we showed Breckinridge the pile of cash in the closet, his eyes nearly jumped out of his head. A million bucks was quite the windfall to a young patrolman, I was sure, and we carefully counted it out and put it all in a garbage bag before we left it with him, taking a receipt for the amount with us. No offense to the young officer, but almost anyone would have been tempted to solve their financial woes by pocketing some of it, and I was very clear when I took the piece of paper with the full amount written on it and put it in my coat. Reed did the same, and we left Breckinridge with the cash, trusting that his personal integrity would be backed up by the knowledge that the three of us had perfect, precise counts of how much money had been recovered at the scene. I suspected he would watch that money like his career depended on it, because the odds were good that it did.

"It was tempting, though, wasn't it?" Reed asked me in the back of the cab, staring out along Lake Shore Drive as we headed back toward downtown, the sun already up.

I yawned. "Not really."

He gave me a look like I was a sucker. "A million bucks and you weren't even tempted?"

"I prefer to make my money the honest way," I said, staring out at Lake Michigan before I fumbled for my cell phone and checked the time, "by beating the hell out of scoundrels for a government paycheck." It was half past seven.

"Take us to Northern Illinois Technical University," I said to the driver.

He made a low grunt and turned the car around at the next intersection. We had been heading to a hotel downtown, one booked for us by Phillips's secretary in her unfortunate after-hours, no overtime work session.

"I was so looking forward to getting a shower and fifteen minutes of sleep," Reed said, yawning.

"No rest for the wicked," I said pointing to me, "or the weary," and I pointed to him. "The campus is probably opening up right about now, and we've got to get a clearer picture of the vic." I called him the 'vic,' like I was in one of those hardboiled cop shows.

Reed made a face at me. "You know you're not much of a detective, right?"

"Shhh," I said, as we rolled down Lake Shore Drive's residential street, "let me live the fantasy. I'll need a bottle of bourbon and a forty-five, naturally."

Reed sighed. "If this keeps up, I'm gonna need the forty-five to blow my own brains out later."

We pulled up to Northern Illinois Technical University a few minutes later. It was a little north of downtown and the campus was surprisingly green and lush considering that spring had not exactly sprung around here just yet. The trees certainly weren't showing signs of new life, but the grass appeared to be stirring out of its winter doldrums. There wasn't any ivy growing on the brick buildings, but the whole place had an old campus feel to it, with tall, red-brick buildings crammed into a smaller area than they would have occupied if the college had been built out in suburbia with more land to strew itself over.

There were actual gates, too, wrought iron, a perfect sort of illustration that this campus either meant to keep the peasants out or knowledge in. Or maybe they just meant to send a message to keep vagrants out, I dunno. Either way, it didn't look super welcoming.

I led the way up to the campus administration building,

helpfully labeled as such by a giant sign that was visible from where the cab let us out. I could see worker bees moving around through the glass lobby doors, and when I pulled the handle I found it unlocked. We stepped through a glass entry and into the lobby itself, heat blasting down on us as we came in. It was a nice hedge against the morning chill, and I made my way to the front desk with a purpose.

"Good morning," said the chipper woman behind the desk. "How can I help you today?"

"Who's in charge here?" I asked, leaning an elbow against the desk.

"Of the reception area?" she asked, still bright, blue eyes shining. "Me! How can I help you?"

"I need to speak to the person in charge of the campus," I said.

Here I saw the first trace of gatekeeper resistance start to show itself. "I'm afraid President Breedlowe has appointments all day—"

I flipped my badge out and saw her smile flicker then fade. "Tell the president to start cancelling. This might take a while."

The lady looked from my badge to me, and her gatekeeper instincts were fighting back hard. "Can I tell her what this is about?"

"Sure," I said, feeling just the tiniest bit of relish at ruining this lady's day, and by extension, her boss's. "One of your professors, Dr. Carlton Jacobs, was murdered last night." I didn't smile. I'm not that ghastly.

"Oh." The receptionist faltered, standing up and almost tripping over her chair. "Oh ... oh my."

"Yes," I agreed. "Oh, *you*, indeed. It's all about you. So ... when can we speak with this ... President Breedlowe?"

"I'll ..." She pointed behind her, to the warren of corridors I could see extending back behind the open administration area. "I'll just ... go ... talk to her secretary and ..."

"Yeah, you do that," I said, nodding as she ran off down the hall.

Reed sauntered up behind me. He'd kept his distance during my exchange with the receptionist, but I could see the disapproval on his face. "You are like a contagion of negativity, you know that, right?"

"I just can't help myself," I said, staring down the corridor where the receptionist had disappeared. "I see these happy, peppy people, and I just want to pee all up in their Corn Flakes." I looked right at him. "I'm working on it with Dr. Zollers, but frankly, it's down the list a ways."

"Why?"

"Why am I working on it or why is it down the list?"

"Why do you do it?" Reed asked.

"Because misery loves company like you love snarky, mean-spirited Italian doctors," I said.

"I only love the one," he said, a tower of disapproval. "Is it really so bad to be a happy person?"

"Not if you keep it to yourself," I said. "But the minute you try and move me out of misanthropy, I view it as a little act of war, your positive energy versus my negative. And you know how competitive I get on these things."

"Yeah, you'll ruin a day for someone in a jiffy," Reed said, sounding more dour than surprised. "Have you ever thought about maybe embracing a more positive outlook on life? See if it changes things for you?"

"I did think about it," I said, "but the minute I tried, my brother decided to rain on my parade by saying that the only legitimate job offer I had was clearly some sort of scam or scheme designed to entrap me. I mean, I bring all this positive thinking and optimism to the equation and he just goes and—"

"Whatever," Reed said, going from older brother to teen sister in a second, his expression growing darker as I grew more amused. "Fine. You've got a healthy skepticism most of the time. Why not on this one thing?"

"Give me a little time, maybe I'll get there," I said. "You are talking way more about this thing than I am, by the way, and assuming lots of feelings and thoughts from me that I haven't voiced to you. I could be super skeptical and you wouldn't know because you're too busy badgering me about this to give me enough space to think it over before I really start steering in one direction or another."

Reed grunted in a way that made me think he needed a bathroom imminently. "You're a weird contradiction."

"Thank you," I said sweetly as the receptionist emerged from the corridor behind the desk, arms folded in front of her like a shield and a stunned look on her face. I wondered if the news of Dr. Jacobs's demise had finally made it through to her or if she'd received even worse news on her journey through the labyrinth. "I'm feeling really optimistic all of a sudden," I said to Reed.

"You're not just a vampire of souls," Reed said under his breath, "you're also an emotional one, draining peoples' positive emotions in order to sustain yourself."

"Even you telling me I suck isn't going to bring me down right now," I said brightly as the receptionist came back to the desk. "Will the president see us now?"

"Yes," she said, deflated. "She's just … follow me." She said the last bit like she'd been utterly defeated and turned to lead us back. I had crashed the gate. BOOM.

I followed her back into the hallway, Reed a few steps behind me. We made about fifty turns that I couldn't keep track of, and went up a flight of stairs. I hummed as we went, and the receptionist turned around to give me a funny look. "I'm having a good morning," I told her, and she scowled at me, "like you told me to, remember?"

Needless to say, we did not speak again. She ushered us to President Breedlowe's office, where the president's secretary, a man in his thirties, wordlessly gestured that we should go through the open door to his left. I entered President Breedlowe's office to find a middle-aged woman with greying hair sitting behind her desk with a stunned look on her face, staring out the window behind her across the pretty, expansive campus.

"President Breedlowe?" I asked, and the woman jerked her head as she came out of her grief coma or whatever. "I'm Sienna Nealon. This is Reed Treston—"

"I know who you are," she said, coming to her feet. She offered a hand and I took it. I couldn't tell if she always shook hands like her wrist was broken or if it was just the surprise, but it was a weak grip, even for a human. "Anna told me that you're here about Carlton. I'm Corinne Breedlowe."

She shook hands with Reed, and it looked much more like an even match. My brother, so compassionate ... it was like they were holding a contest to see who could grasp each other more delicately. He put on his best sympathetic face (I must have left mine at home, with the suitcase and all my clothes) and said, "I'm so sorry for your loss, Ms. Breedlowe. Were you close to Dr. Jacobs?"

"No," President Breedlowe said, shaking her head. "He was one of our premiere ... acquisitions, I say somewhat crudely. Dr. Jacobs came to us from a short stint at CalTech after a longer tenure at Lawrence Livermore labs. He was quite a brilliant man and had published several papers on a variety of subjects that had brought us scads of much-needed attention following our founding only a few years ago."

"You're a new institution?" Reed asked, cutting me instantly out of the conversation. I let him, because I figured he'd ask delicate questions and I wouldn't, and indelicate questions tended to end conversations, so it was best to save them for last.

"Yes," President Breedlowe said, nodding. "Only a few years old but we're already establishing a reputation in the engineering and science worlds. Carlton was such a fixture in our faculty. To lose him now is ..." She blinked, and I could see tears lingering in the corners. "Well, it's quite a blow."

"But you didn't know him well on a personal basis?" Reed asked, probing gently. Such a sweetheart, my bro. Must have all been used up by the time I came around. Or maybe I'm just my mother's daughter.

"No," President Breedlowe said with another shake of her head. "We certainly dealt with each other at any number of school functions, but I don't believe he ever even attended the yearly Christmas party at my home."

"Was he invited?" I asked, throwing a cup of cold water on the proceedings.

"Of course," President Breedlowe said, stiffening like I'd insulted her. I was bad cop; this was my jam. "The whole faculty was invited."

"Did you know of any professional rivalries that Dr. Jacobs might have cultivated?" Reed asked, the delicate surgeon to my ... well, to my Sienna Nealon, master of disaster.

Breedlowe blinked in utter surprise. "You must be joking."

"Often, but not right now," I said. "I know it doesn't seem like it with that simpering expression on his face, but he's being serious." Reed shot me a dirty look that wiped the simpering one right off. Mission accomplished.

"You think a professional rivalry could lead to this man's murder?" Breedlowe asked incredulously, ignoring our adorable sibling interplay.

"Well, it wasn't robbery," I said, "so, unless a metahuman was lying in wait for a random person and happened to kill him by chance, there was some personal motive at work here, yes."

Reed softened it up. "Unfortunately, we can't rule out any possibility, no matter how unlikely, at least not yet. Dr. Jacobs died under extremely odd circumstances."

"Oh, goodness," Professor Breedlowe said, sitting back down in her chair heavily. "I ... I don't ... I mean, I've never heard so much as a whispered rumor against the man." She looked up at us. "I'm sorry. I don't think I can be of much help. His record was spotless, and I'm afraid I don't know of any—" She paused, thinking about it. "Now, hold on. I suppose there was one critique of his work of late that comes to mind, but ..." She laughed, way fake. "I'm sorry. The thought of someone disagreeing academically and it spiraling into murder is simply unfathomable to me."

"It's true," I said, nodding along, "human beings never kill each other for anything less than perfectly solid, logical reasons. Never petty, vain, selfish, stupid ones. Not ever—"

"What my sister means to say," Reed came in behind me and wallpapered over my attempt to be a sarcastic asshole, "is that we can't rule anything out at all, even something so small as what I'm sure is a very professional argument. No stone unturned," he said, almost apologetically, smiling pleasantly at President Breedlowe. "As an educator, surely you understand the need to pursue truth at all costs."

I thought he was laying it on a little thick, but I watched President Breedlowe eat it up like puppy chow right out of his hand. For my part, I kept from making a fake vomiting motion.

"Of course," she said, nodding, the wall down. "Dr. Jacobs had a disagreement across several academic journals with a— yes, a professional rival by the name of Dr. Marabella Stanley."

"What was the nature of their disagreement?" Reed asked, with a little pen and paper out and everything, like a real detective. I was sitting picking my nails, trusting my pretty decent memory to hold this probably irrelevant nugget, and he was all Columbo over there, sweet and unassuming.

"Oh, it was very technical," Breedlowe said. "I'm not sure I can adequately explain. Dr. Jacobs had written a paper about encoding of DNA—"

"Yeah," I said, cutting her off. "You know what? You might have to forward that one to us for later reading." With an expert providing layman's commentary, and another expert distilling it down even further, since I had topped out at home-taught high school chemistry and Reed was way more of a language arts and social studies guy than a science whiz.

Breedlowe nodded. "Of course. If you'll leave your contact details, I'll have the full text of both Dr. Jacobs's paper and Dr. Stanley's rebuttal sent to you immediately."

"About Dr. Jacobs," I said, elbowing in to ask my

questions. I glanced at Reed, but he seemed done. "Who here would know him better? Maybe on a personal level?"

"His department head," Breedlowe answered. "Dr.—oh." She looked past me at the open door, which I had not closed on my way in, for whatever reason. "Well, he's right here. Dr. Gustafson?"

I turned to see a middle-aged guy with big black glasses, a diminutive stature, and a face that looked like someone— maybe me—had punched him in the stomach. "I'm sorry to interrupt," he said, about two steps shy of tears, sad-looking enough that even I felt sorry for him, "but I just heard … is it true?"

"I'm afraid it is," President Breedlowe said. "Ms. Nealon, Mr. Treston … this Dr. Art Gustafson, the head of Dr. Jacobs's department."

"I wasn't just his department head," Dr. Gustafson said, running a hand over his curly black hair, "he was my friend. And if there's anything I can do to help you catch the person responsible for this …" his eyes hardened, "… I'll do it."

7.

"The thing you need to understand about Carlton," Art Gustafson ("Call me Art," he'd told us on the walk back to his cluttered office) said, "is that he was a genius among geniuses in the academic world. It's not normal for someone to cross disciplines. At a certain point, you buckle down and really work hard to become an absolute expert in one arena." He leaned against the top of a cluttered desk that would have put Jacobs's coffee table back at his apartment to shame. "The scientists of the movies, the ones that are—you know, Tony Stark, expert in thermonuclear astrophysics overnight—that's a myth. That's purest fiction. At the top level, science becomes so complicated that in order to become a foremost expert of the sort that does groundbreaking research, you have devote your life to that area of study and it alone. You don't pop in and out from DNA coding to astrophysics and back again, not at the expert level."

"But you're saying that Dr. Jacobs did?" Reed asked. Gustafson had yet to hit us with any dense, techno-gobbledygook, which was to his credit. I was sitting across from him in a chair I suspected was usually occupied by either his students or other faculty members, padded along the armrests, back and seat rather nicely. The office smelled of stale coffee.

"He did it more than anyone else," Gustafson said. "He was conversant—which, I mean a lot of us do this, you know, watch other fields with a casual eye. But his heart, his expertise was in his research, the science of DNA, with a little … call it extracurricular focus on engineering, on creating mechanical interaction."

There was the techno-gobbledygook. "In practical terms," Reed said, asking so I didn't have to, "what was Dr. Jacobs looking to do?"

"Nothing, yet," Gustafson said, a little forlornly. "He hadn't moved into practical applications. He was still experimenting with … you know, I don't think I can adequately explain it. He was dealing with DNA markers of a sort that most people don't … it was an area of research most people didn't touch because it doesn't have any immediate practical application. It was really oriented toward helping us understand ourselves better."

"President Breedlowe was telling us about a professional rivalry," I said, "between Dr. Jacobs and a Dr. Mirabella Stanley—"

"Marabella," Gustafson corrected gently, pushing his glasses back up on his nose from where they'd fallen.

"Knew I should have written that down," I said with a smirk. "Do you know anything about their feud?"

"Look," Gustafson said with a broad shrug that didn't even force him to unfold his arms, "people in our field disagree. There was no heat between Carlton and Marabella. They'd met, they were professionally friendly; calling it a feud would be giving it too much credit. They disagreed on an area of study, it was all polite, written into academic papers published in the biggest journals. It wasn't like a—" His arms came up now as he searched for a way to explain, "it wasn't a knife fight, you know what I mean? No one's reputation was on the line. No names were called. The blood didn't come up—"

"Cold blood runs the hottest of all," I said then wondered what the hell I was saying. I mean, I knew what I was saying, but I doubted my words reflected it.

Gustafson frowned at me. "That's … poetic."

"Yeah, it's right up there with 'a smile can hide evil intent,'" I said and smiled at him. "Look … we've got nothing so far on why Dr. Jacobs is dead. Nothing was taken from him in spite of him carrying a wad of cash, and he had a boatload of money in a safe at his house, he was living high on the hog," I watched Gustafson writhe very subtly. "How much was he paid by the University?"

"Not nearly enough to afford his apartment, if that's what you're asking," Gustafson said. I could smell the discomfort wafting off of him.

Reed smelled it too. "Do you know why Dr. Jacobs would have been in an alley off State Street in the middle of the night with a roll of hundreds in his pocket?"

"He had a gambling—" Gustafson put his face in his hands and grasped at the black ringlets at the top of his growing forehead. "I guess it wasn't a 'problem,' because if you saw the safe, you know he wasn't losing." He brought his eyes up and looked at us. "Like I said, he was brilliant."

"What, he was a card counter?" I asked.

"Crudely, yes," Gustafson said. "I know one of his favorite haunts was a gambling den off State Street. Played cards, whatever he could that allowed him to bet little or nothing when the numbers were against him and bet big once the odds were in his favor. It's how he spent his nights. The man probably had a full night's sleep once a week. The rest of the time? You could find him with cards in front of him at one of those green felt tables."

I exchanged a look with Reed. "Maybe Dr. Jacobs fleeced the wrong sucker."

"It wouldn't be the first time," Gustafson said warily. "At least last time he just got … put out of commission for a couple weeks."

"He's been attacked before?" Reed leaned forward.

"Yeah," Gustafson nodded. "A couple years ago, when he first started here. Some thugs put him in the hospital. Seems somebody didn't take kindly to his winning streak. After that, he was more careful, managed his winnings in smaller spurts." Gustafson looked rueful. "Said it was bad for his wallet but better for his health. I guess it didn't work."

I stood up. "Thanks, Dr. Gustafson. You've been a huge help."

"You're welcome," he said, taking business cards off his desk and handing one to each of us. "Carlton was an invaluable member of our department and our faculty, and he was a good friend." Gustafson's jaw hardened. "Anything else you need, you let me know."

"Could you distill down the essence of his argument with Dr. Stanley for us poor, unfortunate morons?" I asked, throwing in a little self-effacement.

Gustafson's eyes widened as he pondered it. "I can try. I don't think there's anything there, but if you think it'll help—"

"It might," I said, forcefully.

"Then I'll see what I can do," Gustafson said with a nod. "It might take a couple of days. The subject's pretty dense, and I'm not the biggest expert in Carlton's field."

"Just get it to us," I said, nodding at him. "And thank you."

"Yeah, you were a big help," Reed said, taking to his feet and shaking Dr. Gustafson's hand with a little more gusto than I could, given the time constraint I had on touching people. Wouldn't want to steal his memories, after all. I hated to think which agency I'd get a cease and desist letter from on that. "Thank you."

We wandered out of Gustafson's office, keeping our self-imposed silence until we made it outside, the gloomy grey clouds hanging over the city of Chicago, the skyline visible in the distance under the iron sky. "So our vic's got a gambling problem," I said with smug satisfaction.

"Stop saying 'vic,'" Reed said. "And you heard Gustafson. It's not a problem if you're always up at the tables, is it? Because if so, that's the kind of problem I want to have."

"It certainly beats the hell out of *our* current problem," I said, giving him a side-eye as we headed back to the road in the distance, hoping to catch a cab. He looked at me questioningly until I answered. "Too many theories and not a speck of evidence so far."

"Yeah," Reed said, shoving his hands into his pockets as we walked, a newfound determination running over him. "Let's go find this gambling den and start taking care of that problem right now."

8.

Harry

The waiting man's name was Harrison Graves, but no one called him Harrison and only a few people called him Graves. Almost anyone who knew him called him Harry, and if any of them had been asked if Harry was the sort to murder a man in an alley with his bare hands, not one of them would have believed it possible.

Harry Graves stood on Oak Street Beach, the Drake Hotel looming behind him, Hancock tower rising above that building, cup of plain coffee steaming in his hand, staring out across the white-capped waters of Lake Michigan. It was a gusty day on the lake, not the sort he'd want to be on a boat for. To his left and right there were concrete quays running on either side of the sandy beachfront, water spraying over the top with violent force. The wind rushed over Harry where he stood on the top of a dune, just looking out.

He hadn't been able to sleep after punching the professor to death in the alley. It wasn't that he was beset with a regret. He didn't regret it any more than he regretted spilling coffee on the walk over here. It was just a thing that happened, an inevitable result of the fact that the barista in the too-fancy coffee shop decided to fill his cup to the brim. Predictable and unavoidable unless he'd either dumped some coffee out or sipped it before it was cool. He valued his tongue not being burned more than he worried about the drip running down the side of the Styrofoam, and so here he was, wet fingers, sticky cup, and standing on the beach contemplating, very idly, the unavoidable thing that he'd done last night.

"Shit happens," he said to the air in front of him. A lady walking her dog behind him heard it, though, and made a face. She was distracted for just a second and stepped in a small dune in the sand, a pit a few inches deep—just deep enough to turn her ankle. She swore and stumbled before recovering her footing.

Harry had already moved on, though. He turned and headed back down the path toward the underpass leading under Lake Shore Drive and back to Michigan Ave. He walked briskly, still not ready to sip the blazing hot coffee yet. That way probably lay pain, though he couldn't be sure without testing it himself.

He made his way down the walkway ramp toward the underpass, studiously trying to ignore the WWII-era painting of Uncle Sam pointing his finger right at Harry. He'd ignored that particular call at the time that it was first issued and hadn't really regretted it. As he descended down the concrete walkway toward the covered underpass, the smell of urine practically jumped out at him. The ground was wet. It probably wasn't all piss, since it had rained a lot lately, but there was enough of it to cause the strong scent to crawl up his metahuman nose and linger there.

Distracted by the stink, he came around the corner and bumped into a guy in running clothes. Harry was walking at normal speed, human speed, and when he collided with the runner, Harry didn't move much. The runner, though, bounced right off as Harry set his feet by instinct.

"Hey," the guy said, headphones plugged in, talking artificially loud as he pulled his butt off the pissy, wet concrete in the underpass, "watch where you're going."

"Sorr—" Harry started by instinct, burning coffee running down his fingertips—

And suddenly ... he wasn't sorry.

"Yeah, yeah," the runner disregarded him, getting off the ground, his lime-orange shorts and grey tank top spattered with coffee and other liquid. "Asshole." He brushed his hands off and started to go around Harry.

Harry reached out and shoved him lightly with the tips of his fingers, smearing coffee onto the grey shirt as he pushed the runner.

"What the—" The runner fell down again, rolling hard, his legs and ass coming up over his head. He landed on his knees like he'd done a backwards flip, and Harry hadn't even tried very hard. He just wanted to stop the guy for a second, by instinct. The guy's face had scuffed on the concrete, and he had road rash on his cheek. "What the hell are you doing?" the guy asked, more outraged than scared.

Harry just stood there, coffee cup in hand, and then he sighed, decision made. He threw the coffee cup sideways and it splashed out of the cup and out of the tunnel. Harry took two sharp steps forward toward the runner and grabbed him around the jaw. The guy couldn't avoid it; he wasn't strong enough and he wasn't fast enough, not nearly.

"What the—" the guy started to say, but he barely got even that out before Harry twisted, hard and fast, and broke the runner's neck, turning his face around a hundred and eighty degrees and guaranteeing death.

His work done, Harry pushed the runner's body away, disgusted. He shook his own head considerably more conservatively than he'd just shaken the runner's and sighed again. He looked sidelong at his wasted coffee, and his ears perked up as he heard the sound of a telephone dialing behind him.

"911 Emergency," came a faint, faded voice. "Do you need police, fire or ambulance?"

Harry spun to see a woman in her mid-twenties, dressed

for a jog of her own, yoga pants and a tight-fitting workout shirt running down her wrists to where she clutched her cell phone. She wore a horrified look and her phone had fallen away from her ear. Her breaths were coming in sharp gasps. "Oak Street Beach—the underpass—there's a murder—ohmi—"

He hadn't even heard her coming, hadn't sensed her behind him, hadn't been paying an ounce of attention the whole way until the runner he'd just killed had jarred him out of his self-imposed reverie and forced him into action.

Harry looked right at the woman, and she looked right at him. Her cell phone still squeaked, the speaker blaring, but quietly enough that only his meta ears picked it up at this distance. "Ma'am? Are you still there?"

"Shit," Harry said.

9.

Sienna

I was on the phone with Detective Maclean, in the back of a cab rolling toward downtown, listening to the skepticism in his voice as I went over what we'd found. The air in this particular cab reminded me of a school bus I'd once looked over in the course of an investigation in Utah. It was weird and grossly rubbery smelling, like they'd made the seats out of recycled poop cut with plastic.

My conversation with Maclean was starting to feel as if it were manufactured out of similar components. "There's a gambling den off State Street," I told him. I could hear him breathing disapproval on the other end of the line. "That's where Dr. Jacobs was coming from when he got popped."

"Uh huh," Maclean said, his faith in my investigative skills shining through in his tone. "A gambling hall right off State Street. Of all the places someone could put an illegal operation, they chose there. Sure. I'll get right on investigating that."

"If I wanted to make up fibs, I'd come up with something better than that," I said.

"Sure you would," Maclean said.

"Listen, ass," I said. The cabbie's head turned around sharply. "Not you. This is Illinois, all right? How many of your former governors have ended up behind bars?"

Maclean grunted at the other end of the line. "I think we're running four out of the last seven at the moment."

"See, in most places, that would defy belief," I said, "but here, it's just 'the Chicago way,' right?" Maclean ground his teeth. I could hear it through the phone. "Also, I fly and can shoot fire from my fingers. Time was, that would be believed impossible. Now we just accept it as fact. So ... why are you having so much trouble believing me when I say there might be a gambling hall off State Street?"

"I'll talk to Vice," he said, still nonplussed. "See if they've heard any rumors. Where are you going to be?"

"Downtown at my hotel. Thanks," I said. I heard a rustle in the background behind him as I hung up.

"I think technically 'the Chicago way' is, 'He sends one of yours to the hospital, you send one of his to the morgue,'" Reed said, looking out the window at the Gold Coast scrolling by on our right.

"Cops get antsy when you say that kind of thing to them," I said, looking out at Lake Michigan on the left. My phone rang and I answered before I even realized it was Maclean. "Go."

"We just got a 911 call from someone at Oak Street Beach," Maclean said. "Down on one of the walking paths. They said 'murder.'"

"That's ... usual, right?" I asked cautiously, trying not to be too much of an ass.

"No, it is not usual for people to be murdered in Streeterville!" he shouted at me through the phone.

"Oak Street Beach is right over there," Reed said, pointing out the window ahead of the driver.

"Pay the cabbie," I said and hung up as I threw my phone in my pocket and opened the door.

"What the f—" the cab driver shouted in accented English as I stepped out onto Lake Shore Drive at fifty miles an hour.

I know, that was dramatic. But I'd had my fill of riding around in cabs for a while, honestly. This shit was tiresome. I zoomed out of that door, slamming it behind me, but kept low, about ten feet off the ground, hoping the FAA wouldn't notice. It's not like they were that put out about those commercial drones all over the place nowadays, after all. Or if they were, they hadn't issued a million cease and desist orders yet.

I blew over the northbound lane of Lake Shore Drive, heard what sounded like a million horns but was probably closer to five blaring at me obnoxiously for flying over them. I shot over a chain-link fence toward the beach and zoomed over a sloping ramp that looked perfect for pedestrian traffic. I could hear faint, hyperventilating gasps coming from ahead, so I swooped down the ramp and found a woman dressed in way-too-tight yoga capris, holding her phone in her hand like it was her lifeline.

"What happened?" I asked, hovering about a foot off the ground just outside of the tunnel she was staring into. I didn't want to just race around the corner in case the murderer was lurking there.

The woman swung around to look at me with her jaw already down around her skinny knees. "Mu—muh—muh—" she said, incapable of getting anything else out.

"So you made the 911 call, then," I muttered and drifted past her. There was definitely a corpse here, and it looked like one of her fellow fitness buffs. The guy's head had been completely turned around on his shoulders, the neck at a sick angle. He should have been face-down on the concrete but he wasn't, thanks to the anatomical rearrangement that the murderer had performed. "Where's the killer?"

I wasn't expecting a cogent answer and I didn't get one. She pointed, though, down the tunnel behind me, and I was off, zooming past the corpse.

I came out on a walkway that overlooked a road. There was no one ahead of me, so I shot onward into a park complete with a wire-frame gazebo and racks full of those rental bikes that looked so ergonomically uncomfortable I felt like I'd need to be coerced at gunpoint into getting on one.

Then again, if the FAA kept me grounded much longer, one of those sturdy bastards might just become my preferred means of transport, ET-style.

I flew off the ground about ten feet and caught a glimpse of a guy who'd gone down the path ahead, toward the crosswalk to downtown. He was hoofing it, walking at a speed that betrayed him as not so much human. He was right at the corner of Lake Shore Drive and another road, next to what looked like a closed-off tunnel that headed under the street. There was a ramp leading down to it, all walled off at the bottom with cream-colored painted plywood, but he was above it at street level, looking back at me, clearly trying to plot out his next move.

"Halt!" I shouted at him, and he knew I had him. I know this because he froze for a second, and it gave us a moment to get the measure of each other.

He was a medium height guy, probably 5'10", reasonably tan for being a white guy at the end of winter in the Midwest. He certainly wasn't as pale as I was, with my bleachy Nordic skin. He had his hands in the pockets of an old, worn black jacket that looked at least a decade out of style. His jeans were the wrong cut for this century, too, and they were worn in a lot of places. Not threadbare or hipster-faded, either, just well used. He had dark, short-cropped hair parted cleanly over in the style of guys that were in their forties or fifties or older. Everything about this guy screamed, "Vintage!" except for his skin, which was a really good sign that he was an older meta.

He looked at me, and I looked back at him, hovering, ready to strike. I couldn't see his eye color from here, but I could see him making the calculation: Should I run?

He ran.

Actually, he didn't so much run as he pitched himself sideways over the railing and dropped the ten feet or so down the onto the ramp below. He landed adroitly and then sprinted into the faded wooden planks that blocked off the pedestrian walkway under Lake Shore Drive. He smashed right through them without letting it slow him down and disappeared into the darkness within.

"Why is it always idiots they send me after?" I wondered aloud. That wasn't really true, though. I'd run across plenty of people who hadn't been idiots, who had in fact given me a run for my money in the badass department, that had laid well-crafted traps that had occasionally cost me limb and once even life. Still, I had this thing in me where I couldn't let myself quit, so every time someone ran from me, I would doggedly run their ass down and refuse to let them escape, even if it caused me pain. Which it often did.

I shot after him and blasted through the hole in the wood with a fury. I figured he was panicked, running, maybe he knew my rep for chaos and destruction and would wisely want to get the hell away from me regardless of how dumb running from someone who could fly actually seemed on a logical level.

But that was before I flew headlong into his fist, which was waiting for me on the other side of the wooden barricade, along with the fugitive himself.

It halted my momentum in a flash, that punch, took me from sixty to zero in about 3.2. It was like a clothesline from hell, and I felt it on my chin, my jaw, my cheek, and all along the rest of me as I spun off and hit the concrete wall after busting some more boards with my legs.

I landed in a heap, stunned, with more than a few broken bones. If I'd been able to speak, I might have said, "Well, that was stupid." Because it was.

Instead I lay there, on the edge of consciousness, not quite able to summon up Wolfe to heal me, when a shadow appeared above me, looming with a grey sky behind him, the light silhouetting him and robbing his features of clarity.

"You're going to die," he said, his voice low and quiet, and my eyes fluttered closed.

10.

Harry

Harry stared down at Sienna Nealon, who was bleeding out of her nose and her ears, her right leg broken and pointed off at a sickening angle. A cavalcade of emotions thundered through him as he stood there, but stunned horror was probably right at the top of the list.

The fact that she was here, in Chicago, was not unexpected. The fact that she was here, right here, right now, where he was—that was alarming, concerning, worrisome—he was pretty sure he'd need a thesaurus to fully express the level of UH OH he felt pouring over him.

She was out, that much clear by the fact that he was still breathing, but the fact that she was there, that she could—she could heal, she'd be fine from this once she woke up—that was … well, he was down to disquieting.

None of this was any good.

The professor had needed to die last night. Needed to. But this? He stared down at her, scarcely trusting to believe his eyes. This was …

Frightening. Disturbing. Where was that thesaurus?

Harry didn't even know what to do, but he could feel help coming. He looked back and knew it was seconds away. He jumped over her insensate body and ran, smashing up through the walkway on the other side with perfect timing as her backup came in through the ramp on the other side.

She'd caught him because he'd been moving too fast on foot. Well, he wouldn't make that mistake again. He surveyed the area for a second as he burst out onto Michigan Avenue and then walked three blocks, casually, before stepping into a store for five minutes. He meandered, he browsed, and then he stepped out to find police cars, ambulances and fire trucks swarming near the park. As expected.

He raised his hand and hailed the first cab he saw, popping in the back. He gave an address in the Loop and then leaned back to think.

When he'd been in the store, he'd been focused on the next move and the next move only. Harry could only concentrate so far into the future, planning it out. Now he knew he was safe for a little bit at least, and he could open his mind to the next move. He looked back and saw the lights flashing behind him, red and blue and white, and he sighed again. A simple bump-off in an alley wasn't supposed to get this complicated. This was going to require ... desperate measures.

11.

A hard hand slapped across my face, snapping me out of a sweet, blissful nap and back into a world of pain and discomfort. I ached all over, and my face was sticky with blood. I could smell it, the pungent scent flooding into my sinuses and threatening to overwhelm me.

"Owwwww," I said, looking up at Reed's deeply concerned eyes. He was crouched over me, in silhouette, pretty much like my attacker had been when I'd gone out. I wanted to make a joke about the Mack Truck that had hit me, but for all my much-vaunted superiority, my own stupidity had been the culprit in this particular injury.

Wolfe, I moaned inside.

Yesssss, Wolfe said, already working on it. *You shouldn't go charging into—*

"Spare the lecture," I said for the benefit of my psycho and also my brother. Two for one. My wounds started to knit themselves together and my right leg jerked back into alignment as it healed itself. "Yowwwww."

"What happened?" Reed asked, voice thick with worry.

"I thought the bad guy was running but it turned out he was lying in wait," I said as I got up and dusted myself off. It required a lot of dusting.

"You didn't consider an ambush to be a possibility?"

"I consider a lot of possibilities," I said, trying to brush some particularly stubborn wood dust off my knee. "The most likely one when I see someone running from me is that they'll continue to wisely haul ass away, not take the 1.2 seconds I give them to escape as an opportunity to bushwhack me without so much as a weapon at their disposal." I turned my neck and heard a crack as bone set back into place. "That guy said he was going to kill me."

"I heard him run off as I caught up," Reed said. His eyes flared with anger. "You know, if you'd waited for me—"

"If I'd waited for you," I said, breaking into run toward the opposite end of the tunnel, where light was flooding down from my assailant's likely exit, "I'd feel like I was running with weights on my legs."

"I caught up with you, didn't I?" Reed snapped, hurrying after me.

"Because I had to stop and try and converse with a witness who had been so traumatized by the sight of a corpse that she couldn't construct a sentence with heavy machinery. Talk about a drag on your speed."

I burst out of the walkway at the other end of the street and shot into the air, scouring the sidewalk for hints of my foe. The streets weren't exactly packed, but they were damned busy, and it seemed like every fourth person had dark hair and a black jacket. "Son of a ..." I muttered.

Reed drifted up next to me, only fifteen feet up or so, his hands throwing off massive amounts of wind in order to keep him levitating. "See anything?"

I sighed as I looked in all four directions. I saw something, all right. Desperation. My own desperation and about a hundred people of medium height in black coats, only half of whom were actually looking at me at the moment. "This guy's gone," I said, letting myself slowly drift back to the ground at the corner of Michigan and Lake Shore. "He got away."

12.

Veronika
San Francisco, California

It was a dismal day outside Veronika's mother's window, her little view of the world shaded darkly by cloud and sky. The sun was just barely up, hiding somewhere behind the layers of clouds. It wasn't that unusual for San Francisco at this time of year, but it could have been better. The clouds threaded across the sky in layers, deep and thick, blocking out the sunshine and making it feel like a cold, damp winter had settled over the whole world.

Veronika Acheron was used to feeling like this when she came to visit her mother, like a wet blanket had been draped over her, even in the summer, and it was why she tried to stay away as much as possible.

"Are you getting enough to eat?" Veronika asked. The smell of something roughly approximating chicken hung in the air in the nursing facility. Veronika's hands were clutched together under the coat she had hung over her arm. It was long, and velvety, and it felt reassuringly heavy hanging there.

She waited for an answer from the woman in the bed before her. Her mother had always been strong, always been … unbreakable, resolute of will and tireless of body. Now she reclined in the bed, sitting at a forty-five degree angle, propped up by pillows, eyes lazily pointed at the window, looking about thirty seconds from drifting into sleep. This was how she always was nowadays.

"Of course you are," Veronika whispered. There was no reaction from her mother. There never was. She'd seen her fed; it was a messy ordeal, not terribly unlike watching a toddler eat against their will. How funny, that she tied this period in her mother's life with the earliest days of her own. Helplessness lay on both sides of life's spectrum, Veronika supposed. She found no humor in that thought at all, just a cold, burning fear that she'd live long enough to see it visited upon her again.

The ringing of her phone was a welcome interruption from the stink of the food and faint, lingering scent of disinfectant that couldn't entirely cover the smell of bodily functions. Veronika coolly went for her phone and turned away from her mother and the window on the cloudy world. "Excuse me for a moment," she said to her mother in a quiet voice before pressing the key to accept the call.

"Go," Veronika said. She was precise in her professional life. She had to be. She brushed her straight, long red hair back behind her ears. She rarely let it loose, except when she wasn't working.

She listened carefully to the voice at the other end of the line. With something that might have been pleasure from any other person, but from her came out cool steel, she said, "It's been a while."

She listened again, that pleasant voice threading through her mind. "No, I wouldn't mind working," she answered, turning her head subtly to look back at her mother. "I wouldn't mind at all. Do you have a contract for me? Perhaps something a little more in line with my regular … yes …"

A prickle of fear mingled with anticipation ran down the back of her neck, like someone had opened the window to let the day in. "Sienna Nealon? I can …" She paused to let the voice speak again. "Chicago? I can be there on the next … yes, that'll be fine. I'll catch that flight. Am I the only …? No, of course not. That's all right, I don't mind a little competition." She paused, listening, and gritted her teeth for a moment before replying. "Oh, they get a head start, do they? All right. I can work with that. You give them first crack, and when they screw it up, I'll do the job right."

She ended the call and turned back to her mother. Or at least the shell that was her mother now. "I have to go," she said, coolly. "Something's come up, but I'll be back in a few days." She forced a smile, let it faintly tug at her lips, and pressed them to her mother's cheek. "Take care while I'm gone."

She watched for any hint of reaction, any sign of the woman who had once inhabited the wrinkled and tattered body on the bed. When she saw none after a few seconds, she turned calmly away and left to go kill Sienna Nealon.

13.

Reed and I went back to our hotel, a tower in downtown only a few blocks from Oak Street Beach, and I slept for like an age. Not one of the short ages, either; we're talking one of the long ones, enough time for humans to go from crawling on the earth like slugs to talking on cell phones and posting wombat videos on the internet.

I awoke in a dim room, hints of dull light streaming in through the edges of the blinds that shrouded my window. I had a mild headache, the sort of thing that seemed to follow using Wolfe's power sometimes. He could fix drastic injuries, but even the healthiest human being had occasional headaches, and that he couldn't cure. I squinted in the darkness, wishing for it to go away, but my request went unanswered.

I looked past the foot of my bed where a set of double doors with foggy glass waited, cracked slightly open to reveal the yellow light of a lamp on in the room beyond. I'd left Reed out there, hanging around on the couch when I'd come in here to crash. He had his own room, presumably because Phillips's secretary had been decent enough not to make him try and sleep on a sofa, or maybe because government regs just allowed for a two-room suite. I could hear him moving around faintly, sniffing like he had a runny nose.

I rolled out of bed and flexed, looking around the room. It was small, as one might expect from a downtown hotel room, but it was nice and clean, and the bed was soft. I took a deep breath and caught a faint hint of very light perfume in the air. Not enough that anyone but a meta would have noticed it, but just enough to cover some of the other smells a room like this might accumulate given enough time and people parading through.

The smell reminded me of something, and I remembered in a flash that I'd smelled rosemary on the killer. I'd been too distracted when he'd battered me in the ambush, but the smell had been in the air, though faint. Yeah, the guy who bushwhacked me was definitely the same one who had been lingering behind that dumpster to kill Jacobs. Or if it wasn't him, they used the same bath products. I assumed it was bath products that resulted in the pronounced smell that hung around him. He could have been an executive chef for some restaurant, I suppose, and carried spices in his pockets.

I cracked my neck as I opened the door, and Reed grimaced as I entered the living room. Whether it was from the sound of my vertebrae realigning or his surprise at my sudden entry, I didn't know. He sat under a lamp, the orange light shining down on him, the blinds down in here as well, TV flickering from where it was mounted on the wall to my left. "Whassup?" I asked casually.

"Just watching the coverage," he said, nodding at the TV. I glanced over to see the paramedics wheeling a gurney with a black body bag on it out of Oak Street Beach Park. Naturally, there was a big, emblazoned ticker running down the bottom of the screen: "Murders Downtown Shock Locals."

"Of course it shocks the locals," I said, yawning. "We wouldn't want any murders to occur outside of their duly appointed murder zones, after all."

Reed smiled faintly. "You know, there just might be some truth to that."

"It wouldn't be funny if there wasn't," I said, stretching. "If fifty murders occur in one area, the one we expect murders to occur in, it's all shaking the head sadly and wondering, 'What can we do?' But the minute they cross certain borders …" I waved my hands. "Freak out." I yawned.

"You given any more thought to this job offer?" Reed asked, and I could tell he'd been holding it in since I entered the room. All of five seconds, wow. My brother was almost as poorly restrained as I was, but his temptations seemed to run in the direction of annoying people with his strongly held beliefs. Mine ran to assault and homicide.

I rolled my eyes. "No, because I was, in fact, sleeping. But I have thought of an exciting new career path for you— Veterinary Dental School."

He frowned. "That's not a thing. And no."

"Then stop trying to perform amateur dentistry on my gift horse," I said, slumping my shoulders and walking toward the window.

"I thought we decided that saying came from the Trojan horse?"

"We don't really get to decide these things," I said, scratching an itch just below my collarbone. "It's not like we were there for the origin of the saying. I mean, I guess we could ask Janus—" I tugged on the chain to raise the blinds. It wasn't really a blind, per se—more like a solid window shade that rolled up. When I finished, I looked out through a second shade, this one more like a mesh that blocked light and prevented people from clearly seeing into the room. They probably had a good view of my silhouette, though.

Lake Michigan lay a few blocks away, and I could see it surprisingly well through the screen, down one of the avenues, white caps raging on its surface from the stiff wind blowing off the lake. There were a few buildings between us and the lake, dark towers with black-glassed windows, the occasional lit room in them the only signs of life.

"Looks cold, doesn't it?" Reed asked, nodding at the window. "And cloudy. Kind of depressing, which was why I left the shades down."

"I just wanted some natural light," I said. "And yes, the lake looks cold." I pondered it for a second. "At least I didn't end up in it this time. Or naked."

"What?" Reed had a look of WTF upon his face. The TV was still playing faintly in the background, just noise, a string of jabber.

"Never mind," I said, and started tugging at the mesh shade's chain, raising it up. I heard something on the television that made me turn—

"—the first victim, one Dr. Carlton Jacobs, was a noted professor of research on the genetics of humans and metahumans—"

—just as a bullet crashed through the window behind me, hitting me in the side.

I dropped to the ground and yelped in surprise and pain. I threw a hand out and grabbed Reed by the ankle as I came down, shattering the glass coffee table and ripping him off the sofa. "Get down!" I shouted once I had let out my initial cry of pain and had my wits about me again. *Wolfe*, I said inside my mind.

Working.

"What the hell?" Reed muttered as I dragged him closer to me, under the shade of the wall below the window. I looked up and could see the hole the bullet had made as it entered our hotel room. It was not small, and if I hadn't moved, it might have ripped my heart out. Could I from heal that? Very possibly, if the shot hadn't rendered me unconscious from sheer shock, but it wasn't the sort of thing I wanted to try just for kicks.

The sound of glass shattering was followed by the sound of bullets impacting against the wall and the couch that Reed had been sitting on earlier. Stuffing filled the air like we'd walked into a plush animal strip club and some douche-bro was making it rain. Uh ... internal organs of the ... you know what? Never mind.

I tensed, dust and stuffing wafting through the air, ready to move, and Reed laid a hard hand on my wrist as I started to rise up, prepared to zoom across the distance between us and the shooter. I was going to find them, rip the gun out of their hand, and then thread the barrel into a very uncomfortable orifice for them. It was going to be great.

"Don't," Reed said, voice firm.

"I can dodge bullets when I know they're coming," I said.

He shook his head and pointed right at the couch. I looked through the stuffing that was starting to settle, and my eyes widened.

Whoever the shooter was, he'd carved a perfect P into the sofa with his shots, only about three inches tall. The nearest tower was at least a hundred yards away, and this guy or gal had done their work with a rifle with much less than a second between shots.

That … was pretty metahuman accuracy.

"What the hell?" I muttered.

"A deadshot," Reed said, his hand on my shoulder, keeping me down. "Like Diana, remember?"

I remembered Diana. As in Diana, goddess of the hunt. She'd been Reed's companion in an adventure he'd had in Italy. She was also our old friend Janus's sister. Her powers were something on the order of extreme muscle control, which made her able to aim a gun so precisely she could just about give a haircut with an Uzi from a mile away. Plugging my stupid ass full of holes as I flew at her would be a breeze. "Shit," I said.

"Just be glad this assassin's not using a higher caliber," Reed said. "They could splatter us right through the brick facade." He eyed the wall nervously. "Actually, they still could if they wanted to work hard enough for it."

I pushed him to one side and myself to the other, throwing us apart. Reed slammed into the wall closest to his room; I slammed back-first into the one closest to mine, leaving a fifteen-foot dead space between us. I listened, waiting for the crack of the rifle. "Why don't you think they're doing it?"

"A meta just tried to sniper-shoot you in your hotel room," Reed said, staring at me across the glass-covered floor between us. "When you fought that guy in the tunnel, did you get a sense he was a deadshot?"

"If he'd been a deadshot, I think he would have shot me instead of busted up my jaw," I said, eyeing the broken window warily. The glass was broken in a nice pattern, but there was still a lot of it framing the edges. This guy had been precise, all right.

"This is someone else, then," Reed said. "A deadshot could throw a knife and kill you at a distance. He could have capped Carlton Jacobs with a paper clip at ten yards, put it right in his brain."

"You think our killer is bringing in outside hitters?" I looked up at the broken window. "That's reassuring."

"It answers why he's not shooting through the wall," Reed said with a tight smile. "He'll need to confirm the kill, and it's kinda impossible to do that through brick."

"Well, damn," I said, lying against a baseboard in my own hotel room, not really sure what to do next, "this day just keeps getting better and better."

"Hell of a last hurrah," Reed said, smirking slightly from where he lay across the room, and I didn't have it in me to disagree.

14.

Phinneus

Phinneus Chalke had been wielding guns since before they'd reached their modern form. He'd carried a musket during the American Civil War, when he'd been a Union officer from 1861–1865. The clouds of smoke those things let loose when fired in tandem had been enough to keep anyone from noticing exactly how good he was with one, but he'd done more than his fair share for Uncle Sam during those years. He'd believed in the cause. Freeing the slaves had been a plenty good enough reason for Phinneus to pick up a rifle.

After that he'd gone west, like a lot of the survivors of that war. He'd picked up a Colt Peacemaker and a Winchester 1873 lever action rifle, and had done his part to win the west, establishing a homestead out in Montana territory. It had been quite something, taming the rough and rugged land, dealing with the associated difficulties in placing a homestead in a far corner of the US. He surely wasn't proud of some of the things he'd done, but he'd done what he'd done, and he didn't make any apologies for it now.

Settling the west had burned some of the belief out of him. Manifest Destiny hadn't quite manifested what he'd thought it would, and when the time came to pick up a rifle again, this time in 1917 when the US joined the Great War, Phinneus wasn't so sure. The lines were less clear on the good he was

73

doing; he'd heard the rumors that there was some behind-the-scenes meta jockeying underlying that particular war, making it a less clean fight than the Civil War had been. But he'd picked up the M1917 American Enfield they'd issued him and done his duty again, this time being noted as one hell of a shooter.

When World War II had rolled around, Phinneus was the first to sign up. He'd had it in his mind to put a bullet in Adolf Hitler's skull, and while he'd fallen short of that goal, he'd inflicted the fate upon a large number of Nazi soldiers instead. He'd carried an M1 Garand into battle, changing with the times unlike some of his sort, placing bullet after bullet where he intended them. It was a reflex action for him, and the weapons had gotten so good that killing a man had become easier than taking a breath for him.

He'd let Korea and Vietnam pass him by without signing up for either. They'd feel like slaughter to him in any case; World War II had already felt like that, or near enough as not to matter. Phinneus wasn't into cold slaughter. He missed the uncertainty, the chance, the hard quarry that made for a difficult kill. There was something elegant about using a musket, something that left the odds just slightly unpredictable, out of his hands, especially at the longer ranges. With a modern rifle, Phinneus could kill a man from miles away even with an unfair wind, no scope required.

Which was why he'd put his skills to only occasional use, didn't carry a modern weapon, and did his craft for a rather tidy profit every time he was called to work.

The man who'd helped win the West had traded in his spurs for building a ranch on his old homestead in Montana, a spread he didn't care to leave unless the paycheck was lofty enough. But he still needed things, still had bills to pay, and while he certainly had a surplus of money at his disposal, Phinneus had no wish to have to draw down his resources.

So he kept working, and when he'd gotten the call about this particular contract … well, he'd already been in Chicago anyway, so it was almost like he was fated to take it. Besides, Sienna Nealon? Now that was a challenge akin to making a musket shot at a mile. She was a dangerous quarry, and he could feel the thrill …

… at least until he'd seen the window shade go up. That had been a disappointment.

But she'd moved at the last moment, and he'd seen the bullet hit her in the side. It had prompted him to grin, the end delayed, the gauntlet thrown. Because now she knew someone was trying to kill her. He pumped the couch her brother had been sitting on full of lead, signing his signature "P" on it. He hoped she'd notice, wondered if she would come flying all willy-nilly into his sights. That'd be disappointing. That'd end things a little too quickly for his taste.

Phinneus sat there, peering over his Winchester's open sights, parked in an office a hundred yards away, his lips pursed nervously. This was the thrill he'd missed in the last few wars, that sense of peril. The most dangerous metahuman in the world was waiting just over there. He'd gone all over the world on hunts, seeking some of the most dangerous prey, and had given up somewhere in the mid-1900s because the thrill was gone. Plugging a hole in an unfaithful spouse from half a mile away with the Winchester for fifty grand hadn't held any excitement. He'd begun to think his chosen profession was simply … dull. No new worlds left to conquer and all that.

Well, now the thrill was back. Phinneus's palms were sweating on the wooden gunstock. He was still carrying the old Winchester, and his Colt Peacemaker was on his hip, hidden under his coat. He licked his lips, wondering if she'd pop her pretty little head up.

No. She was too smart for that. Phinneus ducked behind the desk and hurriedly put the Winchester back in the shoulder bag he carried. This moment was lost, and if he waited around, she might find a way to turn the tables on him. While that could be potentially fun for a very limited period of time, it wasn't the way he wanted to engage his quarry.

No, this moment was lost, and Phinneus knew it. The hunt would go on, though, he thought as he ducked down the staircase, his boots clapping against the tiles as he came down in a fearsome hurry. It wouldn't be too long before he'd get another shot, though.

And the next time … he wouldn't miss.

15.

Sienna

I'm not used to being rescued by the police. Interrogated for a statement, sure. But rescued? Not so much.

However, in this case, that was exactly what happened.

Before Reed or I could decide on a course of action, cops came bursting into our room, kicking down the door. Naturally, we presented our badges and suggested that the officers should perhaps crouch, maybe avoid the sniper fire that could be incoming at any time. It didn't come in, though, and while we were suggesting politely to the first patrolmen through the door to get his ass out of the way, he got a radio call saying that "the scene was clear" a few blocks away in an office building where the assassin had left some bullet casings behind after shooting at me.

I lowered the shade, lifting myself up just enough to do it, keeping my body arched at a strange angle just in case our shooter decided to take a shot through brick. He didn't, and I got the shades down. I took a breath in relief, and it came out in a gasp of tension, my muscles relaxing like they'd been forced to hold a hard flex for hours. I sagged into a chair and stayed there for a few minutes until I felt my strength return.

"That shot could have killed me," I said to no one in particular. Reed heard me and nodded, then beckoned to me in a motion that indicated we should leave, and now.

We grabbed our limited amount of luggage, which basically boiled down to a couple plastic bags filled with toiletries, and dragged ourselves out into the hall. We met Detective Maclean just outside the door.

"Funny running into you two at a crime scene," he said, not looking amused. Every cop I met was like this, in every city. It's almost like they resented having to deal with the chaos I provided them.

"Hey, the crime was against us this time," I said.

"We are hell on hotel rooms," Reed mused aloud.

"Must be something genetic," I said.

"Someone took a shot at you?" Maclean asked. Like he didn't already know.

"Yeah," I said. "A meta, no less."

"Was it the guy you clashed with at Oak Street Beach?"

"Someone else," I said. "Probably an assassin hired to kill me."

His eye twitched. "Who'd want to kill you?" His jaw tightened. "Other than me, for dragging this trouble into my city."

"Dude," I said, "you have like one of the highest murder rates in the US. Don't lay your baggage on my doorstep." I waved my little bag of toiletries that I'd gotten at the front desk in front of him. "I travel light."

Maclean suppressed a response, and I could tell it was almost killing him to do so. "You were … right about the gambling den, by the way. There's one right off State Street. Vice has been watching it for a couple weeks, looking for an opportunity to move in."

"The good news is, I've provided that for you," I said brightly. "Or I can, if you want, because I need to ask some questions all up in that area and I can call your vice department in after I discover that there's gambling going on in that establishment."

"Yeah, sure," Maclean said, looking at the maroon hallways of the old-school hotel. "Any idea who was shooting at you?"

"Whoever it was," Reed said, "they stitched a 'P' into the couch cushion with some seriously sharp shooting. I gotta believe that's not a common MO."

Maclean raised an eyebrow. "You got that right. You gonna have your people run it through a search?"

"We don't so much have people anymore," I said, thinking of J.J. "Our agency support is ... limited."

"I can't imagine why you're pariahs," Maclean said.

"I know, right?" I nodded. "We're just such lovely, jolly people, spreading cheer everywhere we go."

"Well, why don't you go spread some of that cheer at the gambling den?" Maclean said, waving us off.

"You don't need a statement?" I asked, watching him curiously.

"You were in your hotel room and someone shot at you," Maclean said, shaking his head. "Anything more to it that's not represented in the physical evidence?"

"Not really, no—"

"Then I don't need the details of what you had for lunch or what you were thinking about when a bullet came winging in through the window, no," Maclean said. "Go. Leave me in peace."

"Well, okay, then," I said, cramming my little plastic bag of toiletries into my pocket and adjusting the bloody rip where the bullet had passed through my blouse. I pulled on the coat I'd had hanging over my other arm, ignoring the ruin I was doing to it by getting it bloody. "I guess we're off to cause more chaos." I watched Maclean cringe. "Don't sweat it. This time it'll be vice's problem!"

"I don't think that was very reassuring for him," Reed said as we headed for the elevators.

"If you think it's bad for him," I said as the elevator dinged and I stepped inside, "wait until you see how it turns out for whoever gives me so much as a hint of lip at this gambling hall." My face tightened in resolve as Reed hurried in after me and the doors started to close. "Because now ... I am in a bad mood."

Reed swallowed audibly. "Heaven help us all."

16.

The doorman at the gambling den went tumbling through air without regard for gravity until he came smashing down on a craps table. It was snake eyes for him, though, and his rolled back in his head like a reverse slot machine display.

I stepped into the long hall and took a look around. It was clearly not opening time yet, which worked for me. The building was roughly the size of a six-stall garage, tight and compact, ringed with slot machines and complete with tables for other games in the middle of the floor. A few closed doors broke the bright, jangling slot machine monotony that edged the room, and gave me hope that other recalcitrant assholes like the man at the door would be within, like defiant piñatas, waiting for me to work out my frustrations on them until they spilled their secrets like candy.

A quick glance revealed no sign of security cameras. Naturally. It's not like you want to have obvious surveillance of your illegal gambling operation. Probably tends to make the customers skittish, and it'd be a bonanza for the cops if they raided the place.

"What's going on out here?" A guy at least a foot and a half taller than me stepped out of the nearest doorway sideways. He came out of the door sideways because he couldn't have fit those muscles through otherwise. He looked like a proper thug, a mook of the highest order.

"Yay," I said, "we have another player."

He took in the guy on the craps table in one good look, and with a flick of his wrist he deployed a spring-loaded baton. Double yay. I'd been wanting one of those for a while. "You don't belong here," he said.

"I know, I'm way too classy for this joint," I said, strolling in, eyeing the guy whose ass I had already kicked, passed out on the table as I went past. "Still … I don't see anyone here big enough to throw me out."

He looked at me with jaded eyes. "I know who you are."

"Oh, good," I said, and my smile evaporated. "Let me tell you a few things you don't know. One, I'm not in a happy place, mentally, right now. Two, you're going to answer my questions—"

"No, I'm not," he said, clutching the baton in front of him like it could protect him from me or something.

"Three, I don't like it when people interrupt me, because it's really rude," I went on. "And four … I'm thirsty."

"There's a bar just down the street," he said.

"There's a bar in the corner," I said, nodding in the direction of a big wooden bar. "A gentleman would offer me a drink."

"I'm not a gentleman," he said, "and you're leaving."

"I'm going to enjoy beating the truth out of you," I said, pushing my lips together in a feral smile as I raised my fist and cracked my knuckles. "It's going to be the highlight of my day."

He sauntered out from the doorway, baton in hand. "I don't think so."

"Reed, get me a drink, will you?" I asked. I put on a ham of an accent. "I need to teach this degenerate some manners. Momma always said that hanging out in places like this produced some bad habits, but … I just didn't believe her …"

The thug smiled. "You think tough talk is going to scare me?"

"No," I said, smiling coyly, maybe a little psychotically, "but watching your blood drip out as I break lots and lots of your bones probably will. And if that doesn't work, scattering your body parts all over the city will probably do it. And if that fails … well, I'll come up with something even more creative."

"Holy shit," Reed muttered, making his way behind the bar. He was watching in a distracted sort of way, like he didn't want to see what happened next.

"Tough talk," Thuggy said, still smiling. "Let's see what kind of action you can take to back it up, cop."

I swept in at him as he raised a fist, baton in hand, and I punched him, ramming my knuckles right into his. It made a fearsome cracking noise that echoed through the makeshift casino. It took a second for the force of the impact to run through Thuggy's nerves, and then he flinched, dropping the baton. I drew back a pace to see how he reacted.

He pulled his hand back, a pained look on his face as he cringed. "Ungh!" He clutched at his wrist.

"Yeah, that's not going to fix the problem," I said. "Wanna talk now?"

"I ain't saying shit to you," he said, still holding his hand.

"Ooookay," I said and wound up again, bringing my hand behind me very theatrically.

He didn't even cringe away, though he had to know something horrible was coming. I shrugged and relaxed, instead leaning forward slowly to flick his ear. He started to relax until my fingertip snapped against his lobe and the damned thing ripped off and went flying across the room like Tyson had just bit it off.

"Augh!" Thuggy shouted as he grabbed for his damaged ear with both hands.

"One of your regulars was murdered just down the road last night," I said as he bent double, blood dripping from between his fingers. "His name was Carlton Jacobs. Dressed pretty snappy, tended to win pretty big."

"I don't know nothing about that," Thuggy said, his face creased with pain. "I don't know nothing about nothing!"

"I believe you when it comes to grammar," I said, "but I'm

finding myself more skeptical when it comes to Dr. Jacobs." I raised my hand again, positioning my fingers for another good flick. "Come on. I'm hurting you almost as little as I can, here. Work with me."

He scowled at me through gritted teeth and suggested I do something to myself that was very impolite, so I kicked him in the knee and watched him fall down. I probably broke something, maybe the patella, maybe the shin, I wasn't really sure and I didn't care. "If only I could," I said, almost commiserating to him. "Unfortunately, someone destroyed my hotel room, and since I'm not a fan of exposing myself in public, I guess I'm just going to have to keep effing you up instead."

Thuggy grunted. I'd clearly added to his list of woes. "I'm not saying ... anything." At least his grammar was improving. I felt like that was my contribution to society, and you're very welcome.

"Suit yourself," I said, and kicked him in the gut. It was more of a push than anything, sent him flying up on the craps table, where he landed next to his already unconscious buddy. "Hey Reed? How's that drink coming?"

Reed had poured himself something dark and straight up. "It's not. You never told me what you wanted."

"Pineapple juice and coconut rum. Make it a tall glass, one third rum, two thirds juice. I need something sweet, but still a little boozy."

My brother shook his head in clear disapproval, but he kept it to himself, turning to scour the bar in order to fulfill my request.

"Now ..." I said, strolling over to the craps table, "... where were we?"

Thuggy had his back to me, rolled over facing the door we'd come in through. "I wasn't telling you nothing," he said, back to bad English and sounding strained. With that, he rolled over, a Glock in his hand, and pointed it right at my face. His finger was on the trigger.

17.

I sighed as I ripped the Glock out of Thuggy's hand, taking his index finger up to the first knuckle with it. He was dazed, woozy, like someone had kicked him around pretty good, and thus using metahuman speed to dodge around him and twist the gun out of his grasp with a standard disarming move was like taking candy from a baby. A drunken baby.

"Why do I have a feeling you're the sort of guy who's barred by law from possessing a firearm?" I asked, instantly releasing the magazine and pulling the slide back to eject the round in the chamber. "I'm guessing you've got priors. Lots and lots of priors."

"Screw you," he said, and it was the politest thing he'd said to me in the last few minutes, so I decided to work with it. By snapping him lightly in the mouth. His head hit the table, and when he opened his lips, his front four teeth were missing.

I took it easy on him, I swear.

"Sienna," Reed said, hiding his face behind a hand, "I don't know if you've forgotten this, but human beings don't heal the way we do."

"You may not realize this," I tossed back at him, "but when people pull a gun on me, I give oh-so-much-less than a damn how hurt they get. Now, if you'll excuse me … I'm going to do some leg work here." I straightened up, slipping out of my jacket and tossing it onto a nearby roulette wheel. "By which I mean I'm going to break his legs." I leaned down to look

Thuggy in the eyes. "I bet you're familiar with that kind of work, aren't you?"

He just grunted, and before I could make good on my threat, or do much more than raise a hand, Reed caught my wrist. He didn't catch it hard enough to stop me, just enough to get my attention. "Cool off," he said, a yellow drink in his hand.

"Is that for me?" I asked, and he pushed it toward me, sloshing a little over the rim of the tallboy glass. "Okay. Why don't I tag out and you can play good cop for a few minutes." I looked back at Thuggy. "I'm going to drink this, and let me tell you, I'm a mean drunk—"

"You're a mean sober," he spat back at me, complete with blood from those missing teeth.

"Yeah, so imagine how much worse I'll be when I finish this and it kicks in," I replied, remorseless. "No, really. You think about that. It didn't have to go this way. You could have just told us about this dead professor, maybe hinted at anyone who would have wanted to do him harm, and we would have left when we were done, no broken limbs, no bloodshed. But you had to prove what a big man you are." I smiled sweetly. "I have this thing about big men who decide they want to prove how badass they are by going knuckle to knuckle with me. Maybe it's a blind spot, maybe it's just pride, maybe it's my competitive streak—"

"Or your mean streak," he said, drooling red.

"Could be," I agreed. "Because that's a big damned streak. But whatever it is … it guarantees that I'm not leaving until one of us breaks. Care to guess which one of us will break first?" I relaxed my hand before I broke the glass I was holding. "Because when my desire to inflict pain in order to get you to talk collides with your willingness to take it in order to keep your mouth shut, I'm going to tell you right now that you'll lose, and it's going to be an open question whether you ever walk again when this is over."

"Big … talk," he said, but he wasn't nearly as confident as

the first time he'd taunted me with that one.

"You've got a lot of bravado for a guy missing four teeth and a finger," I said. I strolled over to the nearest slot machine before I yielded to my temptation to stick fingers in his nose and start ripping.

I stared at the little row of cherries on the machine, two above the line and one below, and wondered if that meant the last person to play here had won. I doubted it, and even if they did, I suspected the slots here didn't pay much. I cast a look around the room and saw Reed leaned in close to whisper to the guy I'd worked over. They were both looking furtively at me, like I was going to stalk back over and skin them both at any moment. It could happen, I suppose.

I took a stroll toward the door at the far end of the room that Thuggy had come in through, kicking it open. I found a back room of the sort you might find in a warehouse, roughly the size of a single garage stall, but this one was filled with booze in boxes, and a few kegs that probably went under the bar for the stuff on tap. No one was back there, and I listened for a second just to be sure no one was hiding behind one of the crates, waiting to ambush me with an AK-47 or something.

I headed to the next door and knocked it open to find an office. It was an old-school office, paper everywhere, with nondescript scrawl on everything. I read the top few sheets, and they all had stuff written on them that looked like this:

J. MAGNUSSON—5k—GB v. CHI—BEARS BY 7.

I rolled my eyes with a supreme lack of caring. Thuggy out there was so busy protecting his turf that he probably didn't realize I didn't give a damn about his illicit activities. He didn't strike me as a strong listener in any case, but I suspected it was going to take a lot more infliction of pain to get him to pull his head out of his ass and open an ear to me now. In spite of what I'd said to him, I had mixed feelings about beating the hell out of some low-level douche who probably didn't have any connection to my case. I mean, my feelings were mixed between, "Sure, why not kick the crap out of him for shits and giggles?" and "If you beat him enough, information will come out like wine or blood" … but they were mixed.

OH, FINE. Guilt was settling in for beating the crap out of a guy who couldn't possibly hurt me, discounting the time that he pulled the gun. I sighed, loud and long, and was about ready to move on to the double doors across the room to give them a quick look-see when I realized they said "Exit" above them and were right on the side of the building. Because naturally an illegal casino should adhere to the fire code.

"I think we should call vice and head out," said Reed, pretty tightly, from where he stood over Thuggy. I gave a look at the guy on the table, and … yeah, I'd done a number on him. His shaved white head was streaked with red from all the places blood had spattered and run.

"He's not talking to you, either, huh?" I made my way over to find Thuggy leering at me from between bleeding lips. I was actually surprised he wasn't being more of an asshole, considering the circumstances he was in. I would have thought more swearing would be in order, but maybe he was too concussed to think properly.

"You can knock every tooth out of my head," he slurred, blood running out of his lips, "break every bone in my body, rip out my organs—"

"Don't go giving me ideas," I said.

"—I ain't saying anything." Blood bubbled out from between his lips. "I'll go to my grave screaming in pain, but I won't say a word about nothing."

"I admire your loyalty," I said, not rolling my eyes for once.

He blinked at me. "Wh … what?"

"I believe you," I said, shuffling my feet and looking down. "You're tough, I'll give it to you. You're a real badass among humans. You not only don't scare easily, I think you might be the first person I've met who maybe doesn't scare at all, and I salute you for it." I came up and looked right at him for that bit.

He looked at me with bleary eyes, like he was trying to

work out a puzzle on my face. "H … uh?" He couldn't even put together a word out of that, I'd messed him up so bad.

"Take a nap, Thuggy," I said and gently reached over to put my hand on his forehead. He swiped at it futilely, smacking his palm against my wrist, but I didn't let loose. I pushed his head back against the table, slowly but forcefully, and with more strength than he could resist. I didn't press against his nose or block his ability to breathe, just pushed him back to restrain him, pinning the back of his head against the green felt table.

Clouded though his mind was, he figured out what I was doing pretty quickly and tried to buck his body to escape my hold. He didn't have any luck, and when he brought his hands up to try and rip mine off his forehead, I batted his attempts away with my free hand while I waited for my power to work.

The burning at the tips of my fingers followed a spit of red that came geysering out of his mouth and splashed across the back of my hand. Eww. A tingling sensation ran up from my fingertips into my hand, and suddenly I felt like I'd pushed through his skull and was falling down into his face, sucked into a vortex where my fingers met his skin—

This was hardly the first time I'd used my powers to invade a person's mind. I didn't like to do it very often, because in my experience, a guy as rough as Thuggy wasn't exactly hiding happy memories of sunny days spent with his parents watching parades roll down an idyllic, small town main street. When it came to the bitter memories and broken dreams that made a person violent and unpleasant, I had plenty enough of my own without diving deep into the heads of others searching for surplus. And if there weren't already enough traumas in my own past, I had six other damaged people in my head in addition to the stolen memories of who-knew-how-many others just waiting to be sifted if the mood struck me.

I am not damaged, Zack said with more than a little irritation.

I am, Bjorn said, really owning it. He sounded proud.

I dove into Thuggy's mind and found just about what I

expected, plus or minus a little childhood abuse. The requisite neglect was there, along with a strong father figure in the form of a local criminal that gave him an outlet for his shitty and unsatisfying family life.

I vacuumed up those memories almost accidentally on the road to my objective. I doubted the lack of them would make him a better person, but why not at least try? You know, for science or humanity or in the name of a better Chicago or something.

I zipped past a bunch of memories that had zero practical application to what I was doing and popped into one that was exactly what I was looking for. Thuggy's name was David Sadler, and in his work life, he wasn't just an enforcer for this casino, he was actually a front-of-house guy, the face of the gambling hall and a manager. He greeted customers, schmoozed, and took pride in being the secret-keeper for the establishment. He acted like a bartender, sucking up patrons' secrets and keeping them to himself, which felt like an odd attribute for a crook, but there it was. He didn't use any of the personal information he gleaned in the commission of his job against his customers. Ever.

I plopped into the memory of the middle of his evening last night, the casino rollicking, filled with people. I was led to this memory almost unwittingly by Thuggy's own mental guidance systems, like he knew what I wanted and was trying to so hard not to look at it that he brought me to it by mistake.

Thuggy wandered between patrons, sidling up to the poker table, where I saw Dr. Carlton Jacobs looking very much alive, with sunglasses on to hide where he was looking. He was playing Texas Hold 'Em, and had a big stack of chips in front of him.

"Mr. Jacobs," Thuggy said in a silky smooth voice. I sensed that Thuggy always used the silk, unless he had to intervene with a customer who had reached his credit limit. "Always a pleasure to see you." I realized that Thuggy was calling him "Mister," not "Doctor," and it wasn't because he didn't know his title. It was because he didn't feel the need to extend that information to others who might be eavesdropping. The table was full of other players, and most of them didn't have near the stack of chips that Jacobs did.

Only one did, in fact. A guy who wore a black coat that was decades out of date and had his hair parted crisply down one side in a style that no one but Captain America really wore anymore. It was our killer, and he was sitting with his own fat stack in front of him, fingers resting on the two cards lying on the green felt table.

"Mr. Graves," Thuggy said to the murderer in greeting.

Mr. Graves looked up, giving Thuggy just a hint of a smile. "How's it going, David?" Graves—our murderer—asked.

"Exceptionally well, sir," Thuggy replied, moving down the line to slap him lightly on the shoulder in a friendly manner. "And for you?"

"This guy keeps cockblocking me," Graves said, nodding to Dr. Jacobs, smile widening slightly. "Other than that ..." I shuddered mentally as I realized that the murderer had just said that about his victim.

"It doesn't look like you're doing too bad," Dr. Jacobs said, smiling faintly himself. He reached over and gently clapped the murderer on the shoulder—

And Graves got a look in his eyes like something happened, a thousand-yard stare that penetrated into the distance.

I watched for another few seconds, but Graves pulled himself together, stammering when the bet came to him, and folded before cashing out. He looked rattled, but when he got up to leave, clutching his money, Thuggy caught a glimpse of the look he gave Dr. Carlton Jacobs as Graves left the table.

It was hard like steel, unyielding, a glance that ran over him as he got up to go—there was a decision in it that was as plain to me as it had been to Thuggy when he saw it, even if he hadn't understood what it meant until later, when he'd seen the cops milling around the alley like flies to a carcass.

Graves had decided to kill Jacobs right then and there.

18.

I came out of Thuggy's head with my usual feeling of *ugh*, like I'd just taken a dip in a slime pit and come out covered in slick green algae. Also, my headache was not improving by doing the mental version of a dumpster dive, and as I let loose of Thuggy's forehead, I grasped my own and moaned softly.

"You all right?" Reed asked, and I assumed without looking that he was talking to me.

"Yeah," I said, my voice kind of low, "just wish I could get into a decent person's head for once, maybe see what it looks like when people have a normal, well-adjusted childhood."

"Scott didn't have a normal childhood?"

"I didn't steal his childhood memories," I said, squeezing an eye open to see Reed looking at me with judgy eyes. "Just the adult ones." Very, very adult ones, in some cases.

"You know what they're gonna call you if anyone finds out what you just did here?" Reed asked, lowering his voice either in case there was surveillance in place or because he thought I was suffering from a brain-drain hangover. It was a considerate move, either way. "A vigilante."

"That's next week," I said, shaking my head to rid myself of that ugh feeling. "This week I'm just another overreaching, possibly incompetent government employee that they can't seem to fire."

He gave me his best jaded look. "Why is it we're leaving government service if they can't fire us?"

"Because our jobs are relocating to the malarial swamp that is Washington DC, duh."

He pursed his lips in disapproval. "Look, I don't want to rehash old arguments—"

"Then don't."

"—but," he went on, apparently undeterred, the bastard, "but what you just did there was—"

"Cruel, I know," I said.

"Unconstitutional," he said.

"I'm pretty sure the law isn't settled on taking someone's memories, since the framers probably didn't have that in mind when they were drafting—"

"You deprived that guy of his rights," Reed said, folding his arms, looking more disappointed than anything. "No trial, no—"

"Yeah, I did," I said. "But I caught him operating an illegal gambling establishment, so—"

"That's not an excuse for what you did to the guy," Reed said, looking at the mess I'd made of Thuggy. He had a point.

"What the hell?" Four guys came sweeping in through the exit doors on the side of the building. None of them were as big as Thuggy, but they weren't small, either. They looked like the casino's security detail, and they filed in with angry looks on their faces as they took the sight of the two of us and their co-workers on the craps table next to me.

"He did it," I said, pointing at Reed as someone else came in the main door. I turned my head to look and it was a woman in a grey pantsuit with a pink halter-top looking shirt underneath it. She had long reddish-brown hair and wasn't carrying a purse or anything. The look on her face said she was not someone's girlfriend, or the concierge, or a bartender.

Her face said she meant business, a tight smile and dark eyes that were focused on me and me alone.

"You might want to save the lecture on violence for later," I said to Reed. "You take the guys and I'll dance with the lady?" I caught his nod of agreement out of the corner of my eye.

"Hi, Sienna," the woman said, easing toward me, arms awkwardly straight at her side.

"Howdy, stranger," I said, watching her, "I love your look. It's says, 'I'm here for serious business, but I'm ready to party, too.'"

"I like your look, too," she said, nodding at the bloody mess just beneath my jacket on my side where I'd been shot. "It says I'm not too late … to kill you myself."

19.

Veronika

There she stood, Sienna Nealon, plain as day, looking righteous and defiant all at once. It was a pretty common look on her, at least judging by the press photos. Veronika hadn't paid her that much more attention than she paid to any other celebrity, just enough to know that everyone thought of the girl as some kind of cross between a superhero and a supervillain, depending on who you were asking and when you asked.

Veronika didn't feel a need to ask. She didn't care. Hero, villain, it was all the same to her. She needed to reduce the girl to a corpse to collect on the contract, and anything beyond that was just noise.

Still, caution was warranted.

"You know who ruined my shirt?" Nealon asked, pointing at the bloody stain and rip at her side, hidden beneath the dark fabric of her coat. Pristine, pale skin showed from the hole in the cloth.

"It was probably Phinneus Chalke," Veronika said, stepping a little closer as she peered at the sight of the former injury. "He uses this Old West rifle, one of the ones with a lever on it." She made the motion like she was holding up a gun and racking it the way she'd seen Phinneus do it when they'd been in competition for another job once. "He's an

Artemis. Good shooter." She looked back to Nealon's blue eyes, glowing like ice under a winter sky. "I honestly didn't think he ever missed."

"He couldn't put me down," Nealon said, sounding a little too pleased with herself.

"Never send a man to do a woman's job," Veronika said, a smile twisting her rose-red lips. Nealon's brother was off to deal with the thugs who had come in through the other door. From the way the voices were rising, it sounded like the tense standoff might be about to break out into violence.

"You said it, sister." Nealon smirked at her. "I can't say I've ever met a woman who could go toe to toe with me, though. Most don't even try. The last couple that did? One was a Russian lady that just got out of prison—she begged me to kill her mercifully. The one before that ..." She put a finger to the side of her lip as she thought it over. "I think she was Czech? Russian trained, though. Stabbed me a bunch of times. Regretted it, probably, before the end."

"I didn't realize we were going to summarize all of our battles in an epic recitation before we fought or I would have brought a list, maybe taken some time to compose it into a poem," Veronika said, still smirking.

"I kinda like you," Nealon said, smiling. "What's your name?"

"Veronika."

"It's going to be a real shame when I have to kill you, Veronika."

"I was just thinking the same thing, Nealon," Veronika said, leaning forward slightly. "Shall we?" She spread her arms wide.

"This is the way things should always be settled," Nealon said, matching her motion. "Let's."

Veronika raised a fist at the same time Nealon did, just behind her ear. "You know, that guy over there just tried this," Nealon jerked her neck slightly to indicate one of the toughs that was bloody and insensate on a nearby table, "and it didn't work out very favorably for him. You sure you want to go bareknuckle with me?"

Veronika smiled and struck, and Nealon came right back at her. They clashed, fist to fist, and the force of the impact threw them both back. Bottles shattered behind the bar, and the glass in the slot machines ringing the room burst from the shockwave of their collision.

Veronika slid back ten feet, skidding to a stop on carpet that ripped under the soles of her shoes, and she looked up to see Nealon staring back at her in a similar posture, surprise obvious in the girl's eyes. "Yeah," Veronika said with amusement, "I do."

"Well, okay, then," Nealon said, looking a little disoriented, shaking her hand. Hints of blood welled from her knuckles. Veronika didn't bother to check her own, she just charged forward again.

Veronika came at her straight on, and Nealon dodged right. The girl was fast, Veronika would give her that, faster than anyone else Veronika could recall fighting recently—

Veronika traded punches with her; Nealon landed one to her side, causing Veronika to gasp, Veronika planted one solidly on her jaw and felt bone buckle from the impact. They both flew off to the side, Nealon rolling over a roulette table and sending it skidding ten feet, Veronika slamming into the bodies of the two suited thugs draped across the craps table.

Veronika shook off her landing in a hot second, springing back to her feet as Nealon sat up, Frankenstein-like on top of the roulette table. Her eyes looked faintly dazed, and she muttered, "Wolfe," so low it was barely audible. Her jaw pulled back into line and her eyes cleared in a second. "Gavrikov," she said, "let's end this."

Veronika watched Nealon stick out a hand. The girl smiled as it sprang into flames. She hurled a burst of blazing orange fire right at Veronika—

And Veronika stuck out her own hand to intercept it, springing to life with cold, blue fire. The orange burst curved right into her hand and disappeared, absorbed right into her palm like it had never even existed.

Nealon stared at her, her jaw slack even though she'd just fixed it. "Uh. Okay."

Veronika just smiled and faced her down. This was the most fun she'd had on a job in decades. "What else you got?"

20.

Sienna

Uh oh.

My mom was always fond of saying that there's always someone badder than you out there. It was her all-purpose reason to keep training constantly, like a motto designed to blow away all my excuses about why sleep or television were more important than going down to our basement dojo and getting slapped around by her meta-powered ass for a couple hours per day.

The truth was, since I'd learned what an unleashed succubus could do and really gotten a grasp on how to fully use my powers, I'd been in peril a lot of times, but I hadn't met very many people that I would have considered even remotely as badass as I was. Oh, sure, they had powers, but most of them were soft or attacked me when I was down or used some unfair advantage to sucker punch me because they couldn't stand up to me in a head-on fight.

This bitch … if she wasn't badder than me, it wasn't for lack of trying.

There was none of the flinch in her that I'd seen in other metas I'd fought. She knew how to fight, she'd clearly done quite a bit of it, and she had gone knuckle-to-knuckle with me and caused a shockwave in the process. She'd yet to try and run, even though her nose was bleeding just slightly, probably from said shockwave.

She just looked like she was having a ball.

Like me.

As I said before … uh oh.

I wasn't exactly ready to throw in the towel and call it quits, you understand. But it did give me a moment's pause, realizing I was up against someone like myself, someone who enjoyed the fight, someone who prided herself on being a badass.

Eve, I said silently and sprayed a net of light right at this Veronika's face.

It hit her around the eyes and dissolved a second later as part of her face and hair sprang into a cold, glowing blue before dissipating back to reveal her features. It looked a little like fire, but with more substance. I couldn't shake the feeling I'd seen this power before, but I was at a loss to recall exactly when. I'd fought so many metas by this point that I couldn't even remember all of them. I just knew I didn't have anyone with these powers currently stuck in my prison.

Not that that narrowed anything down. I'd killed way more metas than I'd imprisoned at this point.

I racked my brain, throwing a quick look at Reed, who was fending off the four toughs that had come in through the side door. He should have been having an easy time of it, but two of them had guns and he was blasting them around, trying to dislodge the weapons from their hands.

I snapped my attention back to Veronika, who was advancing on me as I flipped back off the roulette table, buying myself a second or two. I yanked my jacket along for the ride, ripping it from where I'd left it at the point of the wheel when I'd taken it off earlier and flung it right at Veronika as a distraction. *Bjorn*, I said as she disappeared behind the leather.

On it, Bjorn said, blasting the warmind at her.

"Ooh," Veronika said, swiping aside the coat and blinking at me, a smile perched on her perfectly red lips. Had she applied lipstick before our fight? It hadn't smeared at all since we started to rumble. "Warmind. I'd forgotten how that felt."

"You seem strangely unmoved by it," I said, kinda glad the

roulette table was still between us.

"I learned mental defenses from a telepath I slept with on and off for a century," she said, dabbing at the little drip of blood on her upper lip. She looked down at her knuckle, tipped with red, and smiled. "The warmind is like a gentle kiss compared to what a real telepath can do."

LIES! Bjorn said, but somehow I doubted he was right based on both her reaction and his.

I'd run through almost my entire gallery of powers and was left with only a few options, none of them awesome.

Please don't turn into a dragon in the middle of the room here, Bastian said.

I'm not going to, I said, *it's downtown Chicago and there are other things in this building besides an illicit gaming house.* If Maclean disliked me now, imagine how he'd feel if I dropped a five-story building off State Street while turning into a dragon. That's not the sort of thing that brings in the tourists.

I'd run through Gavrikov's, Eve's and Bjorn's powers, though, which left me with only Wolfe's, Bastian's and my own to fall back on. Bastian's, for the reasons above, was right out. Wolfe's I had been drawing on from the first punch of this fight, and Veronika's strength clearly matched his pretty well. All that remained was his healing ability, which I would probably need to make copious use of if we kept brawling. It wasn't exactly a game-winner, though.

And neither were my own powers. Assuming I could lay a hand on Veronika, I kinda doubted she was just going to stand there and take it while I absorbed her soul. Most people didn't, and she was much more of a fighter than your average meta.

"Why are you here to kill me, Veronika?" I asked, hoping it would give me a moment's respite.

"Because I'm being well-paid for it," she said with a smile.

"I kinda figured that you were an assassin," I said as we faced off over the roulette table. "I just thought maybe you'd accord me the respect of telling me who wants me dead bad enough to engage the services of a preeminent badass like yourself to get the job done."

"I didn't ask the why," she said, still smiling, "because I don't care. And you should know I'm a professional, so telling you would be … well, gauche."

"Right," I said, and the *DUH!* idea clicked in my head. "Well, I'm a professional, too, and it strikes me that in all this hustle and bustle, what with being sniped and having you get all up in my area, I haven't even had a chance to show you or your buddy Phinneus the tools of my trade."

Her eyes widened and she kicked the roulette table as I drew my CZ-75 Shadow, which I had conveniently nicknamed "Shadow" (because I'm super original). The table hit me in the upper thighs but I snapped a shot off as I dragged Gavrikov into the front of my mind to lift me into the air. Veronika was already moving, using the kick against the table to try and shove herself backward and down. She hit the floor and rolled as my first shots echoed in the gaming hall.

I fired fast; she moved fast. It wasn't exactly a draw, but my visual acuity rated her as a fricking blur as she rolled under the craps table, and I held my fire so as not to hit the dumb lumps of goon that were unconscious upon it. I came back down to steady my aim, holding my pistol in front of me, focused on the table.

Veronika's eye popped up from behind the craps table. She was clearly holding her head sideways, awkwardly so as to spoil my shot. I considered trying to shoot her through the edge of the table, but I was using hollow-points designed to expand when they hit, low velocity rounds that were meant to disperse their force upon impact with targets like walls. It was a hedge, an acknowledgment that while I might be a pretty good shot, sometimes I missed. Using a higher-powered bullet with a full metal jacket round meant those bullets might keep going, killing some poor bastard in the next room. So shooting through the craps table was not a great option.

"That was a quick draw," Veronika said, a hint of pain

apparent in her voice. "And here I thought we could keep it a fair fight."

"Ever been in a fair fight?" I asked, my aim not wavering.

"No," she said with undisguised pleasure. "This was probably the closest I've had to one in a long while. I have to admit, I don't love it, but the exhilaration? Not bad."

"Yeah, I don't love it, either," I said, keeping my aim on her. She'd try and break the stalemate, that I was sure of. I'd known her for less than five minutes, but I was already certain that Veronika was a full-bore killer, and she wouldn't pass up me turning my back, not even for a second.

"Well," Veronika said, still looking out at me, "I hate to sound like your high school boyfriend, but … save yourself for me."

"You missed that one by years, lady," I said, frowning at her. "Oh. You … you meant I shouldn't let anyone else kill me, didn't you?"

"Yeah," Veronika said, amused, "but thanks for making this weird." She ducked back behind the table and it flipped up into the air, spilling both goons and all the assorted dice and sticks and other regalia of the game into the air several feet. I didn't have to step back to dodge it, fortunately, but when it came back down it lay on its side, a perfect bulwark to prevent me from seeing what was going on behind it. I heard a door thump open behind it and a slot machine rattle as something hit it—I suspected it was Veronika on her way out, but there was no way I was going to just trust that she'd fled.

I eased around, flanking the table wide, trying to listen over the sounds of Reed's scuffle at the other side of the room, not daring to look away from where I'd last seen Veronika. I shuffled my feet slowly sideways, bumping my hip against the bar and letting a grunt escape unintentionally. I navigated around it and the half dozen stools lined up along its side in order to get a clear line of sight around the craps table. My shoes crunched on broken glass from the bottles that had shattered when Veronika and I had clashed with our fists, and the sound jangled against my raw nerves. My mouth felt dry and my anxiety rose while I circled.

Veronika was gone. The door she'd escaped through had slammed back shut, and unless she'd deftly hidden around the side of the craps table while I circled around to check on her, she'd run. I saw a decent-sized bloodstain on the ground next to the craps table where she had peered over at me and traced it back to where she'd been when I'd shot at her originally. There was a smaller stain there, still wet, where I'd apparently tagged her with a bullet.

Whew. A sense of relief flooded over me, and I sagged slightly, the adrenaline starting to fade. I leaned back against the bar, collapsing on one of the stools, lowering my gun. That … had been tense.

"What the hell?" Reed asked, shuffling over to me, a pained look on his face and a trickle of blood running from his left eyebrow down his cheek. "Why didn't you help me?" His lip was bloody, and it had smeared down his chin. He also had a thin cut along the side of his head, visible even through his hair, and his clothing was torn in three places.

"Did you see what I was up against?" I asked, looking past him. Bodies were strewn all over the place on his side of the room, including one that looked like he'd been crushed under a slot machine. Ouch. Guess that guy should have cashed out before the stakes got too high for him.

"No," Reed said, his annoyance bleeding out like his scalp wound, painfully slowly. His eyes were all narrowed. "I was a little too busy fighting for my life against four armed thugs." He scaled back the furious judgment a little. "Why? What happened to you? I thought it was only one person?"

"Yeah," I said, not quite ready to return Shadow to its holster just yet. "One person. One highly trained assassin with the power to—I don't even know, generate blue superheated plasma from her skin? She absorbed my Gavrikov fire like it was nothing and burned through my nets. She shrugged off the warmind like I'd thrown a glass of water in her face on a hot day."

Reed's face fell. "You really didn't see any of my fight?"

I looked at him in disbelief. "I almost died, Reed. This woman's a badass, and she confirmed assassins have been hired to kill me." I shook my head. "Why does it matter if I saw your fight? It looks like you came through it okay."

He looked a little … miffed. "I was … I think I was kinda at my best." Hints of pride made their way through his facade. "I showcased my mad skeelz. Figured it looked cool."

I took a long breath, and now that the adrenaline had fled, I felt exhausted again in spite of having just woken up. "Sorry. I'm sure it was awesome, like something out of a John Woo movie—but you know, without the slow mo."

"Are you all right?" Reed asked, staring at me. I brought a hand up to touch my jaw, where his eyes had fallen, and I found blood there. It ached where Veronika had hit me, and my knuckles were covered in sticky crimson.

"Still alive," I said, trying to force a smile. It was all I could muster, considering that for the first time in a while, I actually had someone worthy of being a little intimidated by lurking somewhere out there in the city of Chicago, someone who desperately wanted to kill me.

Someone who had a genuine shot at getting the job done.

21.

The Chicago vice squad showed up to our crime scene a few minutes after we finished our battle in the casino. They picked over the wreckage of the place as Reed and I stood outside, glancing occasionally down the very alley where this had all started, where the man Thuggy had called Graves had killed Dr. Carlton Jacobs.

I still hadn't quite figured out why that had happened. Not that Thuggy had been a wealth of information; his knowledge of Graves had been limited to polite niceties exchanged with the guy, who had been a regular patron of the casino. Detail was in short supply in Thuggy's brain, though, and while he'd certainly noticed the look on Graves's face when the decision had been made to kill Dr. Jacobs, he hadn't seen it for what it was at the time. To him it was just a nasty look that followed Jacobs touching Graves. I only knew what it meant given the benefit of hindsight.

And I still didn't really know what it meant, exactly. Did Graves kill him simply because Jacobs had touched him? I'd certainly known people who would kill for less, but they tended to leave more of a body count. Then again, Graves had already killed someone else today, and who knew how many unsolved murders in Chicago might be attributed to him. There could be tons of them; Chicago wasn't short of unsolved murders. These two had just gotten attention because they happened in an area that murders didn't typically happen, and because the first was so obviously committed by a metahuman that it forced them to call me in.

I had a headache, both from the fight I'd been involved in and all the crap that had flown my way in the last day. So much for a peaceful last week. I didn't even know how to feel about having assassins after me. Clearly someone was upset that I'd come to town on this, and after clashing with Graves and having him tell me I was dead, my list of suspects was limited to just him at the moment. He'd made a pretty clear threat, after all, and I took him at his word that he wanted me dead.

I only wished he'd hired some less skillful assassins. Veronika looked to be one tough lady, and that sniper—Phinneus Chalke, she'd called him—had only missed me because I'd turned around at the last second because I heard—

I smacked myself in the forehead hard enough that I staggered backward, Wolfe chortling in my head as I did. Sometimes my souls liked to play tricks on me like sneaking their powers to the fore right before I did something stupid like hitting myself. I shook it off, using his healing ability to repair the minor damage I'd just done to my skull. "Ow."

"What the hell is wrong with you?" Reed asked, arms folded, a look of irritation mingled with concern causing his brow to furl.

"I just thought of something," I said, straightening up as I caught my balance. "Remember before our hotel got shot up—"

"Hard to forget that."

"—you were watching the news?"

"Vaguely."

"I heard something that caused me to turn around," I said, words tripping out with enthusiasm, or possibly brain damage from my Wolfe-powered smack to my own head. "The reporter said that Dr. Jacobs worked on metahuman research."

Reed frowned. "I didn't hear that."

"Probably because you were too busy ducking and covering for your life in the seconds after," I said. "If that's true, why do you think Dr. Gustafson or President Breedlowe wouldn't have mentioned it to us, metahumans standing in their damned offices?"

Reed thought about it for a second, his head bobbing side to side as he did. "I don't know. It does sound like a pretty big omission." He puckered his lips. "Especially since we knew that his murderer was a meta."

"And we told them that, didn't we?" I racked my brain. "They had to know. It's why they got questioned by us instead of the CPD."

"I'm pretty sure we told them, yeah," Reed said. "They leaned pretty hard on the 'His research is so complex' argument, though."

"Yeah," I said. "Now it kinda feels like it might be a smokescreen."

"You want to go back and talk to them again?" Reed asked.

"Well, I don't have a line on Graves, so—"

"What graves?" Reed asked, look of intense concentration on his face.

"Graves is the name of our perp," I said, realizing I hadn't told him. "I pulled it out of that thug's mind."

He made a face that expressed his disapproval for my mind-theft again. "Get anything else useful?"

"A pretty good recipe for guac."

"… Really?"

"No, not really. I wouldn't want to deprive our illicit casino manager of something useful, after all," I said, heading back through the alley where Graves had killed Dr. Jacobs, intent on catching a cab on State Street. "Now let's go shake a couple of lying college administrators and see what comes rattling out."

22.

We were halfway back to Northern Illinois Technical University, brainstorming ideas between the two of us for other avenues of investigation, Lake Michigan bursting with whitecaps to our right, when my phone rang, the screen lighting up with the name "Andrew Phillips" and a picture of a donkey.

Reed chuckled. "I don't think I've seen that before."

"J.J. taught me how to do it before he left to go work for that—whoever he took that job with," I said, answering the phone. I thought about ignoring it, but I needed to talk to his ass anyway. "Hee-haw."

"What?" Andrew Phillips's, gruff, nearly emotionless voice came through my speaker.

"I'm glad you called," I said, rushing right into what I wanted before he got snared up in chewing my ass, which I was sure was coming. An ass chewing my ass. The irony was not lost on me. "We've just had a couple run-ins with metahuman assassins that have been hired to kill us, so I need you to send Kat and Augustus down to Chicago right now to help me out."

I could almost hear him struggling to shift gears, his desire to just steamroll me over with his own agenda warring with the fact I'd just told him that someone was coming to kill one of his employees. "I can't do that," he said, apparently letting the seriousness of my concern win out.

"Sure you can," I said, "plane tickets to Chicago aren't that expensive and the flight's less than an hour. These assassins are serious and they're still at large. Get on it."

"I can't do that because Kat and Augustus are no longer with the agency," Phillips said, sounding annoyed. "Their paperwork has been processed and signed off on, and they're no longer federal employees. They turned in their weapons, phones and badges at the FBI building in Minneapolis earlier today."

"Well, then hire them back as contractors," I said, letting my need for assistance win out over my desire to just hang up on this twat.

"I can't do that," Phillips said. "I'm not unsympathetic to your problem—"

"Yes, you are," I said. "You are the very definition of unsympathetic. I just told you I've got assassins after me and you basically replied, 'Pound sand.'"

"I did not say that," Phillips replied, his voice strained. "If you need help, you're going to have to get it from the CPD or the FBI, because your team is already dissolved. There is nothing I can do to help you in that regard."

"Well, what the hell good are you, then?" I asked and hung up without further ado.

Reed looked at me with raised eyebrows. "Wow."

"It's my last week," I said with a shrug. "What's he going to do? Fire me? Give me a bad reference? Because I wasn't going to include him on my resume regardless. Now, back to what we were talking about before we were so rudely interrupted—"

"Dr. Jacobs doesn't have any family," Reed said, holding up his phone, which had text displayed on it. "Maclean forwarded me his info. No next of kin listed, and they found a will leaving everything to charities. Parents are long deceased. So it doesn't look like an inheritance bid."

"Okay, so we rule out family," I said, tapping my chin. "Not that I was considering them seriously anyway. Graves, when he looked at Jacobs—it was like he decided to kill him right there, at the casino. I don't think he was working for any outside sources, and I don't think he had anything we'd recognize as a real motive. It was very spur-of-the-moment."

"Killing in the heat of passion," Reed said, nodding. "But just for touching him? That's a little weird, even by our standards."

"It's weird, but it's not like it didn't happen again when that runner hit him at the beach," I said, shrugging. "Maybe this is Graves's MO."

"Because he doesn't like to be touched?" Reed's voice was skeptical. "That's ... well, that's weird."

"I get it," I said, "I don't like to be touched, either. At least not by strangers. Or most of the people I know." Reed looked at me funny. "It's a sensory thing," I said. "Like rough sheets or—"

"No, I was just thinking," he said, shaking his head like I'd misunderstood his look, "your touch does the killing for you if someone takes the liberty. Sorry, didn't have anything to do with the case."

"Yeah," I said, pursing my lips as another thought occurred to me. "You don't think Graves has that thing I do, do you?"

"Like he's an incubus?" Reed gave me a hard look. "Or that he's got a hair-trigger temper for people who piss him off?"

"Mine's not a 'hair trigger,'" I said, a little offended. "It's, uh ... like at least a ten-pound pull."

"Sure it is," he said, looking out at Lake Michigan's churning waters, the sky darkening as the sun sank behind the buildings on the western horizon.

"Whatever," I said, looking out my own window at the Gold Coast skyline. "I've got two assassins plus a murderer to deal with on my own. Whoopee."

"Hey," he said, snapping his head around and sounding like one of my souls.

"Oh, right, I forgot you and your 'mad skeelz.'" That one

drew a smile out of him as our cab continued up Lake Shore Drive for the umpteenth time that day, with what felt like no more answers than when we'd started this investigation.

23.

Veronika

Veronika was flat on her back in a hotel room off the Loop, a situation she cared for almost as little as she cared for television, which was playing in the background as a distraction from the pain that surged through her shoulder. She had been lucky inasmuch as she knew Nealon was a pretty damned good marksman, and the hit she'd suffered had been less than twelve inches from being fatal. Veronika had pulled the bullet out with no anesthesia save for the prattle of the evening news.

The bullet hadn't come out easily, but it had gone as well as it could considering she was performing surgery on herself. Now she was just lying there, waiting for her powerful healing to work. She'd estimated it'd take a little less than six hours for her shoulder to heal. She was in hour two, and it was still a steady, throbbing agony that reminded her she'd been digging a bullet out of her shoulder with her own fingers only an hour earlier.

Her phone rang, another welcome distraction, and a far better one than the early evening sitcom rerun that was yammering painfully on the edges of her consciousness. She didn't even own a TV—she found them aggravating at the best of times—but her phone was her link to the world. She picked it up with her unwounded hand, pressing it to her ear. "Hello?"

She'd taken the hard breath, the gasping one to get out the pain, before she answered.

"Ms. Acheron?" came the polite voice at the other end. She hadn't thought to check the caller ID, she'd been so grateful for a distraction. "This is Sunny Hills Nursing Facility and we're calling about your mother—"

"Yes," she said, sitting up and then remembering suddenly why she'd been lying down as the pain lanced through the muscles and tissue on her right side. She grimaced but did not cry out. "I'm sorry, yes, what's wrong?"

"Your mother seems to have taken a little bit of a downturn today," the woman on the other end of the line informed her.

"What are you talking about?" Veronika spoke slowly, in order to keep from screaming pain and aggravation into the phone. "I was just there a few hours ago and she was fine—"

"She seems to have contracted an infection," the woman said, clinically, as calm as if she were delivering news about a payment going missing. No, she would be more upset about that, Veronika decided. "Her temperature has spiked to 102."

"Okay," Veronika said, concentrating hard, tuning out the stupid TV. "So … what are you doing about it?"

"The doctor caught the infection on his rounds this afternoon," the woman said. "He's prescribed her an antibiotic, and she's being monitored closely. If the fever continues to rise, however, she'll need to be admitted to the hospital."

"Dammit." Veronika shut her eyes, the phone pressed against her ear.

"Ma'am, this is just a courtesy call …"

"Yes," Veronika said, opening her eyes again. "Thank you."

"You're welcome."

"And … please …"

"We'll be in touch if anything else changes," the woman's mechanical voice informed her. The sound of a click followed a few seconds later, and Veronika sagged back to the bed, clutching a bloody sheet and pressing it against her chest.

"I should be there," she said, to herself, breathless as she pulled what had been a clean section of the sheet only seconds earlier away from her shoulder. It was stained with crimson in a pattern roughly the size of a coffee cup bottom. She took in a breath of the hotel room's sterile air, with its hint of perfume that smelled like sandalwood, and looked at the clock.

Four hours to go until she was healed.

Then she needed to find Sienna Nealon, hopefully before Phinneus tracked her down again and collected on this contract. It wouldn't make her feel any better about not being there when her mother was sick, but adding the money to her account would at least help offset the medical bills that were as inevitable as blood on the sheet she'd put to her wound.

24.

Reed and I decided to start at the bottom, with our "dear friend," Dr. Art Gustafson, who had pledged to help us with his good pal Dr. Jacobs's murder. We ushered ourselves into his office to find the good doctor sitting behind his desk, eyebrows furrowed, working on a computer as we entered. He brightened almost as soon as we were in the door, looking up in mild surprise. "Oh, good, you're here," he said before I could angrily slap him with our new info, and he beckoned us to sit down in the padded chairs in front of his messy-as-hell desk.

Reed and exchanged a look that told each of us that the other planned to take the passive approach in this conversation. It seemed like a smarter move, because we could always switch to the aggressive approach later if we didn't like what Gustafson had to say. In fact, I was likely to switch to it even if I did like what Gustafson had to say, because, duh, it's me.

I dropped into my chair and draped my arms across the rests, staring at the doctor, who was back to paying attention to his screen. This was going to get old.

Reed cleared his throat. "Doctor, we've got some questions for you."

"Of course, of course," Gustafson said, holding up a single

115

finger. "Just ... one ..." He tapped the keyboard quickly a few times, and then turned his monitor sideways, knocking fifteen stacks of paperwork askew as he did so. "Okay, so I've got this for you."

I looked at the long, rectangular screen, which contained ... gibberish. "That's ... not going to help me." I looked at Reed, and he shook his head. Nope.

"Oh," Gustafson said, clearly deflated. "Damn. I spent the whole day on this, trying to boil down the key points of his research—"

"Maybe you could just explain it," I said. "You know ... for the laypeople we are."

"Well, that's what I was trying to do," Gustafson said, still looking a little dismayed. "So ... it starts with genetic markers, the things that make us who we are. Jacobs was examining a lot of different aspects of DNA and, uh ..." He seemed to lose himself for a moment. "Well, he looked into a lot of things. That's what separated him from the more ... specific ... no ... specialist ... scientists. Anyway, one of the things he'd been focusing on of late were the ... well, the differences between humans and metahumans at the genetic level."

"And you didn't think to mention this earlier today, when we came here and told you that Dr. Jacobs was murdered by a meta?" Reed asked, perfectly reasonable.

Gustafson blinked. "Well, to be fair ... Jacobs didn't just work on metahuman DNA. It's not like it was even his specific focus, it was just a ... a side avenue that's come up since the curtain was yanked up on your people a few years ago."

I cocked an eyebrow at him. "Beg pardon?"

"It's not his specialty," Gustafson said, looking at us earnestly. "It's something he included in his research because it's very topical and sexy, and he's a—well, he was a lightning rod for funding and attention for the university. Studying genetics, DNA, all that ... the things he does don't have immediate practical application, so he ... well, he played the game to spruce it up." Gustafson looked a little embarrassed.

"'Played the game'?" Reed asked, sounding a little more reasonable than I felt. "This is, he took advantage of the ... what, the media attention on metas, the political interest?"

"All the above," Gustafson said, face a little red. "An entire race of people that we didn't even know about in the wider scientific community until just a few short years ago? Talk about an embarrassment."

"Well, it was actively covered up," I said, not unsympathetic—unlike Andrew Phillips. "There were scientists studying the phenomenon, but it wasn't like they could publish in journals—"

"Right," Gustafson said, nodding, "like for example, this Dr. Ron Sessions, who I believe worked with you a few years ago ..."

I felt a tingle of surprise like someone had just run fingers lightly up the skin on my back, as if they'd hovered them just a few microns above my skin. "You know about Dr. Sessions?"

"Ah, yes," Gustafson said, nodding, adjusting his glasses as he did so. "I actually went to school with him, oh-so-many years ago." He smiled tightly.

"Not a friend, I hope?" I asked, watching his reaction.

"No, just an acquaintance at best." Gustafson shook his head. "He sort of fell off the earth after graduation. I had no idea what he was even working on until a few years ago, after the news broke, and some of the data from your, uh ... Directorate? After that came out in the FOIA requests."

I narrowed my eyes at him. I didn't know that anything about the old Directorate had been made public. "What are you talking about?"

"Some of Dr. Sessions' research was made available to the scientific community," Gustafson said, as though it were no big deal. "Nothing terribly groundbreaking, I'm afraid, but enough to give those of us who wished to study metahumans further—as Dr. Jacobs did—something of a foundation to work with."

I hated coincidences, but the fact was that with our entire race of metas reduced to a population of five hundred or so, crossover was a thing that happened frequently. Still, the idea that this doctor, this random murder victim killed by one of my people had been both killed by a meta and studying them?

Something about this reeked, and I didn't care for the smell of mystery.

"This is weird," I said, voicing my concerns.

"Yeah, something about this isn't tying off," Reed said, shaking his head.

"I guess I could understand if perhaps Carlton had been involved in any sort of active experimentation," Gustafson said, with his own aura of mystery, specifically in the befuddled look on his face, "but he was doing nothing, really, of any consequence. As I said, he threw the meta concept in mostly for show. Even his arguments with Dr. Stanley were more about the nature of human genetics in general than anything to do with metas in specific."

I frowned. I felt a compelling need to talk to this Dr. Stanley, especially since her name had come up several times in this investigation of Dr. Jacobs's career. "Where does Dr. Stanley work?" I asked.

"I just can't see Marabella having anything to do with this," Dr. Gustafson said, shaking his head. He looked at me with earnest eyes. "Are you sure this didn't have anything to do with Carlton's gambling?"

I exchanged a look with Reed. "We're examining all the possibilities," I said.

Gustafson shook his head and grabbed a sticky note pad. He wrote in scrawled handwriting across the top, something not terribly dissimilar from the chicken scratch I'd seen in Jacobs's apartment from his own hand. "She works for a competing university in the western suburbs."

"A little cross-town rivalry, huh?" Reed asked.

"Something like that," Gustafson said, pulling the top note off with a sucking sound of adhesive peeling away. He offered it to us between two ink-stained fingers. "I'll keep working on this, then." He looked at his computer and sighed.

"What's the matter, doc?" Reed asked, picking up the snarky stick for once. "All this translation stuff getting you down?"

"Like I said before," Gustafson looked at us over his glasses, one lens stained with a fingerprint, "I'll do what I can to help, whatever it takes." He sighed again, looking back at the computer monitor. "Some of this, though … it's a little beyond me." He gave hint of a shrug and turned his attention back to the computer. "Check in with me later, if you haven't solved this thing by then. Hopefully I'll have some more boring technical detail for you by then." And he settled back down to go to work.

"Cheer up," I said, taking the snark torch for myself, "you're an educator, after all." He looked up at me curiously until I delivered my punch line. "And what nobler calling could you imagine for yourself than educating a couple of knucklehead federal agents on the finer details of DNA science?"

Gustafson actually snickered with good humor as Reed and I headed out, off to try and figure out how to put together this puzzle that seemed about five hundred pieces short of completion.

25.

I'd been in a lot of cities, but Chicago's traffic was easily the worst I could recall. Of course, part of that might have been that I was seeing it from the backseat of the cab, but I'd recently experienced LA traffic and this seemed at least comparable if not worse. It made me glad we hadn't gotten a rental car, because Reed probably would have been swearing profusely after the last hour spent in gridlock on the westbound freeway.

"This is ridiculous," Reed muttered, glancing up from his smartphone to look at the gridlock in front of us.

"You've been here before," I said, keeping myself from nervously tapping a finger against the hand rest next to me. "Shouldn't you be used to this?"

He shook his head. "I don't think there's any such thing as getting used to this. I mean, we're not even over the river yet. I don't even think 290 starts for another mile or so." The cabbie shook his head, which I took to mean was him saying Reed was wrong, but my brother didn't notice and I didn't bother to point it out.

My phone rang, a welcome interruption from staring at the myriad cars locked in a holding pattern around me. I didn't think we'd moved in minutes, and I wasn't holding out hope that this situation was going to change anytime soon. I was so annoyed with the FAA right now. Not only was I presently costing the US government a fortune in cab fares, but I was stuck in traffic and wasting my precious time. I mean, for crying out loud, you'd think they'd be cool with the tradeoff—they don't have to pay for my plane tickets or ground transport, all they have to do is pick up a Chipotle burrito to replenish the calories I lose by flying myself (it's seriously a hard burn).

I looked at the screen and saw it was Detective Maclean calling. "Hello?"

"What the hell did you do?" Maclean launched right into it. I had a feeling he was that kind of guy.

"I assume vice called you, then?"

"This is why people don't like it when you come visit their cities," Maclean said, seething on the other side of the phone. "We've got six guys heading to a hospital from your little adventure at the casino."

"Hey," I said, a little defensively, "count yourself lucky they didn't end up at the morgue. They got kinda uppity with us."

"Ungh," he grunted. "I have a preliminary forensics report for you."

"From Jacobs?" I asked.

"No," he said, voice sounding a little strangled. I looked out my window across lanes and lanes of unmoving traffic, then turned to look out Reed's. I frowned. He had a view of the river beneath us, stretching out to the next bridge in the line. "From your hotel room, where our investigators are taking seriously an attempt to assassinate two federal agents. It's drawing resources from other cases."

"I'd feel guilty about that," I said airily, "but since I didn't hire assassins to kill myself in your city just to make your life miserable, I don't."

I could almost hear his eyes rolling, or maybe the steam coming out of his ears. "The bullets we pulled out of the wall and the couch were .44-40."

My whole face furrowed so hard it practically folded in on itself. ".44-40?" I asked, just to be sure I'd heard him right.

"Yeah," Maclean said. "I'd never heard of it, either."

"Oh, I've heard of it," I said. My mentor, Glen Parks, had introduced me to all sorts of guns and ammunition in an attempt to prepare me for whatever I ran across out in the world. His instruction had extended to weapons that were archaic and had fallen mostly into disuse. "It's a pistol round that was also used in old rifles—specifically the Winchester 1873. I mean, it was used in other guns, too, but that'd be the most well-known rifle—"

"What the hell are you, a catalog of historical guns and ammo?" Maclean asked in disbelief.

"Just doing my job," I said, thinking about the ammo used in the assassination attempt on me. Parks had had a Winchester 1873, and I'd shot it. He'd showed it to me with pride, after the other trainees—Scott and Kat—had left for the day. It was an old lever action rifle, the kind you'd see in a Western playing on a Sunday afternoon. It was a smooth, fun gun to shoot, but the pistol round meant it wasn't an ideal gun for a sniper. Rifle rounds could go miles. Pistol rounds couldn't travel nearly so far.

"We recovered the shells," Maclean went on, irritation still bleeding through as he spoke. "Early report indicates a probable match with the slugs we dug out of the wall. Shot distance was somewhere on the order of a hundred yards. Looks like thirteen rounds fired in total."

"The Winchester had a thirteen round capacity," I said, puzzling through the information presented. So not only was my sniper old-fashioned, but he was good. The fact that he was carrying a little piece of Americana and trying to kill me with it gave me an awful lot of conclusions I could jump to. That he was a guy who'd been around when the Winchester 1873 had been invented and he'd carried one since, or that he was weirdly attached to the past. Given that he was a meta, the former wasn't at all out of the realm of possibility. "Damn," I whispered, a little stumped. "I guess I'll keep my eyes peeled for a cowboy."

"You do that," Maclean said. "Do I even want to ask where

you're going to get into trouble next, or should I let it be a pleasant surprise?"

"I'm presently on 290 heading out of your jurisdiction," I said, staring out Reed's window at the river again. "But given the utter lack of speed with which I'm traveling, it may be a while before you're safe from my havoc."

"Uh huh," Maclean said. "What are you doing?"

"I'm going to talk to Dr. Marabella Stanley at the Institute of something or another out in Naperville," I said, "who evidently was something of a professional rival to Dr. Jacobs."

Maclean waited a second before replying, and I couldn't decide whether it took him that long to figure out what to say or if he was just keeping himself from saying something snotty. "Academic rivalry sounds like a mighty thin thread when it comes to motive."

"I've got a lot of nothing else," I said. "I mean, I've confirmed the vic met his killer at the gambling den, but that's about it."

"Wait, how did you confirm it?"

"Doesn't matter," I said. "But the killer's name is Graves. Pair that with the sketch I helped your guys at the beach make, and maybe you can get a hit in an FBI database?"

"I'll work on it," Maclean said, and I could hear him jotting furiously. "I'm getting a preliminary report on the second vic put together right now. I suspect it'll be done before you return from suburbia."

"Cool," I said, glancing once more at the dull blue waters out Reed's window. The darkening grey sky was not doing the river any favors, making it look pretty grim. "Maybe we if we can establish a link between that runner guy and Dr. Jacobs, we can ..." I shrugged, even though Maclean obviously couldn't see it. "I dunno. I'm starting to suspect this Graves might just be into random acts of violence on people who cross his path."

"Well, stop by after you get back and we'll hammer through this dossier my uniforms are compiling," Maclean said. "Safe travels."

"Thanks," I said, and hung up. The lack of movement felt stifling, even though the car was actually a little cool. I looked out my window again. There was still no motion.

"Maclean thinks there might be a link between Jacobs and the guy Graves killed at Oak Street Beach?" Reed looked up from his phone to ask the question.

"He doesn't know," I said. "Did you catch that bit about the ammo our assassin used?"

"I did," Reed said. "So we're looking for an old-time, dimestore cowboy?"

"Or something," I said, and something buzzed past my window so fast that it shook the car as it zoomed by. I started, nearly jumping out of my seat, the seatbelt jerking into action and yanking me back down. "What the hell?"

Reed snickered. "I think it was a moped."

"This isn't Europe," I said, now more than a little annoyed myself. "That's not allowed."

"Why don't you go give him a ticket, traffic cop?" Reed asked, clearly enjoying himself.

"Why don't I just give you a—"

Sienna, Wolfe screamed into my mind, *that was no moped!*

The tiny hairs along the back of my neck prickled up as if someone had run an electric current down them. I looked out the window again, staring into a small gap between a truck and car just outside. I could see other vehicles on the other side of them, and the river across the nearly empty lane of traffic heading into the city. "What was it?" I said under my breath.

"What was what?" Reed asked the back of my head.

I didn't get my answer in time, not nearly in time. A flash of green and grey shot through the gap between the truck and car next to us and slammed into the door of the cab, smashing it in like we'd just gotten T-boned. My window exploded, showering me in safety glass. The whole world jerked around me and we smashed through the guardrail and across the three feet of sidewalk, the back end of the taxi sliding first. It struck the bridge rail and kept going, the force of impact and the cab's weight combining to drag us over the edge and down to the river below.

26.

Colin

Colin Fannon was not the patient sort, and he'd discovered it early on. When it came to getting things done, sooner was always better. Hesitation was not only his enemy, but lingering about with a task unfinished was just about the worst thing he could imagine. He was the easily agitated sort, too, not that he'd admit it.

He'd run from Seattle to Chicago after he'd gotten the call. He'd done it at a leisurely jog—for him, anyway—pacing himself somewhere around five hundred and fifty miles an hour. He'd stuck to the major highways, stopping a couple times to enjoy the endless vistas but getting bored in the dull flatlands of the Dakotas. He appreciated nature, but he appreciated the boring parts more from a distance.

He had other irons in the fire, of course. He was the sort that found himself deeply bothered by societal injustices, and he used his powers to rectify as many as he could in his off time. That was the nice thing about this job, though, was that it allowed for a lot of—in his view—do-gooding for a profit.

Take this task, for instance. Sienna Nealon was known the world over for being a self-righteous fist of the US government, a probably unthinking cog in the machine that reinforced oppression and structural inequality. That made her a useful idiot of the establishment at best and the enemy at worst. Therefore, killing her was practically a public service on his part.

And he got paid. That was useful, too.

He'd buzzed her taxi cab once just to be sure it was her in there. It hadn't taken but one pass to confirm that. So then he'd looped around and figured, why not take advantage of the fact her cab was perfectly positioned to enjoy a watery grave? It wasn't likely to kill her, sure, but it wasn't likely to harm his chances, either. Water would slow him down, but it'd slow her more. He'd find it annoying, the resistance of water.

She'd find it impossible to work around. It'd destroy her ability to shoot a gun or burn him out with her fire power. That was a hell of an equalizer in his view.

The cab hit the water and rolled over onto its top. He could hear the river flooding in through the side windows he'd broken when he hit it, carefully aiming himself at the back door, at her. He didn't want to hurt the driver, after all. That guy was a working man, just a poor Joe doing his job. A Henry, actually. He'd seen it on the man's ID as he ripped him out of his own door before the cab had gone over the bridge.

"Wh … what just happened?" Henry asked, standing in the middle of farthest lane of the bridge, where his cab had been only a moment earlier. The car behind him honked for Henry to get the hell out of his way. Colin thrust a bird at the honking car. Where was this asshole's compassion for his fellow man?

Colin had already almost forgotten Henry, disoriented, standing in the lane of traffic. That was the danger of moving fast, thinking fast. "Your car just went over," Colin said, pointing down into the water. "Looks like you made it out in time."

Henry blinked, looking around, shell-shocked. That happened sometimes when Colin moved someone faster than their senses could explain what happened. "I … there were people in my cab." He had a thick accent, sounded Caribbean.

"Oh, yeah," Colin said with a nod, "I'll see if I can save 'em. You wait here." He couldn't have the cabbie following him, after all.

Colin leapt into the river. The jump was annoying, because he couldn't move faster than his momentum carried him, and he hadn't taken a running start. It took a couple seconds for him to hit the water. It took a quarter-second for him to get his bearings, to see through the dim water to the cab, sinking its way toward the riverbed. There was a lot of garbage down there, and it turned Colin's stomach to see it. With a jolt, he realized he'd just caused an oil-and-gasoline filled vehicle to end up down here as well—he'd created his own personal ecological contamination because he'd acted quickly, without fully considering the consequences of his actions. Well, he'd clean it up as soon as he got done. Hauling the car out of the river wouldn't be too hard, and running down the oil and gas leakage shouldn't be too hard for someone with his speed. It'd take a little time, but he could spare it.

After he killed Sienna Nealon.

27.

Sienna

Man, this was not my day.

Cold river water rushed in through my broken window, shocking the hell out of me even though I'd known it was coming. It iced my flesh, my nerves screaming from the frigid chill. "This way!" I shouted to Reed as I ripped my seatbelt off before the water could completely surround it. The cab started sinking very quickly, and I paused before preparing to swim out the window, casting a last look back at Reed to make sure he was following me.

He wasn't.

His neck was limp, his head slumped against the side of the cab. I looked for his seatbelt. It wasn't fastened.

I grabbed him by the arm, clenching my chilled fingers around his sleeve and yanked him toward me as the water poured into the cab, now at face level. His eyes didn't even flutter, he was so out of it. I pulled his head back so he could take a breath, then ripped him out of the cab as fast as I could, swimming clear of my window against the force of the water rushing in, and then tugged him out, my feet perched on the dented-in door.

Man, I hoped the cab company didn't make me pay for this wreck.

I freed Reed from the cab and readjusted him in my grip. I

could see the hint of the grey skies above as the cab continued toward the bottom of the river. I'd been inverted, upside-down, but I'd found my bearings again, the hint of light streaming from the surface tipping me off as to which way I should swim.

Then something hit me in the back, hard, and I tasted blood.

Speedster, Wolfe had whispered in the seconds between when we went off the bridge and when the cab had hit the water. Those were the seconds when most people would have been screaming, but I was too busy bracing myself and wondering where the hell the cab driver had disappeared to, because he sure as hell wasn't in the vehicle anymore.

You mean like Akiyama or Weissman? I asked Wolfe.

No, he said. *They played with time itself. This is a meta who simply goes* fast.

Great. Figures I'd get the evil Barry Allen up my ass at a time when I already had Graves, the Dimestore Cowboy and Veronika on my tail. (I had no insulting nickname for Veronika, because truthfully, I had a feeling that if she hadn't been hired to kill me, we might have been BFFs.)

My back spasmed in pain. Someone had hit me in the lower ribs on the right side, breaking at least two, if not three of them. It had been done quickly, and with full intention, I knew as I felt those bones push inward and clip the bottom of my lung.

Wolfe! I screamed in my head and sensed his assent as he went to work trying to fix the problem.

I spun, Reed clutched under my right arm and preventing me from using my hand to shoot a net blindly on that side, my left arm working feverishly to move me around, along with my legs. I wasn't that good a swimmer, having not left my house until I was seventeen. Kinda hard to learn to swim in the bathtub. I basically used my considerable strength to flail enough to get the job done, but it was not pretty or efficient.

My flight power will help you, Gavrikov said, and I sensed the ability surging through me, preventing me from sinking further. I spun with the power, doing a zero-radius turn without needing to splash around to achieve it.

A blur moved through the water, slower than the one that had buzzed and hit the taxi cab. I still had Reed under my arm, and both he and I desperately needed air. My brother was still limp in my grasp, and I had a speedster planning to kill me. The speedster turned in the water, looping around, his limbs moving impossibly fast, and came at me again, dodging and veering so fast I couldn't have hit him with a net if I'd tried.

Guns were out.

Fire was out.

Nets were out.

Strength was useless until he got closer, and he'd probably dodge whatever punch or kick I could throw at him.

I turned my body so that it was between the speedster and Reed, and I took another crushing hit, this time to the left arm and side. He hit me so hard my breath left me, eight ribs shattered like I'd been flattened by a battering ram and my arm was rendered useless in an instant.

Wolfe!

It will take several seconds to heal, Wolfe said, and I could hear the panic.

We don't have seconds, I said as the speedster turned to come back again, my good arm still holding my brother and my left immobile and nowhere near fast enough to catch my foe before he pounded me into stuffing.

He came at me again, like a shark but much faster, and all I could do was watch helplessly as the last of my air left me and the assassin bore down, ready to finish me—and my brother—for good.

28.

Colin

Colin could smell the triumph. She could heal fast, but not as fast as he could come back around and deal some more damage. Truth was, she was fighting a losing battle with one hand virtually tied behind her back since she was holding her brother in it. Even if she'd dropped him, though, Colin wasn't optimistic about her chances. Nets wouldn't stop him; he'd faced those faerie lights before and burst right through them with a concentrated shake of his speed.

Her gun was useless, and none of her powers were working for her. What was the best word to describe her in this state?

Oh, right: helpless.

Colin scissored his legs hard, coming around again for another pass, and saw the last of the bubbles leave Sienna Nealon's mouth as she started to choke. Now she was drowning, and that'd make this all the easier, like a spiral down to death. She couldn't fight without air, and the weaker she got, the more he'd hit her. A vicious circle that'd carry her body all the way to the bottom of the river.

He surged toward her, eager to finish the thing. Maybe he'd even make it home in time for dinner.

29.

Sienna

The last of my air left me without a ton of options. I tried to move, using Gavrikov's flight, but it was slow, the water resistance keeping me from steering very fast. The speedster was coming right for me, and I was twenty yards from the surface and already badly wounded.

I wasn't going to make it in time. I knew it, he knew it, and I could see the smile on his squarish face even through the cloud of bubbles separating us.

Perhaps I can be of assistance, Bastian said, pushing himself to the front of my mind.

Unless you've got some wicked good tactical advice for an underwater battle, Roberto, I said in my mind with an aura of panic, *I don't think you're going to be of much use right n—*

Oh.

Yeah, he said. *It's time.*

I drew upon the power of Roberto Bastian, something I hadn't done in years. It wasn't a pretty thing, what Bastian could do, which was why I'd only used it once.

It was, however, a perfect time to try, I thought, as my clothing shredded and my skin turned hard and scaly.

The speedster hit me a second into the transformation, and while I still felt it and it still hurt, it was nothing like what he'd done moments earlier to my unguarded skin. He smashed

133

against me and rolled off, swimming away for another pass. I'd seen his wide eyes before he turned, though. They were about all I could pick out of his blur of a face.

He was startled, to say the least.

My body distorted, lengthening, my legs joining together into a tail, my neck stretching like a snake and my face and jaw widening. My arms lengthened and turned flat, growing greenish-blue under the tint of the water. I kept my right carefully wrapped around Reed and left Gavrikov up front in my mind with Bastian and Wolfe, pooling my powers so I could use them all at once. The transformation took seconds, seconds in which the speedster churned water in front of me, hurrying to attack again before I could finish.

He didn't.

I burst out of the water using Gavrikov's flight power rather than my own wings, one of which was busy keeping Reed from drifting down to the bottom of the river. It must have been quite a sight, a sixty-foot-long, snake-like dragon with wings shooting out of the Chicago River during rush hour. I took a breath and roared, blasting into the sky and skimming the bottom of the bridge as I rose, the hard concrete and metal scraping against my scaly skin.

Screw the FAA, I thought, leaving the traffic and the river behind. I also left behind the speedster, my gun, my cell phone and my wallet. My toiletries, too, though the likelihood that I was ever going to use a toothbrush that had been submerged in the river was less than zero. I was disappointed that I'd lost Shadow, though. I loved that gun, and it wasn't exactly a common weapon.

Water streamed off my back as I headed west, my tail dangling behind me. I let it roll a little, slithering in the air. This was the way to do it, I reflected as I soared over the city, heading west. I let the sky carry me away from the assassin, away from the skyline, and hopefully away from the troubles that were dogging me, at least for a little while.

30.

Colin

Colin watched Sienna Nealon shoot out of the water before he could so much as land another hit, and he cursed himself for his foolishness. He'd forgotten about that dragon power, probably because she hadn't used the damned thing since that first video had revealed her to the world. Out of sight, out of mind and all that, and it had been out of sight for a damned long time.

He swam back around, breaking the surface for a quick breath. He looked up and caught sight of her soaring west, her long, blue tail dangling behind her. It was kind of majestic, really, at least as majestic as watching a snake with wings defying gravity could get.

He sighed, and water burbled between his lips. He wanted to chase after her immediately, but his sense of social responsibility held him back. The cab was, after all, surely leaking oil and gas by now, and right into the river. Gritting his teeth, he steeled himself to get to work on that. He'd catch up with Nealon again later, and this time he wouldn't screw it up and make a mess when he went to kill her. He'd just get the job done.

31.

Sienna

I squeezed Reed under my wing and he coughed, water dripping out of his mouth. His eyes fluttered and I watched him, turning my head sideways on my long neck to observe him. I wanted to make sure he was okay, of course.

He opened his eyes and saw me, and I immediately realized that I'd made a tactical error.

"Holy sh—!" he screamed as he came back to consciousness tucked under the wing of a giant dragon flying over west Chicago. My wing was scaly and slimy from being underwater, and he was wearing wet clothes and had meta powers, so he promptly slid out of my grasp, blowing wet air all around as he did so.

He dropped out of the sky, flailing his arms as he fell. I darted around like I was chasing my own tail, trying to catch him. I went into a hard dive, using Gavrikov's flight power to execute, and pushed my wings back as I did so.

He plummeted toward the earth, now only a few hundred yards from the ground, twisting and spiraling as he fell. I came right after him. He was probably already at terminal velocity, I judged, which meant he wasn't getting any faster. I, though, came with flight abilities that allowed me to exceed 187 miles per hour.

I was about to catch him, only a hundred feet from the

earth, when he pointed both hands down and started spraying air out of his feet. His shoes blew off in an instant and his socks shredded like my clothes had when I'd gone dragon mode. He looked up at me as I zoomed toward him and gave me a look that was irritated rather than furious. "What are you doing, Sienna?"

"Trying to save you?" I asked, the natural menace in my throaty dragon voice somewhat undermined by hesitation.

"I'm fine," he said, floating to a halt a foot above the ground, using his hands to stabilize his flight. He settled on the earth like he was stepping gently off a curb to cross a street.

"I—" I started to say, still a couple hundred feet up, but the roar of a jet engine drowned me out. I turned my head a hundred and eighty degrees to see a commuter jet with a Delta logo on the tail fin making an abrupt and ugly turn. I looked in the opposite direction and saw runways a few miles off. "Oops," I said.

"That's why the FAA doesn't want us flying," Reed yelled up at me.

Dammit.

32.

I spent the next twenty minutes coiled up behind a mini-mall in suburbia as Reed went and bought me new clothes and shoes. Fortunately my scales kept me warm as I lay on the cold pavement. A car came around the corner once and saw me draped in a giant mass at the rear of the mall. I lifted my head to look and let my forked tongue slide out to hiss at them. Needless to say, they hit reverse and peeled out, never to return.

Reed came back with an armful of stuff in a plastic shopping bag. He was still dripping, his hair plastered in an unflattering way across his scalp. He nodded toward a stand of bushes nearby and I floated toward them, shrinking back into human form and diving behind them for cover as my scales turned into naked skin.

"Here you go, Eve," he said, and tossed me the bag. "Women are not easy to shop for, by the way."

"I told you I don't care what you got me," I said, tugging on a t-shirt first on the assumption that if the cops came wheeling up to investigate reports of a giant snake menacing shoppers, it'd be more workable to tug the tail of the shirt down to cover myself than to try and do so by tugging up on an underwear waistband. Priorities, people. I tore into a three pack of cotton panties that wouldn't have looked out of place on a grandma and held up one of them so Reed could see it. "Okay, I'm revising that. Really?"

"It was cheap," Reed muttered, glancing at me, clearly trying desperately to give me some small measure of privacy even as he nervously watched the road. "Hurry up. I want to go get replacement phones so we can call an Uber."

"A what?" I halted, my granny panties halfway on. I shivered in the cold April air. The midwest clung stubbornly to winter, breaking only occasionally for breaths of spring. I didn't find it at all reassuring that Chicago was just as schizophrenic as Minneapolis in this regard.

"Uber," he said, kicking at the pavement, scuffing his shoes and causing dust to cling to their leathery black surface. "It's this whole new thing replacing cabs."

"Why couldn't we just get a cab?"

"Stop being such a stick in the mud."

"Listen, brother o' mine, there's only one of us who almost became a stick in the mud, as in river bottom mud, and it wasn't me, okay?" By now I was floating my way into my too-tight jeans and hoping he'd gotten me shoes that fit.

"I'd be more excited if we hadn't gotten dumped in the Chicago River to begin with. Why does this shit always happen to you?"

"Like you're blameless. I seem to remember Phillips being pissed off about having to try and settle with some Chinese buffet you tore up in the north metro during your manhunt for Anselmo Serafini—"

"Fine, whatever," he said, trying to shut off the conversation before I went and hammered him with any of his own countless acts of destruction. "Just get dressed and let's get our phones."

"No time," I said, pointing to the darkening skies. "We need to talk to Dr. Stanley before she leaves for the night, remember?"

Reed sighed, a deep, rumbling noise of discontent. "How do you know she hasn't already?"

"Because I called and made an appointment under a fake name," I said, trying to force my wet feet into tight socks. A seam tore loudly. "Shit."

"Take it easy there," Reed said.

"Whatever, I've got like two more pairs of socks." I won the battle with the clinging cotton and then slipped on the shoes he'd bought me. There was at least half an inch at the toe, and the damned things had a heel on them. "Who were you shopping for? Your girlfriend?"

"I did the best I could," he snapped. "You threw like ten sizes at me—"

"Yes, one for each article of clothing—"

"Well, it's a lot to remember." He was red. "And, I, uh ... was in a hurry. It's awkward shopping for women's clothes."

I emerged from behind the bushes, wobbling on the shoes he'd gotten me. I wasn't going to be able to fight in these, not easily anyway. "Why?"

Wearing black dress pants with a yellow t-shirt, I teetered on my new shoes as I put on a cheap brown suede coat with no belt. They were just low enough to guarantee that if I had a tramp stamp at the base of my spine, the world would have seen it below my jacket. "Oops," Reed said mildly, looking me up and down once with a pained expression on his face.

"Yeah, I look like I've been dressed by a man," I said, putting my arms out. "A blind man. With no fashion sense. This is a new low, even for me."

He looked at my hair, and I saw a subtle grimace that told me everything about how I looked. "Yep," was all he dared to say.

"Let's go, you ass."

I could see the grin he didn't quite bother to hide out of the corner of my eye. "Sure you don't want to try and—"

"No." I hit a steady clip, walking with a little more care and with a little less steam than I normally would have, because of the shoes. "We need to question the doctor, and now. I want to get to the bottom of this case ..." I let my voice fade off dramatically then finished by muttering. "... so I can go home and dress myself in a manner that doesn't look like I've just raided a psychotic clown's wardrobe."

33.

Phinneus

Phinneus set up at his vantage point after having crept across the campus, hiding his weapons under his coat. The pistol was easy; the rifle took a little more work, but he pulled it off. Pretty soon he had a nice view through a big-ass window of an office building on a campus out in the suburbs.

He'd gotten the tipoff as he'd been pondering what to do next. He'd considered making calls to all the hotels frequented by government employees downtown, but he didn't want to do that. Not only was the success rate low (Nealon was unlikely to check in under her own name after an assassination attempt) but it'd involve sitting on the phone like one of those damned telemarketers for hours.

Yeah, getting this tipoff from the guy who'd hired him was way, way better, even if he might have to deal with a little competition in the process.

Plus, now he had a side job to complete.

But for the moment he was just sitting, watching the window a few hundred feet away, seeing the mousy little doctor lady behind the desk pecking away at her keyboard. If the man who'd hired him was right, Sienna Nealon would show her pretty face here in just a few short minutes. Phinneus looked over the iron sights of his Winchester and took a deep breath. Now there was nothing to do but wait.

34.

Sienna

"I still say we should have gotten phones and Ubered it over here," my brother groused as we stepped out of the cab at the campus where Marabella Stanley worked, me still in my clown clothes and him still dripping slightly.

"Stick with the classics," I said as he collected his credit card from the cabbie.

"You are the very enemy of progress," Reed said as the cab headed off down the tree-lined drive and we headed up into the administration building. "You're like an angry old man ranting about how that newfangled television thing is ruining the world."

"It does rot the brains of you whippersnappers," I agreed as I opened the door for him. He frowned and went inside.

After getting assistance from a weary-looking undergraduate who seemed like he had better things to do, we headed on a short walk across campus toward the science building, a flimsy little visitors' map in hand. The campus was lovely, if a little chilly, and Reed was shuddering by the time we'd reached the science building and climbed the three floors to Marabella Stanley's office.

It wasn't difficult to find, being clearly marked and all that. The frosted glass-paned door was propped open to the outer office when we got there, revealing that Dr. Stanley shared a

142

receptionist with about six or seven other professors. The waiting area was clean and carefully maintained, suggesting that either janitorial was on top of things in this building or the receptionist was some sort of neatnik. I looked at the desk and saw not a paperclip out of place. A nameplate with "Stephanie Bruszek" written in white lettering was perfectly squared off, equidistant from each of the sides of the desk, giving me my answer.

Reed led the way to the lone office with the lights still on, a frosted glass window with Dr. Stanley's name printed on it in gold letters telling us we might just be in luck. He rapped lightly on the glass. I let him because I still had a tendency to break windows by accident.

"Come in," Dr. Stanley said in a brusque tone, and Reed opened the door and stepped in. I followed him a moment later and caught her frown as she took us both in with a glance. He, still dripping slightly and shivering, and me dressed like an idiot and wobbling on these heels. "Oh my," she said. It fit.

"Dr. Stanley?" I asked, wishing I had my badge to flip out. I was going to surrender it in less than a week anyway, and everyone knew who I was by now, hopefully. "I'm Sienna Nealon. This is Reed Treston—"

"Yes, I know who you are," she said, and I sensed a pinch of nervousness in her reply. She didn't ask us to sit down, she just sat in her chair, suddenly looking like she wanted to crawl out the window onto the darkening campus.

Marabella Stanley was a larger woman. Her plus-size blazer was draped over the back of her chair, her pale arms, made visible by her sleeveless maroon blouse, showed more than a hint of loose skin on her upper arms. Her auburn hair looked like it fell past her shoulders a few inches, she had a very classy looking gold chain around her neck, and she was certainly dressed in a much more flattering manner than yours truly, even on my best days. She had one mole just above her left eyebrow, and a bead of sweat positioned opposite it on her right eyebrow.

She also looked like she'd rather be anywhere else at the moment, maybe including at the bottom of the Chicago River. I wouldn't recommend it, personally, but that was the kind of nervous she looked.

"We've got a few questions for you, Dr. Stanley," I said, lingering at the door. I was polite enough not to just barge into someone's office, after all.

"What about?" she asked, and her voice was just about taut enough to break a vocal cord.

Reed and I traded a look. Was this just nerves at having us show up unexpectedly? Or was it something else? Something like ... guilt?

I took another step inside her office. She was right in front of us, the streetlamps shining into her office's windows behind us. The door blocked me from a full view of the campus out her window, but I could see movement out there, just past the door hanging open, as students wandered around on the concrete pathways below, presumably on their way to evening classes.

I focused my attention back on Dr. Stanley as Reed took up the interrogation with the obvious question. "Is there some reason you're breaking out in a sweat right now, Doctor?" Reed asked, walking slowly across the office to stand at the other side, against the overstuffed bookshelves that ran between her desk and the windows.

"No," she said, the only person in the room who couldn't see how obviously she was lying.

35.

Phinneus

Dr. Stanley was talking to Sienna Nealon and her brother, and it was obvious to Phinneus even a building away that whatever she was saying, she was lying through her teeth. It was written all over her face, which was breaking out in a flop sweat of the sort Phinneus hadn't seen since his days of sitting in ratty old wooden casinos out on the Western frontier with a shot of whiskey in his hand and his Colt Peacemaker still warm in his belt from the killing he'd done.

He could just see Nealon's shoulder through the window. The office door was between her and him, in addition to the glass window of Stanley's office. It wasn't an optimal shot, but if he wanted to start a fight and not necessarily finish it with one bullet, this might be the way to go about it.

Naw, he decided, there were others on the job now. As much as he wanted to have a real shootout with this girl, there were others involved at this point. He'd heard it was Veronika Acheron, that cold-blooded bitch, and Colin Fannon, that damned sprout-loving hippie. However badly Phinneus wanted a solid fight, a real shooting match, he didn't want it badly enough to let either one of those Johnny-Come-Latelies pull the contract right out of his hands.

"Bad luck, girlie," he whispered over the open sights. This time he wouldn't miss.

36.

Sienna

Reed turned his head to look out the window to my left about two seconds before it shattered. His hand was already up when it burst, and a gust of wind shoved me like someone had grabbed me and flung me out of the room, slamming the door to Marabella Stanley's office behind me. The frosted glass window with her name on it burst into a million pieces and showered down on me courtesy of Reed's wind, causing a dozen superficial cuts.

"The hell!" I yelled at him, even as my brain started processing what had just happened. That window I'd been standing in front of had broken, and a crack had sounded over the roar of his wind blast.

Dimestore Cowboy had just tried to kill me. Again.

"You okay?" Reed called from inside Dr. Stanley's office. I could tell from his voice that he was on the floor, hiding with the brick wall between him and the shooter. So was I, for that matter, flat on my back in the reception area, a window above me with the blinds shut.

"Fine," I said, rolling to my feet and crouching beneath the window. I didn't have Shadow, thanks to speedster dropping me into the river, and my desire to return fire was rising by the moment. I'd seen a building not a hundred feet away out Dr. Stanley's window, a perfect perch for a sniper. Clearly,

Dimestore Cowboy had either been waiting for us or he'd set up remarkably quickly for his shot. I suspected the former.

"What now?" Reed called through the broken door. "My gun's all wet, and, uh—"

"You're not that good with it anyway," I finished for him.

"Hey, I'm all right with it—"

Something sparked in my head about our situation. We were under fire—

… under fire …

I grinned in what could only be described as a feral manner as I decided on my next move. I readied both my hands and called out in my mind. *Eve, Gavrikov …* I felt them respond, putting themselves at my disposal.

"What are you doing?" Reed asked, probably getting the hint from my silence that bad things were about to unfold.

I made little play guns out of both hands, index fingers up, the rest of my fingers knuckled into a fist, just like the kids get expelled from school for doing nowadays. "Nothing," I said innocently.

Then I fired a net of light from my left hand as I spun away from the wall. It hit the solid white blinds and jarred them, jangling them—

Giving Dimestore Cowboy motion for a target.

The return fire from him was immediate, and by the sound, as well as the holes in the blinds caused by my net of light bunching up the vinyl to form cracks, I knew exactly where he was as I crouched, peeking up with my right finger extended.

I opened fire with a concentrated burst of Gavrikov's power, a sizzling blast of superheated air the size of a bullet that punched through the glass in front of me, heading right for Dimestore Cowboy on the rooftop opposite us.

37.

Phinneus

He'd been a little too itchy on the trigger, he decided after he landed a solid shot in that glowing spot in the blinds. The first miss had been honest, after all; her damned brother had gone and blown Sienna out of the room as he'd shot. He didn't usually miss, but this wasn't a circumstance under his control. He chalked it up to an oops and moved on.

The second shot, though, that had been a little clever bit of red cape twirling on Nealon's part. She'd put it out there, whipped and twirled it right before his eyes, jetting out one of those nets of light into the blinds, and he'd shot before he thought, putting a round right through the middle of the anomalous-looking shape without waiting to see if it resolved into a person shape.

Whoops, twice. Probably a mark of his eagerness to get this job done. He'd already accidentally finished the side job, after all.

The first burst of fiery heat hit the knee-high brick wall that encircled the rooftop, right in front of his damned face. It didn't take him more than a second to realize what it was, because it made a hot, hissing noise when it smacked the brick, and glowing shards of superheated clay and mortar burst everywhere.

She didn't stop with one shot, either. That damned girl

blasted his position with a good half-dozen bursts of concentrated heat. It burned the air, singeing Phinneus's mustache and beard, filling his nose with a smoky smell. He squinted his eyes shut, but too late. Chunks of hot brick had already got him, burning his eyes, burning his face.

Phinneus fell to his side and hissed through gritted teeth. It burned like hell, like sin, and he pawed at himself in panic, dropping the Winchester, rolling to the side as fast as he could manage, hoping that the cover provided by the brick lip of roof would keep her from drawing a bead on him and peppering him with more of that hell.

Phinneus could feel the burned skin, and knew blisters would be rising pretty quick. He could barely open his eyes, pulling the lids apart only enough to see a hazy sky above him—and he knew the haze had nothing to do with the sky and everything to do with the damage Nealon had just done to his face.

Dammit, she'd near-blinded him, at least for a little while.

More shots demolished the brick in front of the vantage he'd been occupying only moments earlier with a hard, cracking, hissing sound, and Phinneus didn't really want to chance going back over there, not even for the Winchester.

Shit.

It was a little bit of a tug-of-war between his rifle or his life, and he knew which one he valued more. It hurt powerfully, though, the thought of leaving that beauty behind for the cops to lay their grubby, unappreciative hands on. Still, the choice was clear to him even through his clouded eyes, and he looked for the door to the stairs and started crawling on his belly toward it, pride as forgotten for the moment as the thought of killing Sienna Nealon. He'd get back to both, though, and real soon. That was for sure.

38.

Sienna

I probably went a little overboard shooting at the brick that ringed the top of the building across the way, but I didn't want to take any more chances than I had to that our sniper would get away to menace me again later. I didn't know that I was having any luck at it, but I was damned sure trying to spatter his position with enough literal fire to keep him from returning his lead-filled version of it my way.

I stopped after about five minutes, having demolished a good ten-foot section of the rooftop barrier. The brick all around it was smoking, my efforts creating a wicked, compact, outdoor version of a kiln to glass the edges. They glinted in the lamplight, revealing a bare section of rooftop, bereft of human occupancy.

"You think he ran?" Reed asked, shouting at me from inside Dr. Stanley's office.

"Like a rabbit and without a single look back, if he's smart," I shouted back, crouched under as much cover as I could beneath the now heat-shattered window in the receptionist's office. Man, Stephanie Bruszek was going to be pissed when she got to work tomorrow.

"Anyone there?" a voice called out from the roof that Dimestore Cowboy had presumably been standing moments earlier. The voice sounded youthful, tentative, and understandably nervous.

"My name is Sienna Nealon and I'm a federal agent," I called out the window. "Who are you?"

"Uhh … Greg Strucker with campus security," came the voice in reply. "Are … are you really Sienna Nealon?"

"Step up to the edge, Greg," I called back, and he did, very hesitantly, step out where I could see him. He was probably in his late twenties, big glasses, a few extra pounds. He had a Taser gun gripped in his hands, and he was peering across the void at me.

I stood up, staring out at him through the massive hole I'd burned in the blinds and the window. It was like looking out a small tunnel. "You see anyone else over there, Greg?"

He looked around, pausing at the damage to the roof's edge. "Gahhhh," he said, his neck falling limply down in surprise, his glasses going straight to the end of his nose. He caught them with one hand. "Oh, man. That's …"

"Stay with me here, Greg," I said. "No one's on the roof with you?" I could see his campus security uniform, and there was no sign of a gun anywhere on it, not even under his canvas coat with the fuzzy interior that stuck out on his lapels and collar.

"No," he said, turning around in a complete circle. "There's a gun here, though." He peered down at the last few inches of surviving brick where Dimestore Cowboy had been crouched. I'd only destroyed it far enough down to be sure that no one was hiding there, I hadn't leveled it all the way to the roof. "Old one, with wood … uh, handles and stuff."

"It's called furniture, Greg," I said, stepping over to Dr. Stanley's office and pulling open the door. Reed was crouched down in the far corner in front of me, his Glock 17 in hand. Even after all the practice we'd done, he still looked uncomfortable being in the same zip code with it, let alone holding it. I started to step up onto the broken window's ledge, but a girlish scream from across the way stopped me.

"What the—" Greg cried. "Dr. Stanley!"

I turned, one foot already up on the glass-covered ledge, and saw what had caused the campus security man to cry out. Dr. Marabella Stanley sat in her chair, arms hanging limply over the sides, her maroon blouse now crimson red just above her left breast, her face slack and pale, guaranteed not to answer a damned single question now that she was dead.

39.

"As far as last weeks on a job go, this one has to be a record-breaker of some sort," Reed opined after we'd given our statements to the Naperville PD.

"I feel like it deserves a superlative," I agreed. "'Most Sucktacular,' maybe?"

"That's a winner," he said with a nod.

We were standing outside the crime scene because there was no reason to stay in the thick of it. Neither one of us were forensic pathologists, after all, though the paramedics were already carting Dr. Stanley off in a black bag, the gurney rattling as it took up her weight. We'd positioned ourselves in Stephanie Bruszek's reception area, figuring it was already good and shot to hell, and that it was unlikely that just by lingering on the couches in the corner we'd do any damage to the one piece of evidence in the place. It was the bullet Dimestore Cowboy had shot at my light net, and it was in the far wall, having torn through Stephanie Bruszek's copy of an Ansel Adams photo. Personally, I hoped she would invest in a nice Chagall print to take its place, but based on what I was seeing of her workspace, I doubted it would fit with her personality.

"So, we've got another dead end," Reed said, like I didn't already know that.

"Yes," I said simply, since I had pretty much nothing to say to elaborate on that obvious fact.

"So …" Reed said, "… what do we do now?"

"Well," I said, "it seems to me someone set us up here."

He frowned, then the furrow in his brow lightened as he got it. "Dimestore Cowboy was waiting for us."

I winked at him and made a clicking noise with my tongue. "You got it. Who knew we were coming here and has a severe irritation with us at the moment?"

"Detective Maclean?" Reed asked. Now he was back to frowning. "I don't know about that."

"He also knew where we were when the speedster assassin attacked," I said.

Reed shifted uncomfortably in his chair. "Say … you don't think the speedster is waiting out there, do you?" He paused. "Also, we should probably come up with a name for him."

"I didn't see him, otherwise I'd be all over it," I said. "But between him, Dimestore Cowboy and Veronika—"

"Wait," Reed said, "is Veronika the one that smacked you around the casino?"

I stared at him with a look of lead-melting intensity before I answered. "Yes."

"Three assassins after us," Reed said, not looking too thrilled. I couldn't blame him. "Yay."

"After me," I corrected. "Dimestore Cowboy has passed up on the easy kill on you twice now. I think we can rule you out as a target."

He pursed his lips, eyes moving back and forth as he processed that. "I don't know whether to be grateful or insulted."

"You're alive. I'd just sort of be glad about that, personally." I took a deep breath. "Maclean was promising to talk to us about Graves's other victim before we headed out here."

"Dr. Stanley was looking awfully guilty about something before she caught a bullet to the chest," Reed said.

"You called this a dead end," I reminded him.

"Well, we should get some paddles and see if we can

resuscitate it," he said.

"That doesn't work," I said, shaking my head.

"I know it won't work," he said, like he was explaining things to an idiot. "I watched them work on her with the paddles for like ten minutes—"

"I was talking about your metaphor," I said, rolling my eyes. "You can't revive a dead end, it's an inanimate object, like a cul-de-sac. You'd need to make a new exit out of it, maybe go off-roading—"

"You've got three assassins after you but you take time to nitpick my metaphors?"

"Just because death is hounding my footsteps doesn't mean I'm going to pass up on opportunities to remind you that I'm smarter than you—"

He chortled at that. "As a younger sister should. Seriously, though—what do we do?"

"Well, try as he might, Gustafson didn't seem to be too helpful in shedding light on what Dr. Jacobs was up to," I said. "And he's still working on that, so I feel like asking him to decipher whatever the late Dr. Stanley was working on is just going to be more of the same sort of pain in my ass."

"So you're looking for a new type of pain in your ass?" Reed smirked. "We need another expert. They're dropping like flies." The paramedics rolled by with the gurney carrying Dr. Marabella Stanley's earthly remains. "You think Dimestore Cowboy killed her on purpose or was it an accident?"

"Accident," I said quickly. He looked at me funny, and I knew I wasn't going to get off that easy. I took a breath before explaining. "You blew me out of the room—"

He closed his eyes hard as he got it. "My gust sent his bullet off course."

"Ricocheted right into her, yeah," I said, trying to be as gentle as possible. The angle had been all wrong for Dimestore Cowboy if he'd been trying to plant Dr. Stanley on purpose. He'd definitely been aiming for me; she'd just been collateral damage, dragging whatever she'd been stonewalling us about with her into the grave.

"Shit," Reed said, putting his face in his palms.

"Don't worry about it," I said. "Worse things have happened."

He raised his face out of his hands to give me a look of disbelief. "Not to her!"

Well, he had a point.

"So what's our next move?" Reed asked, resignation settling over him.

"We find out who Dr. Stanley's closest colleague was and get them over here to answer some questions," I said, resolute, "and then after that, we go take Detective Maclean up on his invitation …" my face hardened, "… and ask him a few questions of our own about how these assassins keep figuring out where we're going."

40.

It turned out that Dr. Stanley's closest colleague actually lived in Milwaukee and commuted to Chicagoland only twice a week, on Tuesdays and Thursdays. The campus administrator, Jeffrey Parker, an obsequious man in wire-framed glasses and a tweed jacket, was incredibly apologetic about it, and gave us this Dr. Erin Hope's number and left a message for her that hadn't been returned by the time we were ready to leave the campus. He'd given her our numbers as well, of course, but as neither of us had a functional phone at present, it wasn't going to do us a hell of a lot of good.

"If she doesn't answer our message by tomorrow," Reed suggested as we were hiking out to catch a cab, "we could always drop by and surprise her."

"Or we could go to Milwaukee tonight and pay her a visit," I said. "Maybe have local PD pick her up and hold her until we get there."

"Yeah, get the long arm of the law after her," Reed said, by now nearly dry but still shivering, his hands thrust deep into his coat pockets against the vicious, chill wind whipping through the campus, rattling the trees around us. "Nothing like a little fear and intimidation to get the little people to cooperate."

"Dr. Stanley was hiding something," I said, not immune to the freezing ass cold myself. Minneapolis hadn't even been this cold when we left, had it? "I've got no reason to believe her colleague isn't in on it in some way."

"You've got no reason to believe she is," Reed said, giving me one of those superior looks that I hated on him, like he was making a reasonable suggestion or something.

"Whatever," I said, blowing him off. "We need phones. First stop, that. Second stop, we grill Maclean. Third stop, if we haven't busted this thing wide open by then—we go to Milwaukee."

"Well all right, then, Sam-antha Spade," Reed said, falling into step next to me, smirking at his own joke. "Let's go solve this thing. After we get new cell phones, of course."

"Maybe some dinner, too," I said, prompting Reed to smile even wider. I was glad he was feeling happy again. I damned sure wasn't. All I wanted to do was find this Graves bastard and put him in one of his own before anyone else got hurt.

41.

Harry Graves

It wasn't in Harry's nature to run from a fight, but then, it wasn't in Harry's nature to get in a fight in the first place. Fights were for idiots, for people who couldn't see any way around them. They got in the way of good fun, and if you knew someone was going to be a problem, it was better, in Harry's opinion, to just ice them quietly rather than let it become a long, drawn-out scuffle that attracted noise and attention.

Of course, he'd violated his own rules a few times lately, and that was the genesis of his current problem. Back to following the rules, Harry thought to himself glumly as he walked down the quiet alley in West Chicago.

He'd retreated out of downtown when Sienna Nealon had come. He'd long had a safe house of sorts in Chicago, a place he'd picked up on the cheap in the fifties and had never quite abandoned. He'd blow through town every couple years and stay there. It was worth keeping in his opinion; after all, it'd probably gone up in value a thousand percent over what he'd paid for it, even given the current somewhat sketchy nature of the neighborhood. He had investments like this all over the US, though he never thought of them as anything other than homes without the homey-ness, and he always sent enough to cash to the right account to make sure the lawyer he had on retainer paid the utilities and the taxes.

The nice thing about owning these properties was that it gave him a place to park his car when he was in town. Chicago was a nightmare in that regard. He'd seen the signs for the $15 valets and it made him a little sick. But, then, Harry could remember a time when you could almost buy an acre parcel of land in Chicago for that.

Night had shrunk in around him, and he was walking down the alley toward the back of his own house. They were little houses, a thousand square feet, but he didn't need much space. He tended to travel real light, maybe leave three or four changes of clothes in each of his houses' closets, and bring the ones on his back to the next locale he traveled to. Made packing a nonissue. Of course, some of the TVs in his dwellings weren't exactly up to modern spec. The one here he'd bought in the fifties, with the house, and it didn't even work anymore. Something about digital antennas nowadays. Not like he watched much TV, but it would have been nice to have right now, catch a little news of the manhunt that was probably underway for him.

Although, there were other reasons too. Harry had long prided himself on not paying attention to current events. They had a strange habit of sounding repetitive, the panics of the day. He could almost imagine himself watching cable news and shutting his eyes, harkening back to the day when a tinny voice on the radio was shouting about the impending destruction of the world. Harry had never yet seen it happen. It just wasn't the nature of the world to go and get itself destroyed.

True, people died every day. He'd proven that with his own damned hand the last couple days.

But worldwide destruction? That was a fantasy concocted by a society with too much affluence and too little real thinking to do. Harry had seen the future arrive on time every morning, the change that every generation fearfully predicted would result in the end actually resulting in … not the end. Maybe he'd gotten jaded after all the doomsaying he'd heard in his long life.

He walked through the cold night, hands deep in his pockets, the streetlights in the alley shining down on him. He would have figured more of them would have been broken out, given the status of the neighborhood, but only two out of twenty or so actually were. Those two places were covered in a dark pall, though, and he stepped to avoid them almost subconsciously.

No, Harry had never put much stock in the end of the world. Life would spin on, and so would the world; that was something he could just about hang his hat on, even though he didn't wear a hat anymore.

Harry shuddered against the chill as he walked past a garage that had its door open, loud music blaring into the night. Some damned rock band or another. Harry was all about living in the moment, adapting to modern times—which was why he didn't wear a hat anymore, thank you very much, John Fitzgerald Kennedy—but he'd never gotten into modern music. He could sit at a card table all night long, gambling, smoking, drinking, and be totally at home except for the music. Put some Sinatra on and he was in bliss. It was why he liked steakhouses so much. They were like a retreat into the halcyon days of class, back when Harry could still comfortably and carefully win money hand over fist in Vegas.

Fortunately, the places he tended to frequent didn't put crappy modern music on for the sake of creating an atmosphere. That was the benefit of back alley poolrooms and gambling dens. They didn't rely on loud noise and flashing lights, all sound and fury and crap, for ambience. Harry glanced into the open garage at his left out of instinct and habit more than anything.

There was a guy in there in a wife beater shirt, white but stained with black spots of grease. It didn't take Harry much effort to see the guy was working on a motorcycle. Pieces of it lay on the floor of the garage, carefully placed on blankets spread over the concrete. Harry took the motorcycle in with a glance; it was an Indian, looked newer.

"Hey," the guy in the greasy wife beater said, acknowledging him with a nod. "How you doing?" He said it in that inimitable Chicago fashion, just a hint of challenge under the facade of politeness.

"Good," Harry said, slowing his stroll, keeping his hands tucked in his pockets. "How are you doing?" He had been raised to be polite, and conversation wasn't exactly his bane, though he tried to keep it superficial.

"I'm all right, neighbor," the guy said, giving him a nod. Harry didn't know the guy, but the guy evidently knew Harry. That wasn't a total surprise. By design, Harry didn't pay attention to anything unless it directly crossed his path. It was simpler to remain blissfully unaware, for the same reason he didn't have conversations that went beyond the surface level. Entanglements were messy. "What are you up to this fine, freezing-ass evening?" The guy took a long pull of a lite beer that was sitting on a workbench, and the cigarette in his mouth drifted smoke.

Harry caught a whiff of the smoke and a hint of the beer's scent from outside the garage, and wished he was doing something other than getting in his car and beating a hasty retreat out of town. Sitting in a favorite parlor with cards, a beer and cigarettes in front of him, sounded preferable to skedaddling so Sienna Nealon wouldn't catch up with him. "I was just about to make like a fetus and head out," Harry said. "Looks like you got a long night's project in front of you."

The guy had been leaning casually on his workbench, but he came off it now, beer in one hand, taking a drag from his cig with the other. He left it dangling between his lips as he crossed the garage over to Harry. "You just got into town a few days ago. You're not leaving already, are you?"

Harry kept from narrowing his eyes, but only just. This was the danger of having a fixed residence. He always knew people talked about him in the neighborhoods where he kept houses, always behind his back. He was the ghost of any street he lived on, that was just fact, as inescapable as gossip in a small town.

"Yeah. Spring hasn't sprung quite enough for me, yet. Maybe I'll come back later this year."

"I try to keep a watch on the neighborhood," the guy said, still strolling up to him. "I'll keep an eye on your house if you want, give you a call if I see any of the punks around here doing any damage to it."

"I don't ... keep a phone," Harry said lamely. It was true. "Just call the cops for me if you see someone vandalizing the place."

The guy's eyebrows spiked. "You got it," he said. He seemed affable enough. He left his cigarette dangling between his lips and thrust out a hand toward Harry. "I'm Paul Beckman."

"Harry Graves," Harry said and offered his hand. Beckman was close enough that Harry was practically taking a drag off his cigarette just standing this close to him. He touched Beckman's hand in the course of the shake, and sure enough, he got a flash in an instant. He knew exactly what kind of a guy Paul Beckman was.

"Whoa!" Beckman said in surprise. "You got a mean grip there."

Harry's mouth felt dry. He wanted a beer. He wanted a cigarette. He wanted to be gambling.

But he wasn't.

He was standing in a back alley with a real sonofabitch, and all his attempts to keep his damned head down and get the hell out of town had just fallen by the wayside with a handshake.

Harry didn't like to fight, and he damned sure didn't like a fair fight. So instead of doing something like telegraphing his movement, he just punched Paul Beckman right in the face, hard enough to knock his ass back into his garage. The cigarette fell out from between Beckman's lips as he flew, crashing into his workbench. The impact knocked all the air out of Beckman and Harry watched him fall with dull eyes, utterly devoid of compassion for the hell he was about to put Paul Beckman through.

Harry stooped and retrieved Beckman's cigarette off the wet pavement and put it in his mouth, taking a deep drag. Well, he wasn't gambling or drinking, but at least he had this, he reflected as he stepped into the garage and pulled the door down with a clatter.

"What the ... hell you doin'?" Paul Beckman asked, trying to right himself. He was sitting down with his back against the workbench, trying to stand but failing to coordinate his movements properly.

Harry sidled up to him, cigarette in his own mouth now, dangling lazily from his lips. Harry pushed back the sleeve on his right arm and choreographed this punch so Beckman could see it coming. He didn't put too much into it, just enough to split skin and give Beckman a hell of a shiner tomorrow. He did it again, then again, then once more, holding the man by the greasy shirt with his left hand and pounding him with his right.

"The ... f ..." Paul Beckman wheezed through a split lip, his right eye swollen shut. "Wh ... y ...?"

"Because like that shirt you're wearing, you're a wife beater, Paul," Harry said, looking at him remorselessly. He paused for a moment to take a drag off the cigarette and then lift it into the air with his right hand while he continued to hold Paul Beckman's t-shirt with his left. He exhaled smoked in a thick cloud right into Paul's face, and the man blanched and coughed. Harry put the cigarette back in his mouth and smacked Beckman once, hard, across the lips with a backhand.

"D ... did that ... b ... bitch ... tell ... you ...?" Beckman looked at him with his open eye, blood dripping down his lips and his cheek, and Harry nailed him across the face with a straight punch again, probably only putting ten percent into it.

"She didn't tell me anything, Paul," Harry said, sighing, and punched him again. "You beat her loud enough the whole neighborhood can hear you." He punched him twice more, this time to the body, breaking a few ribs, listening to them snap and pop as he worked the man over. Paul Beckman was more than wheezing now, he was crying faintly, which was why Harry had shut the garage door when he came in here. "Don't you?" He smacked him hard in the newly broken ribs, eliciting a pig-like squeal. "Don't you, Paul? You like hearing her cry. You like the way it makes you feel, you impotent little weasel?" He popped him again, and again, playing the busted ribs like a xylophone. It didn't even take much strength at this point.

"Yes, yes, yes!" Beckman cried, and Harry sensed the man had hit his breaking point.

Harry slapped him once more to focus his attention, and Beckman looked right at Harry with pleading eyes. "You're never going to hit your wife again, are you?" Harry asked him, not blinking, not flinching.

"N-no," Beckman said, shaking his head urgently.

Harry dropped him, left him limp next to his workbench, and then grabbed his beer, knocking a wrench off the bench as he did so. It plopped down perfectly on the middle of Beckman's forehead and knocked him clean out. He'd wake up in the morning with a hell of a headache and a hell of a lot of other aching things, and he'd never say a damned word about this to anyone. He'd slipped in the garage; that was the tale he'd tell the world.

And he'd never hit his wife again.

"I believe you," Harry said to the unconscious Beckman after draining his beer. He tossed the can in the garbage on the way out and pulled up the rattling garage door to step out into the cold before shutting it behind him. There was no one in the alley, and the night was quiet all around.

Harry didn't like fights. He didn't believe in the end of the world, in spite of what every doomsayer in every generation had said. He liked living in the moment, he liked his beer, his cigarettes and his gambling.

But he'd be damned if he was going to just run out of town now. That went way beyond keeping his head down and crossed into the realm of pure chickenshittery.

And that wasn't Harry Graves. Not at all.

With a quick breath that fogged in front of him like cigarette smoke from the butt he'd left burning on the garage floor, he started back the way he'd come. There was only way out of this conundrum, really, at least without running, and he was ready to face it.

He had to find Sienna Nealon. *She's going to die*, he thought, his shoes slopping along the wet alley floor, his footsteps carrying him back toward the city of Chicago and the girl in question.

42.

By the time Reed and I got our phone situation ironed out, the clerk was ready to go home. I sympathized, being quite ready to go home myself, but unfortunately, that wasn't in the cards for me right now.

I had about a million thoughts rattling through my mind, leads I wanted and needed to chase. Okay, I had three, actually, but I wanted to chase them all, right now. I had Detective Maclean and his possible treachery at the top of my list, along with his presumably now-compiled dossier on our second murder victim, the runner at Oak Park Beach. I was toying with ways I could expose Detective Maclean as the person who was siccing metahuman assassins on me, but the problem I was running up against was motive. He certainly had some opportunity, and probably the means, since detectives have access to all manner of unsavory sorts. Usually that's because they're busting them, but plenty of Confidential Informants—CIs—can also arrange for the door the swing the other way.

Unfortunately, I didn't have a plan just yet, other than to sally forth into the precinct house and yell, "*J'accuse!*" right in Maclean's face. He was a hardened cop, had been on the street for a long time. Even having the most dangerous woman in the world yelling at him in French was unlikely to cause the man to break out in a sweat. And while I could have, I dunno, dangled him off a building, that would probably be frowned upon, and the government was unlikely to spare me from prosecution from something like that, given it was my last week. Thuggy they'd overlook. A Chicago cop? Not so much, I figured.

"I know that look," Reed said as we cruised along in the back of his Uber, which turned out to be a Toyota Prius driven by a young lady named Melody who apparently clerked at a local mall and drove people around in her car in her spare time. "That look means trouble."

"So are you two like, a couple?" Melody asked. She had her ears perked up and everything.

"He's my brother," I said, wondering why I was being driven around by a part-time taxi driver instead of just getting a full-time one, especially since the government was paying for these little trips anyway.

"Oh, sorry," Melody said, apologizing. She let that rest for a beat before throwing out her next question. "So are you guys going downtown to party tonight?"

"We're heading to a police precinct, remember?" I was looking at her cock-eyed; none of the taxi drivers had tried to engage me in conversation for more than a few seconds of our ride.

"Oh, right," Melody said, nodding, glancing back at us in the rearview. "Probably not partying there." She chortled, and it sounded a little like a duck quacking at low volume. "What are you going to the cop shop for?"

"We're federal agents investigating local transport licenses," I said, hoping to switch this Chatty Cathy off. "You know, the kind taxi drivers need."

"Oh, cool," she said, plainly not getting the hint. "I bet that's fun."

"Yes, looking into local bureaucracy is totes fun," I deadpanned, then turned back to Reed and lowered my voice. "I was trying to figure out how to trap Maclean so we could prove he's set these assassins on us."

"I don't like Maclean for this," Reed said with a shake of his head. "I think Gustafson is more likely."

"You think Dr. Gustafson has meta assassins in his Rolodex?" I asked, jaw down in disbelief. "I'm sorry, but that just doesn't pass the sniff test."

"What are you guys talking about?" Melody asked from the front seat, way too chipper for this time of night.

"Federal Statute N51047," I replied, making shit up, "the use of personal vehicles for non-regulatory purposes."

"That sounds serious," Melody said. "Are people breaking that law around here?"

"People break every law, everywhere," I said. "That's why we have jails."

"Oh, that sucks," Melody said, like it was such a bummer, you guys. "So are you going to get to do any partying while you're in town?"

I looked at Melody in the front seat and I finally realized something. "You're going out partying tonight, aren't you?"

"Totally," she said, nodding, a big grin on her face, her eyes not so much on the road. "That's what so great about this gig. I picked you guys up, and it's paying for my gas money to get into the city. How cool is that?"

I glared at Reed and he shrugged. "It's cheaper for us, and she gets her gas money paid for to party. That's win/win."

"I feel like *I'm* losing in this case," I said, and my phone buzzed. Apparently my number had finally synched with my voicemail. I dialed it immediately, before Melody had a chance to ask any more scintillating questions about partying or regulations.

The first voicemail came as a little bit of a surprise. I saw Reed stiffen in the seat next to me as it played. "Ms. Nealon, this Jonathan Chang. We met the other night in the bar in Eden Prairie, where I presented you with a job offer to run the local branch of our new metahuman NGO. I wanted to reach out to you to follow up. I know you're in Chicago at the moment on a case, but I've had a chance to look into your problems with the FAA, and I'd like to meet at lunch tomorrow to discuss them, as well as the career opportunities. Please give me a call back at …"

Reed was glaring. "Fer real?" he asked, sounding like a … I don't know, like he was pissed and from the San Fernando Valley.

"What?" I asked, innocently. "I'm totally a hot commodity. Like corn or soybeans."

"You guys aren't doing ecstasy back there, are you?" Melody asked, turning to look at us. I missed the glass partition that separated me from my fellow humans in a cab.

"What?" I looked at her in horror. "What the hell are you—we're federal agents, remember?"

"I figured you guys were making that up because you didn't want to talk to me," Melody said, shrugging.

I stared at her in sheer disbelief. "If you knew we didn't want to talk to you, why are you still talking to us?"

"Just because you're really rude doesn't mean I have to be," she said without an ounce of judgment. She sounded like she was going out of her way to be peppy and nice, and it irked me more than I can properly describe.

"Steady," Reed said, catching my arm. "Don't lose your shit because someone's being too nice to you."

"I'm bucking my nature here, Reed," I said, steaming, "but it's really hard. Zollers says my natural instinct is to separate myself from humanity because I can't take it."

"Yes, the milk of human kindness tastes like ash to you, doesn't it?" he asked with a smirk.

"As you know, I prefer a steady diet of sarcasm, cynicism and thumbtacks," I replied, feeling my urge to kill falling.

"That's a rough way to go through life," Melody said sadly, apparently deciding I needed either commentary or a life coach. "You should try yoga for relaxation. Or maybe some Kegels to work out your stress—"

"I am not doing fucking Kegels!" I screamed in the back of the non-taxi. Everyone fell silent at my outburst.

"You sure?" Melody asked, cutting into the silence like a knife into an artery. "You seem like you need something. Maybe a colon cleanse?"

I sat seething in the back of the car, Reed looking sympathetic but refusing to meet my eyes, a barely-concealed smirk on his face for the rest of the ride to the police department.

43.

Veronika

Veronika had never liked spending idle time while on a job, so the afternoon spent flat on her back waiting for her wound to heal had been like hell itself had risen up from beneath the earth and dragged her down into its fiery embrace. Which totally fit with the pain in her shoulder.

Now she was moving again, though, and the shoulder felt a little stiff but was otherwise fine. Digging out a bullet hadn't been the most fun way to torment herself, but it had allowed the news she'd received about her mother to really seep into her mind and roll around for a while. That was idleness for you; give it a chance and it'd just consume you whole, letting all your doubts and fears play in your head for a while. Yeah, that was hell, but at least it was over now.

Now, Veronika was back on the job, pacing back and forth in front of Chicago PD's headquarters. She'd gotten a message from her employer while she was out, giving her a nice line of sight to perfect ambush opportunities. She knew her counterparts, the competition, had gotten the same chances. She'd read the news reports on her phone, and it looked to her like Sienna Nealon had given Colin Fannon the slip after an ambush at the river, and that she'd dodged Phinneus Chalke again at some college out in the 'burbs.

That damned sure worked for Veronika. She'd had a

feeling neither of those losers would be up to bringing Nealon down. The woman was a badass, first rate, and Veronika recognized more than a few of her own tendencies in the agent. She'd skimmed some of the news articles while she was waiting, confirming a little more of what she'd already suspected. Nealon was the antisocial type, apparently always pushing people away. Veronika could relate.

It didn't interfere with her planning, though. Nealon still had to die; that was the job she was being paid to do, after all. Standing here, staring across at the police headquarters, she just hoped she'd gotten the jump on Colin and Phinneus. After all, Nealon was working with the cops, was an obsessed workaholic, and was almost certain not to call it a night just yet. So unless she'd picked up some other hot lead, it seemed likely that sooner or later, she was going to end up here, consulting with the detectives at the CPD.

Veronika sighed. She'd already been waiting hours, carefully eyeing the front of the building for any hint of Nealon. She'd watched the number of visitors to the precinct diminish as the hours grew late, the night shift dragged in, and the civilian employees clocked out. Now it was getting lonely on her stretch of sidewalk, and she'd taken to pacing back and forth a couple blocks, keeping her razor-sharp meta eyes on the front of the building when she was facing it, and her cell phone camera angled to catch all traffic when she wasn't. It was a pretty clever way to go about it, she figured. Better than just lingering in front of the entrance all night.

She was expecting a cab, so when a Toyota Prius pulled up in front of the entrance, she almost discounted it. But then it stopped to let two people out. Veronika paused and looked back with her own eyes.

Yep. The dark hair, the short stature, the wider hips hidden under coat that was—wait, was her shirt yellow, her pants black and her coat brown? Veronika squinted into the dark, her eyebrows rising. Nealon looked like an idiot had dressed her, but when she passed under a light, Veronika knew it was her, the brother walking a pace behind her.

"Showtime," Veronika breathed, turning around to head for the front of the police headquarters. She was in a hurry, after all. No time to waste.

44.

Sienna

The police department wasn't as grand as I expected. It certainly wasn't ivory towers; just more brick and glass, and when we went inside I found the standard corridors and painted drywall that seemed to be the mark of every bureaucratic institution from colleges to law enforcement agencies.

Detective Maclean's cubicle was on the fourth floor, and Reed and I found it without too much difficulty. Like every other police station I'd ever been in, it smelled of coffee and effort, along with some hints of smoke that had clung to clothing in the chill air, trailed inside by those who'd gone out for their smoke breaks.

Maclean was looking more than a little weary as we came up on him. He'd evidently been warned we were coming, because he was watching down the row when we turned the corner. "Heard you caused some trouble out in Naperville, too," he said, not looking amused in the slightest. "And of course, I assume that flying dragon over the river was you?"

"You get a lot of dragons around here when I'm not in town?" I quipped, simmering rage boiling beneath the surface. Okay, not too deep beneath the surface. Maybe like a micron beneath my surface at most.

"It's not a common occurrence, no," Maclean said, and he

was watching me a little more carefully now. He'd probably picked up on my mood. Like I said, it wasn't well concealed. "We got the cab, too. Looked like someone pulled it up onto the riverbank. Was that you?"

"No," I said, frowning, taken aback. I'd left the damned thing at the bottom of the river. Who would have bothered to dredge it up again? That was just weird.

"I've got this profile for the second vic," Maclean said, apparently choosing to bypass both my surprise at the taxi revelation and my prickly greeting and go straight to business. Normally, I would have approved. At the moment, though, seeing him here, giving me a little dose of shit, I was having a hard time controlling my emotions, which were rapidly breaking in a distinctly hostile and unproductive direction. Thanks to numerous sessions with Dr. Zollers, I was aware of this.

Thanks to the fact that I am a rage-monster of a human being, I also did not presently care.

"These assassins just keep finding me," I said tightly. I could feel Reed stiffen behind me at the knowledge of what was coming.

Maclean cocked an eyebrow at me. "There's more than one?"

"There are three now," I said, faux-chipper, heading toward woodchipper. "A speedster who can move superhumanly fast, like the Flash, a sniper who can't miss—" I paused, "uh, except when he shoots at me, apparently, and a woman who can absorb fire and turn her skin to a burning plasma that's hotter than anything I can produce and also is one hell of a fighter—"

"Yeah," Maclean took this knowledge in stride, apparently not too concerned with either my well-being or the assassins on my trail, because he turned back to his computer screen. "I put that 'Graves' into the database and came up with bupkis. I also looked into murders committed with .44-40 ammo and came up with a little more, courtesy of your friends at the FBI—"

"I don't have any friends at the FBI," I said, steaming. "Only enemies."

Maclean looked right at me. "I can't imagine why."

It took everything in me not to rip him out of his chair and shake him like a party mix. My fists were clenched, my lips were pressing against each other so hard that if I'd ever had collagen injections, they'd be exploding out from the pressure. I felt like someone had twisted my insides, like they'd put a good, solid grip on my guts and were squeezing …

Before I could let fly a raging reply, my phone rang. It played Beethoven's "Moonlight Sonata," which was a song I found soothing, and which had apparently downloaded from the cloud in order to overwrite my new phone's default preferences with the personal ringtone of the individual calling me at the moment.

Dr. Quinton Zollers.

"Hello," I said in a pleasant tone as I raised the phone to my ear.

"You need to calm down," Dr. Zollers said, traces of sleepiness in his voice. "I can feel your blinding rage from here, and it turned a quite pleasant dream into something akin to the St. Valentine's Day Massacre."

"How interesting you picked that to reference," I said, "since I am in Chicago." I was still staring hard at the object of my rage, Detective Maclean.

"I am aware of that," Zollers said with a yawn. "Deep breaths, Sienna."

I took a deep breath in through my nose, out through my mouth. "Okay," I breathed.

"Turn away from the man—it's a detective, isn't it?"

"Yep," I said tightly and did as he asked. I turned around to find Reed watching me with alarm all over his face and his color quite washed out. "Don't look at me like that," I snapped at him. He held up his arms in surrender and took a step back, then another.

"I know it's not as fun as imagining how you'd gut this

man," Zollers said coolly, defusing my annoyance a couple more notches at the absurd reference to me gutting Maclean. I wouldn't do anything that horrific. Smack him around, steal memories, threaten to drop him out of the sky without a parachute, yes, all possibilities I'd considered. But gutting people was a Wolfe thing to do—

It is so delightful, Wolfe said.

—not a Sienna thing.

"Good," Zollers said, soothing. "Now … I know you're heading into a confrontation. Try to imagine what you want to get out of this conversation."

"Information," I said, very neutrally and not entirely honestly. What I wanted was more along the lines of "Detective Maclean crying profusely as he admits to sending three stupid, annoying metahuman assassins after me. While wetting his pants."

"Picture with clarity how you'd like this conversation to go," Zollers said, almost certainly aware of exactly what I was thinking at the moment. "Imagine it without violence, like we've discussed. Try to picture a peaceful resolution, one where you get everything you want without once having to use force. Can you do that?"

I pictured myself grabbing Maclean by the crotch and twisting until he sang in a higher key, bursting into beautiful song and elucidating how he'd hired assassins to kill me. "I'm, like, halfway there."

"Better," he said, though I suspected he was patronizing me, as therapists do. "Now go the whole way. Picture getting what you want through persuasion, without having to raise your fist, or turn a man's dangling bits into a braid, because that is still quite violent. Also, it's the sort of thing that scares away potential dates, just FYI. Don't set fire to that bridge."

I took another breath, and pictured a calm, placid conversation with Maclean in which he admitted to sending assassins after me, and which I finished by punching him through the skull. Whoops. "This is really difficult," I said.

"Imagine if perhaps you're wrong in your accusations against this detective," Zollers said. "Picture yourself killing an innocent man, having his blood all over your hands, his widow crying because you've killed her husband." I felt a cold chill run down my back at the thought of a woman wailing in my ears, at hearing his colleagues talk about what a good and decent man Maclean was. He'd given me shit, and I hated that. It made me angry, especially when I had three assassins after me, not one of which I'd cleanly bested. They were all still out there, and it was hanging over my head—

"That's right," Zollers said, interrupting my train of thought. "You feel threatened. Your anger is leading you in directions that the evidence doesn't fully support. What if you're wrong? What if you beat this man to death with your bare fists and it turns out they keep coming because someone else is responsible for your predicament?"

I took a ragged breath and it stuck in my lungs painfully, like my ribs were still broken or something. The last of my flaming rage died in that instant, and it came out on my next exhalation, along with some of the pain. "You're right," I said, my mouth tasting bitter. I should have eaten before we came here.

"You're in control," Dr. Zollers said calmly. "Don't let these assassins, or worrying about what they're going to do, let you fall out of it. Don't let the blinding rage take over. You're in a mystery, and the only way you can solve it is if you keep in control. Short-term violence may seem like a satisfying answer, but inflicting it against innocent people … well, you know how you'll feel about it later."

That ashen taste in my mouth got worse. Yeah, I knew how it felt to push my rage in the wrong direction. "Thank you," I breathed, still raggedly, and hung up, once more in control of myself.

"You done?" Maclean asked, sounding more than a little cynical.

I turned to answer him, but I never got a chance to say a

word, because the desk next to me exploded as Veronika came smashing through a cubicle wall, her fists aflame with blue, shards of plastic showering me and forcing me to shield my eyes. When I pulled my hands back, she was standing there in a grey pantsuit, looking refined and lethal, her hands smoking blue light as the plasma rolled off of them. She wore darker red lipstick that stood out against her pale face and rosy red cheeks, a smile perched on her lips. "Hello, my dear," she said, "thanks for keeping the assholes at bay until I recovered. Now … let's you and I finish this thing, shall we?"

45.

"Dammit, Veronika," I said, rolling my eyes at her like it was no big deal that she'd just smashed her way into the Chicago Police Department Headquarters, "I'm in the middle of something here."

She looked amused, hands aglow, standing off in front of me, like she was calling me out on my bullshit attempt to push her off balance without beating her ass. "Don't try to play me, kid. I'm a lot older than you."

"You said it, not me," I fired back lightly, and saw a glimmer of amusement in her eyes. "I thought you were very well preserved for your age—"

She came at me, fast, not so much furious as cold and calculating, which was way more dangerous than some unhinged nut. I'd fought my share of unhinged nuts, and they usually screwed up in the heat of passion. Veronika took a swipe at me with her other hand held back for defense, and I could feel the air heat up as her blue, glowing hand passed within inches of my arm, which was up to defend me.

Gavrikov, I said, and drew him forth, flaring both my hands into orange flame, mostly as a test.

"Put those away before you hurt yourself," Veronika said with a smirk, pulling a hand toward herself and snuffing my flames just like that, on command. The fires went out, leaving nothing but smoke to drift off my sleeves where the heat had started to burn my clothes.

Damn. I had no gun on me at the moment, thanks to the speedster causing me to lose Shadow in the flight from the river. In hindsight, I should have taken Reed's, because we both knew it was of way more use to me than him, but I had a problem with taking it away and leaving him nearly defenseless. I mean, his gusts are strong and all, but they weren't exactly intimidating to me. Don't tell him I said that.

"I don't need to hurt myself," I said, "I've got a veritable clown car full of you assholes doing it for me. I hurt your friend Phinneus, by the way. He left his rifle behind—"

"Out in Naperville at that college?" Veronika asked, lurking just out of reach, smiling smugly. So she'd been following my movements, too.

"Yeah, there," I said, ready to take a poke at her defenses. "By the way … while you're here and interrupting me … does the name 'Graves' mean anything to you?"

She reacted to that one with a hard frown. "Graves? Harry Graves?"

"Dresses years out of style," I said. "Likes to gamble—"

"Yeah, that's Harry Graves," she said, blowing me off as she came in hard with a punch, "not that it'll do you any g—"

I clipped her in the jaw as I dropped hard left, finally getting the better of her in an exchange. She smashed into a cubicle behind me, blue hands burning through the plastic and metal like they weren't even there. She spun in a second, her cheeks even redder now, her amusement mingling with anger. I'd stung her pride. "Nice move," she said.

"I've got a few of them," I shot back. "Any chance you want to tell me more about Harry Graves?"

"I'd rather send you to your own," she said, coming at me again, hard. I fell back, cooler than I'd been a few minutes earlier when Zollers had talked me down off the edge of rage-induced madness. I dodged, ducked, dipped, and generally avoided the thrown wrenches that were Veronika's steaming blue plasma punches. The air shimmered with her every attack, the heat coming off her hands becoming a stifling presence in the room.

"Yeah, that's not really a trip I'm looking to make at the moment," I said, going completely non-offensive. Her hands would hurt, I knew, and that'd provide a moment's distraction which might allow her to slip in another pummeling blow when I least needed it. One error would practically beget another, like a normal person in a knife fight, and the compounding pain would send me right to my death. Though I hadn't seen her do it, I could imagine Veronika putting her glowing fist right through my chest and destroying my heart in an instant. Or, possibly worse, my brain. She could set my blood to boiling with a directed burst, if she could direct her plasma the way I could shoot fire—the possibilities were endless.

I was racing to try and figure out a plan of action. I doubted very much that flashy moves would work, but I wasn't averse to trying them if I had the foot space to do it. Unfortunately, I was in a very long, narrow row of cubicles packed so tightly together that I knew the fire marshal must have given this place a pass because it was the cops. Veronika came at me with relentless fury, forcing me to back up.

The one lucky stroke, if you could call it that, was that the cops had taken off. I didn't see Reed, either, which meant he'd probably been the one driving the evacuation, making himself and the others scarce in order to give me room to fight. I didn't know a ton about Veronika, but if she was like me with even less of a moral compass, taking hostages wasn't out of the realm of possibility for her. She'd take any advantage to get the job done.

I retreated steadily backward under her constant physical assault, never letting her land a punch. I was under no illusions; there was no bell to save me, and I doubted Veronika would just politely stop coming to kill me when my back came up against the wall, as it inevitably would. "So," I said, glancing back to see how much more space I had out of the corner of my eye, "Harry Graves didn't hire you?"

Veronika laughed as she threw the next punch. It looked a

little weaker, maybe because she was snickering. "Graves isn't the kind to hire anyone, not even a barber, clearly."

I thought about his hair and nodded. "So … who did hire you?"

Veronika snorted, shortening her punches after swinging wide a few too many times. If I had a speed edge on her, it was a very narrow one. "That's not how it works."

"Oh, come on," I said, "they're trying to have me killed. Fair's fair."

"If you don't stop running and stand your ground," she growled, "I'm going to stop chasing you and just burn you out."

"Well, go on, then," I said, still stepping back. "Have at it."

She paused, narrowed her eyes, and started to concentrate. Her eyes glowed blue, like her hands, like a fluorescent light tinged with otherworldly cerulean, and they started to smoke.

"Uh oh," I said, more than mildly concerned.

She did the full Supergirl, blasting beams out of her eyes as I leapt through the air and into flight. I could almost feel her attack following me a hair behind as I flew around the room. The smell of burning was intense, and when I looked back as I hooked around her like a ball on a chain with her at my center, I could see her energy dissolving the walls where it hit, burning through and consuming everything in its path like corrosive acid.

I doubted she'd had anyone flee like I had for a while, and I had a sudden, uneasy realization about where this was going. I hoped Reed had gotten everyone out, because—

I hooked back around to where I'd started from as I heard the shifting of the ceiling above. I found the nearest window and dove for it, her blasting along, eyebeams ripping behind me right on my tail.

I shot through the window, which she'd already helpfully dissolved with her power, and I zoomed toward the street level below. Cops were filling the avenue, milling around and looking up. Veronika's power was lasering out after my exit in a very imprecise manner. It stopped a couple seconds after I dipped, and I halted, hovering a few feet above the street, waiting to see if—

Yep. That did it.

The fourth floor of the police headquarters came collapsing in on itself. I'd been a little busy when I was flying around, what with rampant, superhot plasma flying in a hard trail just behind me, but I'd seen her destroy more than a few load-bearing columns in her race to kill me. My guess was that Veronika hadn't had to pull out the old eye-beams in a while, and never against a flying target like me, indoors and circling her rather than getting the hell away as fast as possible. In the heat (ha ha) of the moment, I guess she'd forgotten about what happens if you destroy all the walls around you while indoors.

The fourth floor crashed down and a wave of dust and debris came billowing out as the roof dropped. I waited, wondering if the next floor would follow, but it didn't. It held strong, which meant Veronika only had a couple tons of debris on her. Maybe it stopped her, maybe it didn't. I wasn't too thrilled at the prospect of sifting through the mess to find out.

"Why." Detective Maclean was standing a few feet below me, covering his face with both hands, his skin covered with dust from the wreck of his headquarters. He didn't even ask a question, and the desperation was audible in his tone. "Why me."

"Sorry," I said, drifting down to him, keeping a wary eye on the building. Reed came staggering out the front entrance, caked in white from head to toe, and started toward me immediately.

"You ..." Maclean said, just shaking his head. I seemed to cause this reaction in people a lot.

"Is she dead?" Reed asked as he trotted up.

"I doubt it," I said. "My luck's not been that good lately."

"Who was that?" Maclean asked, finally showing his face. It was dust-covered, too, though less so than his hands.

"One of the assassins," I said. I did feel calmer now, calm

enough to ask my most pressing question without blood-spitting rage. "So … did you hire them to kill me?"

Maclean looked at me with his lips slightly parted as he tried to make sense of what I said. I think he got it pretty quick. "I wish," he said. "Because then, if I had, I would have told them not to do so RIGHT AT MY DAMNED DESK."

"That's … a reasonable point," I said, my anger pretty much gone. I was splitting my attention between the building, where Veronika had been buried, and Maclean, who was somewhere between the seething anger I'd seen in him moments earlier and utter surrender.

"Why would you even think I hired people to kill you?" he asked.

"Well," I said, suddenly feeling a little embarrassed, "one of the assassins showed up right after I told you where I was last time. And the next went to where I told you we'd be. And …" I gestured at the swelling look of indignation on his face. "Well, you know."

"Know … what?" he asked me, barely keeping his lid from blowing off. "You think I want to kill you?" He looked at the wreckage of police headquarters and deflated slightly. "Yeah, okay. I want to kill you a little bit right now. But I wouldn't pay good money to have it done—" He looked back at headquarters. "Well, I wouldn't pay my money to have it done, anyway." He gave me a nasty look. "What's my motive, in your view?"

"I dunno," I said, still feeling foolish for having said it now. "Corruption, maybe?" Maclean went red. "What? I know, it's not like cops in Chicago *ever* go bad …"

"I … am … not … dirty," Maclean said, his face wavering with rage again. "Though I am now finding some motive within myself. And you can go screw yourself for suggesting it."

"Everyone keeps saying that to me," I said, feeling pretty mild. The rubble hadn't moved, suggesting to me that maybe Veronika was out of the fight for a little bit. "Like I wouldn't rather be doing that instead of getting shot at, drowned, smacked around, burned—"

I felt a wave of heat behind me and threw myself forward blindly, knocking Reed to the side as I rolled back to my feet. I came up in a defensive stance and saw Veronika waiting right there, her beautiful suit covered in dust. "Burned," she said, really definitive. "I like that. I think that's how we end you." She came at me again, eyes glowing, ready to kill me for good.

"Yeah, well I think—" I started, but something zipped behind me in a rush of air, and I felt a strong hand grab me by the back of the neck. The world launched into a blur of speed before my eyes, and Veronika disappeared as the speedster took hold of me, carrying me away from the ruin of police headquarters.

46.

I got thrown hard and landed on solid dirt, kicked again for
good measure by the speedster as he turned me loose. I hit wet
turf and ripped it up as I scrambled to halt the momentum of
my speedy abduction. I didn't know exactly how fast I'd just
been carried along, but it had been so quick that I was hitting
the ground before I really had a full idea of what was going on.
The disorientation washed over me as I rolled, and I yelled for
Gavrikov out loud and he answered before I even fully had
control of myself. I spun to a stop in the air, hovering with my
feet off the ground and looking into the face of the bastard
who had just manhandled me like I was a sack of sugar he was
taking home from the grocery store.

"This is the crappiest tag team ever," I said, spitting dirt
out of my mouth. I glanced from the speedster, who was
standing there on the grass wearing a flannel shirt and jeans,
leering at me with a smile too wide for his face, to my
surroundings, which were a dark sky and stadium seats that
rose hundreds of feet above me on the three sides I could see
without turning my back on my enemy. "What the … did you
bring me to a football stadium?"

He tossed a speedy shrug and stared at me. It took me a
second to realize why he wasn't making a move. He thought
he'd killed me with the throw, and my neck ached enough for
me to easily believe he might have if I hadn't used Gavrikov
to stop my roll. I was probably about to plant myself in the

dirt headfirst when the power of flight kept my momentum from breaking me in two.

Now he was standing off because ... what? He figured I'd fly off? That was a probably a real danger, actually.

"So ... a-hole," I said, staring him down, ready to zoom skyward, "what's your name?"

"Colin," he said, really soft-spoken. He had a feeling of danger about him, though, that told me I wasn't his first kill.

"So, Colin ... do you know Harry Graves?" I fished. "Or who's trying to kill me?"

He smirked. Shoulda known he wasn't stupid enough to go for that. He was just watching me hover, and I could see his muscles tense. Could I get up in the sky faster than he could jump up and drag me down? I doubted it.

Gavrikov, I said in my mind. The speedster twitched, and I wondered if he could read the subtle motion of my muscles as I prepared to make my move. "Let me show you something," I said. "Nothing dangerous, I swear. Just watch, and if I make a move you don't like, well ... you know."

He stared at me, immediately cautious. "What?"

"Kill me, of course," I said.

He gave me a suspicious look, then nodded. Natural curiosity had overcome his caution. Stupidity is not the exclusive province of the young, of course, but Veronika never would have fallen for this one.

I reached into my pocket slowly, bringing out my cell phone. He frowned at it, looking at me a little pityingly. "That's not going to help you," he said with a shake of the head.

"I didn't take it out to help me," I said, and I glanced around us. "This is Soldier Field, right? Home of da Bears?"

He kept both eyes on me as he answered. "Yeah. I guess so. Why?"

"Because they suck, of course," I said, keeping my phone clutched in my hand. *Wolfe*, I said, and felt him nod in my mind. He'd been up front all along. "Also, because it's the offseason, so ... no one here." I took in the whole place with a sweep of my hand.

"What does that have to do with your phone?" Colin asked, just waiting for me to deliver the punch line.

"Not a damned thing," I said, and I threw my phone straight up into the air as hard as I could. It flew into the night sky and disappeared. I figured I had twenty, thirty seconds before it came back down. "I just really didn't want to have to replace another phone, and I didn't want anyone else to die."

He made a scoffing noise. "The only one who's going to die here is y—"

I exploded in a blast of unrestrained fire that traveled roughly as fast as the speed of light. I saw Colin the speedster disappear behind the leading wave of flame as I went nuclear, Gavrikov-style, my flame and heat blasting the home of the Bears and turning the grass into ash and dust in less than a second. The world went white around me with the heat, with the intensity, with the sheer power of my just-below-atomic blast, and I funneled the energy out hard in every direction.

The sound was the loudest thunder I'd ever heard; the feeling of the flames exiting every pore made the air white-hot around me. My clothes burned off, unfortunately, as they always did, and I cratered the ground beneath me and turned the dirt to glass from the heat.

The explosion faded in seconds, leaving nothing but a scorched field turned to shining glass beneath me, and the stands smoking, infernos burning on the terraced stadium seating above.

My eyes swept the field. I didn't see a smoking corpse, but then, I might not have, even if I had caught him flat-footed. I sank back down to the earth, my skin absorbing the white-hot glass's searing warmth as my feet touched down. I stuck out a hand and my phone plopped hard into it, right on schedule.

"Smoke you, asshole," I said, looking over the wasteland I'd created in Soldier Field. I didn't even care anymore.

Reed was right. I didn't know much about the NFL, but I knew the Bears could probably play just as well in the parking lot.

Suck it, Bears.

47.

Colin

Colin had barely made it away in time, his clothes fried off, his skin badly burned. The air in his lungs had been sucked out and consumed, and he was choking hard, tasting his own blood as he staggered away. He wasn't running but a hundred miles an hour, at best, and he was careening off of objects in the streets because he couldn't fully see.

The bitch burned me. My eyes, my face, my body.

He found an alley and shot down it, slamming into the brick next to a dumpster. He caromed off the wall and landed on his ass, a dirty, disgusting water puddle that stank of refuse soaking through his clothes.

Colin didn't care. He barely noticed. Sienna Nealon had just hurt him more than anyone in his entire life had hurt him, even before he'd gotten his powers. He huddled into a ball and hoped, gagging his lungs out and coughing crimson liquid, hoping that his ability to heal would spare him. And he sat quivering, hiding, worried for the first time that it wouldn't.

48.

Sienna

Veronika showed up a few minutes later, naturally, before the cops could get to the scene. I was fully expecting her, just chilling in the middle of the crater of glass where the force of the explosion I'd made had pushed the dirt down before changing its molecular state. Veronika came into the stadium at a run, at metaspeed but not as quick as Colin the speedster, and she grinned with pleasure when she saw me waiting for her.

"Don't get up," she said, slowing as she approached. She was smiling, probably thinking I'd cleared some of the competition for her. "I take it you wiped Colin's smug face off the earth at the speed of light?"

"Presumably," I said, sitting on my naked ass, watching her. The stadium was still burning on the upper decks, filling the sky with dark, drifting clouds of smoke. I guess I'd torched everything on the lower decks with my blast, because nothing was burning there. "Either that or he ran off, I don't really care which at the moment."

"Yeah, it's not really going to matter soon, is it?" she asked with a big ol' smile. "You didn't even bother to run, which means—" Her shoulders fell. "Ohhh. Nealon. Tell me it's that you've given up. Tell me it's not that you think you can beat me."

"I haven't given up," I said, drumming a bare foot against the bottom of the glassy crater. This would make a real nice hot tub the next time it rained. Maybe the local synchronized swimming team could practice here. It'd certainly be more elegant than letting da Bears keep using it.

Veronika made a tsk-ing noise. "Let's just … run through this. You use fire, I snuff it. You don't have a gun. You try and net me, I burn through. You warmind, I shrug it off. You try and punch me, kick me, whatever, I do the same thing, but with hands that will burn through you." She got an annoyed look. "And if you try and fly off again, I will lead you with my eyebeams and smoke you that way. Don't expect a repeat of the police station. I won't trail you again."

"I'm not going to do any of those things, Veronika," I said coolly as she shuffled toward me, cautiously.

"Oh no?" She stopped about ten feet away. "What's your big plan to defeat me?"

"Well, I like to play to my strengths," I said, and slid my phone across the glassy field. It clicked as it came to rest where the team benches had probably once been. I stood up and brought my makeshift weapons with me. "So I think I'm just going to beat the living shit out of you."

Veronika's eyes widened in unmistakable horror as she saw what I'd done with the time between when I'd torched Colin and when she'd come rolling into the stadium. I came at her like she'd come at me before and she barely had a chance to put up a glowing blue hand before I crashed into her with a giant block of glass the size of a tall dresser. I'd personally pounded it out of the ground near the fifty-yard line, and another just like it for my other hand. It gave me a nice, six-foot reach, was probably not going to dissolve easily, even under attack by plasma, and allowed me to punch right past Veronika's hands and ram it into her face like a truck bumper to the jaw.

The best part? It didn't even shatter when I hit her. Veronika's jaw did, though.

I'd had about enough of this assassin bullshit. I wanted these monkeys off my back. I was sick of them sitting there cackling, throwing feces, and generally dragging me down. I punched Veronika in the face again with a giant block of glass, and her plasma hands didn't do squat to stop it.

Ahh, punching people in the face. I was very much in my idiom here.

Little shards of glass broke off my massive, comically large boxing glove stand-ins. Veronika took another hit, then started to stumble back, trying to avoid my long, powerful shots. It wasn't easy on her; she couldn't fly, she could only move so fast, and I was coming after her with a vengeance, flying, pounding my glass meta-beaters like pistons. I broke her arm, aimed a little lower going for her leg, and watched her try and throw up a fist to go knuckle-to-knuckle with me again.

This time, it didn't end as well.

Her hand glowed blue and it refracted through the glass, making a searing noise and filling the air with a smell of something burning that wasn't quite like anything I'd ever caught the scent of before. The closest I can think of is the smell of water evaporating off of pavement on a hot day. The glass sizzled as I slammed it against her hand. She cried out and her fist sank into the six-foot glass buffer between us, all the way the way up to her elbow.

Naturally, I was merciless. I pounded her in the face twice before she got her other hand up to sink it into my second weapon. This immobilized both of them, but by now her face and body were bleeding from a good dozen wounds created by both my punches and shards of the glass chipping off as I slammed them into her at high speed.

She grinned faintly now that she had my weapons trapped. I could tell by the sizzle that she was burning through, gradually, her arms going hot all the way up to the shoulders, firing her way through the edges of the glass.

Fortunately, I had anticipated this, and I hit her with the big surprise.

Okay, it wasn't so much a surprise as it was me using Gavrikov's flight power to slam her forward into the glassy ground faster than she could push back or burn through the glass barriers between us.

She hit the ground hard, glass shattering for ten feet in every direction. The glass weapons I was using broke from the impact, too, Veronika's glowing hands bursting through and falling to the side, the light beginning to fade in her stunned state. Her eyes were dulled and I was determined not to waste this opportunity.

Because I knew, if our positions were reversed, she damned sure wouldn't.

I snatched one of the biggest shards out of the air in front of me as the glass burst and fell, and I lifted it up high for less than a second, getting momentum behind it.

Then I drove it right through the middle of her.

She moved at the last second, damn her, and I perforated her right through the middle. She screamed in pain and lashed out at me with a freshly glowing hand. It hit me across the face, and OH MY SHIT THE PAIN.

I flew backward twenty feet, all thoughts of flight and fight and anything else pretty much shooting out of my mind as if they'd been blown out with my brains. It hurt so bad I couldn't even assess the damage at first, all I knew was that it felt like she'd ripped off my entire lower face. No, worse than that, actually, because I'm pretty sure my lower face had been ripped off before and it hadn't hurt this bad.

I was moaning on the ground, and when I came back to myself I raised my head to find her doing exactly the same about twenty feet away from me. *Wolfe*, I begged, and he obliged, coming to the fore and starting the healing process. I tried to speak but nothing came out, and the smell of char was everywhere, as omnipresent as the pain in my face.

About ten seconds later, I sat up. "Owwwwww," I moaned through newly forming skin and lips.

"Unnnnghhh …" Veronika said from where she lay, closer

to the edge of the stadium. "I'm not sure this is worth the contract money."

"Youuu shud acks fir a rayseeee," I said, not able to fully form words. Had she burned my tongue out?

"That's a good note," she agreed, letting out a little moan of pain. "I'm adding that … to my … to do list."

"Yu realiiiise, ob course … that dis means warrr."

She sat up just in time to see me flying at her, and she raised a hand just in time to turn me aside with a burst of flaming blue plasma. I dodged back as it burst forward in a blinding flash, so bright I couldn't even see. When my rods and cones returned to normal, the flare of plasma she'd released was gradually falling to the earth, way slower than gravity would have brought normal objects down. It fluttered, slowly, like a curtain dropped but catching a stiff updraft to slow its descent. It wasn't a small burst, either—it was like a blanket she'd thrown at me, three dimensional and tilting wildly toward me on three sides. I flew back ten feet as it fell to the glass and sizzled, burning the already crisped molecules as it ate its way into the ground.

I looked up and found Veronika running, looking over her shoulder as she jumped into the stands. It took me a minute to realize why she hadn't run toward one of the major exits. Then I heard the sirens.

Reed came pounding up behind me, his pistol drawn. Maclean and some other cops were behind him a good hundred yards or more, huffing their way over.

"Reed," I said, drooling as my lips finished healing, "shoot her."

Reed stared at me, horrorstruck. "I can't do that! She's running away."

"Yes," I agreed, wiping the drool off my chin, afraid to pursue for fear she'd toss up another lethal barrage of plasma, "but she'll be back to kill me. Again. And she might succeed next time, so do your sister a solid and shoot her already!"

"But …" I could see he was desperately torn, the barrel of

his gun not even aimed at her. "That's so … that's just so …"

"At some point," I said, losing my patience, "you have to decide whether you're going to let Greedo take that first shot in hopes he'll miss. Because I don't have a crew of visual effects wizards to make my head tilt out of the way in a cheesy, claymation-style effect, which means next time she comes at me, she might just kill me." I stared him down. "Now you have to decide whether you want that to happen, or whether you're going to just *man up and shoot first, Han Solo.*"

My brother blinked at me, then steadied his aim and started firing, running through the whole magazine in about five seconds. I turned my head in time to see Veronika stagger, and I knew he'd pegged her at least once. She jumped into an exit and disappeared. I didn't dare follow her into that blind corner.

"Well," I said, staring after her, "it was a good effort.

"I just shot a retreating woman in the back," Reed said, his voice as soft as puff pastry.

"I'm proud of you, Han," I said.

He gave me a hard glare. "No matter how you say that, it sounds like Vader to me."

I lowered my voice to as close to the James Earl Jones signature hiss as I could replicate. "Come to the sensible side, dumbass, where we don't let murderous assassins take free shots at us in hopes that they have terrible aim."

"What the hell did you do?" Maclean yelled at me as he came running up, breathing heavy. He had a bevy of patrolmen behind him, and all of them, without exception, were looking around at the wrecked Soldier Field like one of their relatives had died, their faces ashen.

"I just delivered an ass-whipping to the visiting team like you would not believe," I said. No one seemed to find it amusing. "What? I'm still alive." No one found that amusing, either. Reed handed me his long coat to put over my naked body. None of the cops was even looking at me; they were too horrified by the destruction of their football stadium to even care that my pretty ass was hanging out. I looked at Reed as I buttoned up the coat, thus closing the gate on any of these guys getting their own sort of free shot.

"You are not part of the home team," Maclean said, grabbing his grey hair and running his hands through it with a clear wish to just tear it out. He looked at the ruin of the stands around him and stomped a foot on the field of glass experimentally.

"My last week in government service is going super well," I said, turning to Reed, who didn't look any happier than the rest of them. "How much do stadiums cost again?"

49.

I slept like the dead. I wasn't dead, fortunately, but I slept like I was. I hadn't been able to leave the scene of the carnage for hours after the Soldier Field showdown, and when I had, it had required me to cross a line of reporters and locals who all looked angry and offended in equal measure, like I'd murdered their mothers or something. I really thought they were going to throw things, but they didn't, which was fortunate. I'd definitely exhausted some rage on Colin the speedster and Veronika the terrible, but my tank wasn't exactly running on empty yet. In fact, an argument could be made that the sun might burn out of the sky before I ran out of furious anger.

The sleep was a beautiful thing, though. Reed and I had retreated to a hotel way on the outskirts of town and told no one, not even Maclean (actually, especially not Maclean) where we were going. Reed wasn't really speaking to me, and I couldn't tell whether it was because I'd convinced him to shoot Veronika in the back as she was fleeing or because I'd blown up da Bears stadium. I doubted it was the latter, but I didn't want to probe.

At least I knew their team colors. I'd burned them right off the scoreboard, and that's the sort of thing I remember. Navy and orange. I doubted that was going to get me any points with Bears fans, though.

I closed my eyes when the sky was dark and didn't open them again until I heard the knock at the door at eleven-thirty in the morning. I knew what time it was because of the clock by my bedside, glowing red right in my face. My cheek was wet with drool, which was something that happened a lot, and I still smelled like something had burned all around me. That smell was impossible to get off, it took like fifty million showers, or maybe a good dip in the Chicago River, though that was a little like trying to get the funny smell out of your house by burning it down.

"Reed," I moaned as the knocking came at the door again, very polite, like someone was just a little too effete to knock like a man.

He didn't answer, and I looked up. The hotel we were staying in was another suite, though smaller and less impressive than the one downtown. I could see his door through the main living room. It was closed, and there was no light coming from beneath it. For all I knew, he was the one knocking.

The knock came again, a little more insistent this time, and I groaned. My head hurt, either from the fight or the untold fumes I'd inhaled last night while I was vaporizing the stadium and flying around a collapsing police station. I exhaled. My morning breath was pure dragon fire, and not of the Gavrikov variety. "Ungh. Reed!"

I still heard nothing from the other room, and the knocking came once more. I sloughed off the covers and wrapped the bedspread around my naked skin (I still hadn't gotten replacement clothes, and I'd be damned if I was going to send Reed to do so again, not after what had happened last time). I padded across the floor of my room and out into the living room. The knock sounded again, still quiet, like the person doing it didn't have an ounce of self-confidence to their name.

No assassin would knock like this, I was sure, and by now I was so irritated that whatever hotel employee was disturbing me at this ungodly hour of nearly noon that I was intending to give them a piece of my mind. I dragged my makeshift toga's tail behind me as I went to the door, ripped it open …

… and my mouth dropped in shock as I saw who was waiting on the other side.

50.

Harry

Following the chaos wasn't terribly difficult for Harry, especially when he was paying attention to the world around him. It was the sort of thing that intruded whether he wanted it to or not, but with a little careful practice, a little effort toward indifference, he'd learned to keep his head down and shut it out, keep it from mucking up his life too much. It wasn't perfect, but it was better than having to see the jangly, sharp edges of the world as he went about his preferred business of gambling, drinking and smoking.

Some things, however, were too much for even him to ignore, and the eruption of a massive explosion at Soldier Field was one of them. Keeping his head down was one thing. Ignoring enormous detonations was another, and Harry wasn't in the business of turning his face away from all danger at his own peril. No, the destruction of Soldier Field would have been the sort of thing to break through his shield of disinterest, even if he hadn't more or less shrugged it off back at the garage where he'd beaten Paul Beckman to a pulp.

No, in his search for Sienna Nealon, the explosion of a Chicago landmark had been something akin to a flashing sign saying, "Here I am!"

He'd arrived on the scene with the rest of the reporters and lookiloos, people who wanted to pick over the carnage and people who wanted to look on in horror at this piece of their life that had been ripped apart. Harry could sympathize with the second sentiment, at least. He used to bet big on the Bears back in the day. Now he tended to bet against them, but the sight of the stadium destroyed, pieces of concrete falling off the sides, the entire exterior fried to a crisp, had caused him more than a small cringe.

When Sienna Nealon had come out clad in a trench coat, he'd noticed her lack of shoes or pants pretty much immediately. Even for Harry, that was a hard detail to escape. He hadn't gotten too good a look at her before, down by the beach, when he'd been working his ass off to waylay her so he could get away. She was cute. More than cute, really, though her hair was kind of a mess. It was kind of a good look on her, though, even though she was scanning the crowd with penetrating eyes. He could see the glacier blue from where he stood, and he nonchalantly dodged a couple times to guarantee she didn't spot him.

It hadn't been the time for a confrontation, after all. He could see the weariness on her, the shuffling way she walked. She was ready to collapse, and he could sympathize with that, too.

Plus, she was naked, and he envisioned any scenario in which he approached her at that moment would end with her coming out of her trench coat, and as much of a dog as Harry was, he still prided himself on being a gentleman of the old school, and making a lady jump out of clothes was not something he cared to do if it didn't lead to a mutually consensual and enjoyable action afterward.

So, instead, he stalked her like a creeper, dimly aware as he hopped a taxi and said, "Follow that cab," that this wasn't likely to end any better if the cabbie got overexcited in one direction or another. Harry sussed out exactly what to say to keep the man calm and do what needed to be done, though, and a hundred bucks in cab fare later they ended up at a hotel in the sticks. Sienna Nealon and her brother, a tall guy with a look on his face like he'd just had a stiff drink right out of a dill pickle jar, walked into the hotel.

Harry had waited twenty minutes and followed, checking in right after them. He'd asked a couple questions of the clerk and got him to go into the back room long enough to get a moment with the computer. He'd fished for the number for Ms. Nealon's hotel room and found it with thirty seconds to spare. When the clerk came back, Harry was leaning with his elbow on the front desk, just smiling politely, a perfectly patient customer.

Harry glanced at the clock when he got to his room. It was a quarter past two. He sighed, staring in annoyance at the non-smoking sign prominently propped up on the desk, and shuffled over to the minibar. He chose two little bottles of the whiskey and got a plastic cup out of the bathroom. He poured himself a glass, a tall one, and settled onto the bed with his clothes still on. He set the alarm for eleven-thirty in the morning, figuring that'd be enough sleep to guarantee a rested, measured response from Nealon, and then waited for sleep to take him.

Tomorrow, he'd see this thing settled one way or another.

51.

Sienna

Graves was outside my damned door, and I was standing there wearing nothing but a bedspread. He had his hands on his hips, his eighties jacket all puffed out around his arms and chest, his old jeans looking ragged and tattered and kinda like they weren't from recent decades, and an indifferent look on his face. His hair was a little messy, too, and his skin had that sallow tone that smokers sometimes get after years of use, like the tobacco was just oozing out of every pore. I could smell it, along with hints of rosemary, and it didn't go well with the burnt scent wafting off my skin.

"You cheeky son of a bitch," I pronounced, dropping the bedspread and raising my hands to fight.

His eyes went south. All the way south. "Whoa," he said, eyebrows heading in the opposite direction.

I did the only thing I could think of to respond to that. I threw a punch at his face.

And the bastard dodged it, not fast, but well enough that I didn't even graze him. He did it confidently, like it was the easiest thing. I, naturally, followed up with another punch as his eyes continued to run unhampered over my naked body.

He dodged it again.

"Hold still, you asshole!" I shouted as I came at him again and the bastard dipped right out of the way just in time. I shouted at him more out of frustration than any actual belief he'd hold still and let me jack him in the jaw.

He sniffed as my arm went flying past his face, and broke into a wide grin. "Is that ... man, it smells like someone lit a stick of Teen Spirit on fire."

I grunted in aggravation as I started to come at him again. He was grinning at me in a sheepish but not really sort of way, like maybe a little guilt but not enough to get his damned searching eyes to stop. "Hey," he said, "knock it off, will you? I'm here to surrender."

I actually did stop before throwing another punch at him. "You're here to what?"

"To surrender," he said, putting his hands up in front of him. "To throw in the towel." He paused. "Actually, if I had a towel I would absolutely give it to you right now—" He waved a hand up and down to indicate me, standing there, in the hallway of the hotel, starkers.

"Get back to the surrendering thing or I'm going to start throwing fire at you."

"Right," he said, nodding and bringing his gaze back to my eyes. "I give up. You've got me." He thrust his hands forward like he expected me to handcuff him. "I yield to your authority, and I am your prisoner."

I just stood there for a minute, staring at him. This schtick was familiar, and I was every sort of suspicious. "Why?" I asked.

"Because," he said, and now he was serious, "you're going to die." He must have sensed my immediate instinct to punch him, because he held the hands up in front of his face to remind me of his surrender. "I'm not threatening you."

"It sure sounds like it," I said, "so you might want to explain yourself."

"I'm a Cassandra," he said, the look on his face at once urgent and clouded with a hint of ... worry? "So when I say you're going to die, I mean it ... I mean that I've seen your future, and I can tell you that somehow, some way, in the next couple of days … you and your brother are going to die … and I think a lot of other people … innocent ones … are going to go with you as well."

52.

Phinneus

Phinneus wasn't quite blind, but he couldn't exactly see real well, either. His vision had certainly improved overnight, and now if he squinted he could make out most of the details on the television screen—the newscaster's pretty face, the outline of the graphic at her shoulder—it was all coming back to him, but a little slower than he needed it to.

Phinneus spun the cylinder of his Colt Peacemaker idly, then spun it again. It was good and lubed up, six rounds loaded, ready for the next fight. Phinneus was ready for the next fight, too, but in a city as big as Chicago, his tracking skills weren't as useful as they'd been on his last job, which had been in West Texas. That had been fun, following his quarry's footsteps like he might have a wounded deer. He'd gotten to use the Peacemaker then, too, which wasn't something that happened all that often.

He sighed in regret over the loss of the Winchester 1873. He'd kept the damned thing for almost a century and a half. It was probably worth twice as much as this job would pay, and he was more than a little sore about it. Yeah, once it was all over, chances were good he'd be paying a little visit to wherever the Naperville police stored evidence. Right now he didn't have the time nor the inclination for a liberation mission, but it would happen. He couldn't let that pass, nossir.

For now, though, he squinted at the TV screen. His next lead was going to have to come from either the one who'd hired him, or else by tracing one of the other assassins. Veronika Acheron didn't tend to leave much of a trail, but a speedster like Colin did, blowing with a stiff breeze and pounding his feet against the pavement hard in excess of hundreds of miles an hour didn't exactly allow for travel without a trace.

Pretty soon he'd be back on the trail, but for now, Phinneus just stared at the TV, his vision improving minute by minute, and visualized what it was going to be like to plug Sienna Nealon with all six shots from the Peacemaker.

53.

"I don't get it," Reed said, staring at our prisoner with a sleepy, befuddled look on his face. "You're giving up? Because the world is ending or something?"

"Because I think the metahumans in Chicago are going to die, yes," Graves said, looking both wary and tired of explaining himself by this point. We were all sitting in the living room of our hotel suite, Reed with his shirt off on the couch, Graves sitting in the desk chair opposite us, and me, uh, still naked under the bedspread I had wrapped around me like a toga. "I've seen it."

"So why are you here?" Reed asked, looking at him through bleary eyes. "Why not just leave?"

Graves looked like someone had poked him in the back with a gun, all resigned and annoyed. "Look ... I don't know what you think of me—"

"That you're a murderer," I said quickly.

"That you're a killer," Reed added.

"That you need an Extreme Wardrobe Makeover, Eighties Edition." I slipped that little knife in at the buzzer.

Graves stared down at himself and frowned, lines creasing his face. "I'm not taking fashion advice from the girl who's currently sporting a look last favored in the Roman Empire."

"Listen, Graves—" I said.

"That's not my name," he said with more than a little annoyance.

"Your name's not Graves?" I asked, raising an eyebrow at him.

"My name is Harrison ..." He paused, looking uncomfortable, "... Harry ..."

"Harrison Wells?" I asked, jumping in.

"He said 'Harry,'" Reed cut him off. "It's Chicago, and he's performing acts of wizardry, disappearing and whatnot. Clearly his last name is 'Dresden.'"

"The hell are you people talking about?" Harry shook his head. "Yes, my last name is Graves, okay? But call me Harry, please."

"How about I call you a coroner van?" I asked, starting to fold my arms in front of me before realizing that it would cause me to flash the prisoner in question. I quickly went back to holding my toga. "Why did you kill Dr. Carlton Jacobs?" I asked, getting right to the point.

He looked like a teenager with his hand caught in the nookie jar. "Well, he needed to die."

"Not exactly selling us on why we should work with you," I said, glancing at Reed, who wore a look of mounting concern.

"Okay, so, here's the thing," Harry said, lowering his head, closing his eyes, and launching into his explanation. "I was gambling with the guy a few days ago—"

"At the casino off State Street," I said, drawing a look of surprise from Harry. "We know."

"Right, well," Harry said, "I try and keep my head down, see? I don't like using my power on people. Cards ... yeah, I use it all the time—"

"Cheater, cheater," Reed said, sounding almost scandalized at the thought of dirty play. Clearly worse than the murder we were after Harry for already.

"—but I don't like to read peoples' futures," Harry said, tapping his finger against his leg like he needed a smoke.

"They're messy. The happy moments don't exactly come jumping out at you; it's mostly the sad and horrifying shit that comes tumbling through your brain when you open yourself up to it. So, I'm gambling with this guy, and he's in my personal bubble, and I'm ignoring him as best I can, and then—boom—he lays a hand on my shoulder and I see it."

I listened, trying to reconstruct the scene in my mind from the memory I'd stolen from Thuggy. It all tracked so far. "See what?" I asked.

"Your professor," Harry said, leaning back in his chair, "he had a lot of deaths in his future. He was going to kill a lot of people, and they were going to die badly." He cringed, the faint crow's feet around his eyes wrinkling. "Now look, I can ignore minor stuff all day long—you know, I bump into someone and they're going to get beaten to death in twenty years … hey, I'll turn a blind eye and go on about my business. But some guy is going to kill hundreds? Maybe more? And it's coming soon?" He shook his head. "That I can't just pass up on. So I waited for him outside, traced his path in my head, and when he came through, I socked him in the jaw and killed him."

Reed and I exchanged a look. "What about the runner at the beach?" Reed asked, still suspicious.

"Oh, that guy," Harry said, making a disgusted sound deep in his throat. "He was a week away from murdering an ex-girlfriend and her roommate. He was a major creepo, a stalker I think they call them nowadays—in my days we just called them creepos—yeah, he was going to break into her apartment and get caught by the roommate, kill her with his bare hands, and lie in wait until his ex came back, then—"

"All right, well, I don't need to hear any more of that," Reed said, standing abruptly. He looked straight at me. "You believe this guy?"

I stared at Harry and he stared back at me. In my eyes, not at my exposed shoulders or cleavage or anything. "You gotta believe me," Harry said, open-faced as any human being I'd ever seen. "I wouldn't be here if this was the kinda thing I could just walk away from. Putting myself in your crosshairs after dodging away from you on the Mag Mile is like the last thing on my list of shit to do. It's more like, 'gamble, drink, smoke, stay the hell away from the law.'"

"That part I believe," I said, not taking my eyes off him. "The other parts, though … how was Doctor Jacobs going to kill people?"

Harry took a deep breath. "That I don't know. When you're looking into a person's future by accident, it all sort of blurs by to the big events. All I could see was the screaming, dying pain of thousands, and it was all tied to this guy's fate. He did it, somehow, that I could see, so I figured removing him from the equation would, you know, change the future. I thought it was done." He inclined his head toward me, once, sharply. "Then I caught a glimpse of you at the beach—"

"And you said, 'You're going to die,'" I repeated.

"Because I could see it on you," Harry said, nodding at me, "that exact same kind of death I saw Jacobs causing, and it was as obvious as your—" he raised a hand to point at my chest and then apparently thought the better of it. "Uhh … well, it was obvious." He turned to look at Reed. "It's on you, too. Screaming, painful death, and it's only a few days away. But I walk down the street, and your average Joe … nada. Their future retains its normal shape, the probabilities are there like you'd see in any other city, any other normal case." He made a face. "Except for a couple, here and there, utterly random. They've got this ticking clock over 'em, too."

"You think they're metas," I said, not looking away from him.

"I do," he said, "because I looked into one of their futures and saw the man very subtly tinkering with the odds at a roulette wheel. This was at another casino I frequent, see—"

"I'm detecting a pattern in your life, yes," I said, frowning at him.

"If you see death coming for metas," Reed asked, thinking about it, "what do you see when you look at yourself?"

"A Cassandra can't look into their own future, sonny boy," Harry said airily. "We can only see the future as it relates to other people or objects. Like, if your sister there wanted to put that TV over my head like a collar, I could see the TV in ghostly motion, along with the probabilities for where it would land based on my reaction, and I'd see her movement, but … I'm left out of the equation." He shrugged. "Fortunately, I can see cards being flipped over before they turn, and a roulette ball settling before the wheel even turns, which horse crosses the finish line before the race starts—you get the picture. Anyway, what the hell else do you need in life, really?"

"A clearer idea of what the hell is going on here, for one," I said sourly.

"Are you believing him now?" Reed asked, shooting me an urgent look.

"Mostly," I said. "He fights like a Cassandra, that's for sure."

"He makes love like one, too," Harry said, a little too full of himself for my taste, "not that you'd know." I just gawked at him, kinda not believing he'd just said that. "I can read the future, see. It tells what I need to do to make a lady—"

"Uh, yeah, that's not cool," Reed said, covering his face like he could blot that image out of his mind.

My phone rang before I could respond, which was a good thing, because I was kind of stunned speechless. I could hear the phone buzzing in my room, and Harry looked at me. "You should get that," he said. "It's important for your future."

"You should get it for me," I replied, the wheels in my head becoming unstuck, "because I'm afraid if I get up my toga is going to fall off."

"I already saw you completely naked." He stared at me for a second before cracking a grin. "All right. It's not going to fall off, but there's a split up the side that's going to give me a great view if you—" He stopped, shaking his head, and then stood, heading to my room. "Yeah, I'll get it for you."

"Are you seriously believing this?" Reed hissed into my ear

the second Harry had walked into my room. I could still see him, and I suspected he could hear what we were saying.

"I'm getting there," I said as Harry returned, bringing my phone with him. He tossed it to me lightly and I caught it in the hand that wasn't holding together my bedspread. "Hello?" I asked.

"Ms. Nealon, this is Jonathan Chang," came the voice on the other end of the line. "I was hoping I might be able to prevail upon you to meet me for lunch today."

"You should say yes," Harry said, giving me an encouraging smile.

"I don't have a thing to wear," I hissed.

"Even better," Harry said.

"I've got a reservation at Carrier Cattle Co. Downtown for 12:30. Can I count on you to join me?" Mr. Chang asked. "I'm about to leave from my office to catch the private jet I chartered, and I'd hate to head for Chicago if you can't make it."

Harry nodded. "Table for five," he whispered.

I looked at him in puzzlement. "Sure," I said into the phone. "I can do that."

"What?" Reed asked, standing up again. "Right now? We're going to do this *now*?"

"What else are you going to do?" Harry said with a shrug. "Let me peer into your future for you—yeah, still horrible death … unless you go to lunch." I looked at him with wide eyes. "Seriously," he said. "The probability of death changes if you say yes to this guy. I can see it." His stomach rumbled audibly. "Also, I'm hungry, and my room's minibar is out of the best kinds of booze."

"That'll be fine, Mr. Chang," I said.

"Excellent," Chang said. "I'll see you at 12:30. Also, I saw what happened at Soldier Field last night. I think I might be able to assist in your current dilemma."

"Great," I said, my voice hollow. "I'll see you then." I hung up. "What the hell are you playing at?" I asked Harry.

"I'm not playing at anything," Harry said, "Carrier Cattle Co. is good eating, always. Also, there's something that's going to happen at this lunch that's going to give us a shadow of hope." He smacked his lips. "I love it when everything comes together like that."

"How much hope?" I asked, holding my phone tightly in one hand, my bedspread loosely in the other. I felt like I'd been whammied, like Harry had hit me over the head with something heavy and I couldn't think straight.

Harry suddenly looked very guilty. "Not much," he admitted, "but it's more than you had before, so maybe now isn't the moment we should get picky."

54.

"I need a gun," I muttered as I walked out of my room with Reed's coat buttoned around me. It was huge, my brother apparently getting all the freakish height in the family and leaving me with nothing when I came along. At least I got the brains.

"I think you actually need clothes," Reed replied, giving me a critical eye, Harry Graves standing next to him shaking his head in disagreement. "Maybe some shoes?"

"I think you look just fine as you are," Harry said, and somehow—maybe it was because he'd probably been delivering this line for a century—he managed to avoid sounding like a gross old man doing it. He actually sounded charming. Not charming enough that I wanted to take my coat off or anything, but charming. Worlds away from his earlier crack about his prowess.

I slipped my phone into the coat pocket and flexed my toes against the thin carpeting on the hotel room's floor. "All right, so we're going to a meeting that's going to give us a slim chance to change this catastrophe that's about to befall the metas of Chicago." I glanced back at the clock. "But that's over an hour away. What can we do in the meantime?"

"I know a gaming hall not far from here …" Harry chucked a thumb at the door.

"Veto," I said and looked to Reed. "I guess we don't have Maclean's second victim dossier anymore."

Reed shot me a look that crawled from me to Harry, filled with great significance. I wondered for a moment if Harry caught it.

"Unless I'm lying about everything," Harry said in a loud, staged voice. Yeah, he caught it.

"How about these assassins?" Reed asked. "I can't imagine we've seen the last of Veronika or—what was the name of the one with the gun?"

"Phinny ... uh ..." I struggled.

"Phinneus Chalke?" Harry asked in sharp disbelief. "You've got Phinneus Chalke after you?"

"And Veronika something or another," I said.

"Acheron?" His jaw dropped an inch. "Holy crap, you've got somebody mad at you."

"A speedster, too," I said.

"A ... what?" Now Harry just looked perplexed.

"Like the Flash," Reed said.

Harry gave him the same confused look, and he pointed at me. "She's going to flash who? I mean, she's dressed for it, but—"

"A speedster," I said, my irritation drawing his gaze back to me, "someone who can run really fast. Colin Something-or-other."

"Fannon?" Harry's eyes closed involuntarily. "Oh, man. Who turned this bunch of hardcases on you?"

I looked at Reed. "Smart money's on Gustafson now, isn't it?"

"Seems likely," Reed said, thinking it over, "since he was apparently soft-stonewalling us on what Jacobs was up to."

"And he knew we were heading out to Naperville," I said. "Probably not too much of a stretch to guess which road the cab would take—"

"That would explain the speedster attack on the bridge," Reed said, tapping his chin. "And the ambush at Dr. Stanley's office. But not the why, really. I mean, if we're leaping to conclusions, I'm guessing he's tied into us dying somehow, in pain … but how and why?" He shrugged. "Maybe it has something to do with that research he didn't want to explain? The stuff about metas?"

"Hmm," I said, nodding. "That's a good, long leap. Well, we've got a line between points, but it's pretty thin, and there's no way we can tie anything to Gustafson. I mean, this could be coincidence so far." Reed gave me a patronizing look. "I admit, it's unlikely, but we need a little more."

"Why not let Gustafson know where you are for something?" Harry asked. "Set up a trap to draw in your would-be assassins?"

I exchanged a look with Reed. If Harry was playing us, getting all three assassins to come at us at once was not going to end well on our end. "Uhm …" I said, not thinking quickly on my feet.

"Oh, right," Harry said, nodding. "You're worried I'm going to betray you. Fair enough." He just accepted it, like that. "Well, here's something for you—these three? Colin, Veronika, Phinneus? They work alone. For good reason, too. Not one of them plays well with others, so you can bet your sweet ass—" He started to point to me and stopped, grimacing partway through, apparently remembering my sweet ass was currently a strong breeze away from being exposed like Marilyn Monroe, "—uhm, that if you get them in the same room together, they're not just going to fight to kill you, they're going to fight each other to be the one to do it. That's how assassination contracts pay. Winner take all, loser sucks tailpipe and chokes on the fumes."

"Taken a few assassination contracts in your day, have you?" Reed asked, his cynicism about Harry bleeding through.

"No, but I know these cats you're talking about," Harry said with a smirk. "Every single one of them got recruited by Century back when you were fighting your war, did you know that?"

"No," I said, frowning. "How did you hear about it?"

"Metahumans that have been around a while tend to form

interlocking circles of acquaintance, let's say." Harry grinned. "Six degrees of separation, right? Only it's less than that, because there aren't that many of us. We all know each other. We run into each other every now again, talk, gossip, the same stuff normal people do. Phinneus, Colin, Veronika—they all said no to Century, and they walked away with their lives, taking at a least a couple Century players each when they did. You weren't the only ones fighting that war."

"Yeah, I must have missed you guys at the five year reunion," I snarked. "Great. They're all badasses."

"So set an ambush," Harry said with another shrug. "Walk them into it. Deal with them one at a time if you need to, let them fight with each other—"

"And have you switch sides in the middle of it?" Reed asked. "Ugh. This is like a morass."

Harry glanced at me. "I'm normally in favor of more ass—"

I gave him a pointed look back; the charm had gone out the window again. "I'm in favor of less, and you're being one right now."

"Fine," he said, throwing up his arms. "What assurance do you need from me in order to feel safe? Because I would think that the fact that these assassins didn't descend on your hotel room in the night, even though I was checked in just down the hall, I would think that would be enough." He spread his hands wide. "What do you need from me? Within reason. I'm not going to go committing seppuku or anything like that—"

"I have an idea," I said, folding my arms over the coat and staring at Harry shrewdly. Reed was looking at me with one eye cocked, probably because a grin was spreading over my face. "And maybe … just maybe … we can roll our problems up in one big ball and get rid of several all at once."

55.

"Mr. Chang," I said, shaking the lawyer's hand as he extended it to me. We stood in the middle of a pretty impressive steakhouse, waiters in white coats bustling around us in a two-to-one ratio. We were standing in front of a booth on the back wall exchanging pleasantries, the view opposite us a window showing a busy street overlooking the river. "Thank you so much for meeting me right now." I stood a little taller in my new shoes, the suit I'd bought with Reed's credit card looking good enough to give me some confidence that I wasn't walking into this meeting naked with nothing but an overcoat.

Plus, Harry had stolen me a gun. I didn't really want to know how, but after we'd gotten downtown he walked off for about ten minutes and came back with a Glock of the sort the cops carried. I didn't even want to ask, but he assured me no harm had come to its previous owner, so I'd taken it from him without much in the way of question.

It gave me a warm feeling to know I was armed as Mr. Chang ushered me into the booth at the far end of the room in the Carrier Cattle Co. The room had dim lighting, perfectly elegant ambiance oozing out of the ultra-soft suede leather that I was scooting across so I could sit in the middle of the booth. The better to see all my angles of attack, before you ask.

"I understand you've had something of a difficult trip," Mr. Chang said, a little stiffly. He pushed a small bag over to me under the table, looking uncomfortable for having to do so. He lowered his voice before he spoke again. "I've brought everything you asked me to."

"Excellent," I said, favoring him with a smile before I turned to see Harry had scooted in to my immediate left. That forced Reed to sit on the outside of the half-circle booth, at my left. His back was to the kitchens, and he didn't looked pleased about it. But, then, he didn't look pleased about any part of this meeting or this plan. I found myself smiling at him. "Thank you for accommodating our requests."

Reed caught my look at him and shot me a scowl. "What are you grinning about?" he asked, apparently unconcerned with showing his displeasure in front of Harry or Mr. Chang.

"Oh, uh," I fumbled for a lie of convenience, "Wolfe just said something—never mind."

Reed's eyes narrowed as he stared at me. "What did he say?"

"That you're mad because you only like to eat Italian," I said, making shit up out of thin air. I sensed Wolfe's approval.

Reed blew air out from between his lips. "Wolfe's idea of a great party is the Donner party, so he can shut right the hell up." He flicked his eyes toward Mr. Chang. "I'm not so sure this little gathering isn't going to turn out like that one, though."

Chang's eyebrows inched up a millimeter or two. "I'm afraid I don't quite follow, Mr. Treston."

"He's just crabby," I said. "Because he's suspicious of your offer."

"I can understand," Mr. Chang said with a nod. "Naturally, this opportunity probably does sound a little too good to be true—"

The waiter, a bigger guy in one of the staff's white coats rolled up, looking a little like a pharmacist, his smile turned to a frown, his gaze fixed on Harry. "Sir, you can't smoke in here."

I turned my head. Sure enough, Harry had a cigarette

between his lips, bronze lighter in hand, about to flip it open. I hadn't even noticed. Harry just looked at the waiter. "Should have seen that coming. You gotta be shitting me."

"I'm afraid I'm not joking, sir," the waiter said. "There's no smoking allowed."

Harry let out a long-suffering sigh. "For a hundred years you could light up wherever the hell you wanted. You know what this is? They make a fascist state and call it progress. Even the damned Nazis let you smoke indoors."

The waiter did not take this well, but he tried. "I'm sorry, sir, but you can't—"

"Yeah, whatever," Harry said, putting away his lighter like he was the single most put-upon person ever on the face of the earth. "I see how it is." He actually sounded hurt.

"Uh, if we may continue?" Mr. Chang asked, clearly trying to delicately shift the focus back to his concerns, "Mr. Treston obviously has his worries, and I'd like to address—"

"Hey, dudes," came a voice from behind Reed, who spun in his seat to see the speaker. I honestly thought it was another waiter at first, but then I saw the thick-rimmed black glasses and the pudgy face and recognition dawned on me. "Reed with mead!" J.J. smirked at my brother. "I was going to save that for RenFest, when you might actually have a cup of mead on hand, but that's, like, September, and I was afraid I'd forget between now and then—"

"What's he doing here?" I asked, caught somewhere between dismay and awe.

"Ah, yes," Mr. Chang said, "J.J. here was one of our first hires for the new working group—"

"I was recruited," J.J. said, pleased as punch. If he'd had suspenders, he'd have stuck his thumbs in them and puffed out his chest.

"That guy's not ever getting laid," Harry pronounced, looking J.J. up and down in appraisal.

Reed looked aghast. "You can read that?"

"I don't need to read it," Harry said, picking up his menu

and turning his attention toward the embossed black lettering spelling out each item, "I can practically smell it on him."

"Not that I'm not happy to see you, bro," Reed said to J.J. before turning his irritable gaze on Chang, "but I thought you said Sienna gets to pick her own team if she does this."

"Of course," Mr. Chang said. "Anyone she wants."

"Well, naturally we want J.J. on board," I said, and the little geek lit up as Reed frowned at me. "Actually," I admitted to J.J., "I've kinda wished you were around a couple times this last few days when stuff came up …"

"Scoot over, hoss," J.J. said, waving for Reed to make room for him. He came up with a small laptop that he'd been carrying out of sight under his arm, and put it on the table in front of him. "I am at your disposal." He looked at Chang. "I am at her disposal, right?"

"Of course," Chang said, looking at me. "Anything you need."

"Convenient," Reed said through gritted teeth.

"I need to know about a Dr. Carlton Jacobs," I said, leaning across the table toward J.J. "He's kind of a science-y sort of geek, like a real Bruce Banner by way of Victor Frankenstein kind of vibe—"

"Sure, sure," J.J. said, staring through his thick glasses at the screen in front of him. "One of those kind, yeah, probably written fifty papers but can't figure out how to log into his own computer." He was actually sneering. It was a cross-geek rivalry. "Okay, I've got his FBI file here, and …"

"You're not with the government," Harry said, frowning, turning his attention unhappily from the glass of water in his hand to J.J. "How'd you get into their watchamathingy?"

"Oh, it's easy," J.J. said. His neck suddenly snapped as he leaned forward abruptly. "Oh. Oh, wow. You're, uh … you're not going to like this, Sienna."

Reed leaned over to look, and his eyes almost popped out of his head, his jaw dropping. "What. The. Hell?"

"Yeah, it's a real ripoff you have to pay for the bread here,"

Harry said darkly, looking at the menu and ignoring anything else going on around him. "You probably have to pay for the tap water, too. I swear to God, next they're gonna start charging for napkins at these places—"

"Sienna," Reed said warningly, looking up at me. "This guy … Jacobs …"

I sighed. I should have known there was something there, something beneath the surface, something that apparently a simple look at an FBI file would have told me. If only there'd been someone helping me who could have frigging done that basic thing. "This is why I'm leaving government service," I said to Reed, who flinched back from the heat of my voice. "Because this is how it is, always. It's like we're being actively shut out, but it's all done very passively, by an utter lack of caring."

"I'm … not arguing," Reed said, looking pale. "You're right. And—I mean, I'm following you for a reason."

"Yadda yadda," Harry said under his breath, still staring at the menu, "kiss and make up already, you crazy kids. You've been fighting with each other all morning and stewing over it afterward. Cain and Abel didn't argue this much."

"What is it?" I asked. "What did we m—"

"Jacobs has an FBI file that's tied to one of your old cases," J.J. said, peering up at me through his thick glasses. "He was questioned last year because his research was sponsored one hundred percent … by Edward Cavanagh."

56.

Veronika

Veronika had gotten the call after she'd had a night of miserable sleep, interrupted by agony from the shards of glass that had been driven into her torso by Nealon, that pain in the ass. There was no doubt about it in her mind: Nealon was one big damned badass, irrespective of her short-stack stature.

Now Veronika was just lingering outside Carrier Cattle Co., surveying the entrance. She'd been tipped that Nealon was coming, but she'd been standing out here for a few minutes and hadn't seen her coming. She was still a little stiff from the throwdown at Soldier Field and the fall of the damned police building on her head, but that wasn't out of the ordinary for a hard beating like the one she'd taken.

At least, she didn't think it was. It had been a long damned time since someone had kicked Veronika Acheron's ass the way Sienna Nealon had. It produced respect and severe irritation all in one. Like a painful rash, she wanted it gone but she didn't want to touch it.

She'd almost steeled herself to go into the restaurant to wait it out when she heard the rumble of a Harley coming down the street. She paused, playing incognito in the thick post-lunchtime crowd clotting the streets, eyes dancing to the source of the noise.

Dammit. It was Phinneus Chalke, riding his damned bike

right up to the restaurant.

He parked sideways, his front wheel touching the curb, sandwiched between an SUV and a Honda, leaving neither room to maneuver in his direction. His grey hair was done up in a ponytail, and—were his eyes red? He smoothed his coat around him as he got off the bike, and Veronika caught a glimpse of his pistol at his side, hidden beneath the tan canvas duster.

She started across the street immediately. No way was Chalke getting first shot at Nealon. She'd been through way too much hell to just let him win now.

57.

Sienna

"Edward Cavanagh," I said under my breath, a kind of muttered curse right up there with the F word to me.

"Yeah, Edward Cavanagh," Harry said next to me, clearly just playing along. "Who the hell is Edward Cavanagh? You know, for those of us who have lives and other things to be doing instead of reading egghead crap off a computer like you kids do nowadays."

"Or read a newspaper, like they've probably been doing since your day," I snarked in return. "Edward Cavanagh was head of Cavanagh Technologies, the company that pioneered an anti-meta suppressant gas as well as another drug that could spontaneously cause normal humans to develop meta powers. He was trying to unleash it on the world when he got caught in Atlanta and thrown in jail by yours truly."

"Rough deal," Harry opined, picking up his napkin from the table and delicately tucking it into his pants.

"It looks like Cavanagh funded him on an ongoing basis," J.J. said. "He was up to the hip waders with Jacobs's research." He scrolled down the screen. "Ooh, and I've got multiple visits by Cavanagh before his death, some lunch meetings the FBI was able to confirm ..." He adjusted his glasses and looked up at me. "Cavanagh might just have been using Jacobs's research in the suppressant and ... uhh ... power ... serum? What do you even call that?"

"Egghead bullshit," Harry said sourly.

"Upsetting the natural order of the planet in a heinous-ass way," I said.

"Doesn't have the same ring to it," Harry said.

"Whatever Jacobs was up to," I said, looking at Reed, "if somehow he or Gustafson were going to unleash suppressant on us, given all the crap we've got coming our way, that could definitely result in a painful death."

Harry looked at me through slitted eyes. "I don't think that's it."

"Well, can you give us something more specific?" Reed asked, voice hushed, elbow on the table. "Because, you know, 'painful death' doesn't exactly narrow things down."

I caught movement across the restaurant, against the background of the grey street beyond. The place was a little empty given it was now past lunch hour. Most of those who remained were the four people hanging out at the bar. I guessed a steakhouse at almost two p.m. wasn't a big draw, even in Chicago.

The motion I saw was a guy in a long, tan coat, striding across the room while sparing a glance our way every few seconds. He had a long, grey ponytail and a mustache, but he managed to wear it without looking like a pedophile, so kudos to him. Without meta senses, it would have been impossible to see him looking at us like he was. With them, it was impossible not to.

"Business is about to pick up," I muttered under my breath.

"I don't think this place is going to get busy until at least five o'clock," J.J. said, his face buried in his computer screen. "I mean, I guess I could be wrong, but—"

The guy in the coat cut across the room toward us, apparently abandoning all pretense of doing something other than coming our way. He slipped back his coat and his hand touched the gun at his hip. "Sienna Nealon," he said from halfway across the room, "I'm calling you out."

58.

"Really?" I looked at him flatly, my hands beneath the table. "Because I just want to call the waiter over. I could go for some steak. I haven't even eaten today—"

Phinneus Chalke looked at me, probably annoyed at my irreverent sass while he was pointing his pistol at my face. "I said I'm calling you out. I got a Peacemaker aimed at your brainpan, girl."

"And I've got a CZ Shadow aimed at your nutsack and a Glock pointed at your heart," I said, clinking the barrels of both the gun Harry had stolen for me and the spare pistol Chang had brought me from Minneapolis against the bottom of the table. "I'm guessing you're pretty high on the power scale, Phinneus, but do you think your balls will grow back after I shoot 'em off?"

A slow smile spread across his face, which I found surprising, since I wasn't bluffing about aiming a gun at his twig and berries. "You're all right," he pronounced.

"As a shot, I'm better than all right," I said coolly. "As a person, I'm hell on my enemies. Harry?"

Harry stirred beside me. "Yep. He's going to die the same as the rest of you."

Phinneus seemed to split his gaze between me and Harry. "Graves, is that you?"

"It is, Phinneus," he said. "I need a scotch."

I resisted the compulsion to roll my eyes because I didn't

want to take them off Phinneus and his pistol, the barrel of which was looming awfully large where it was pointed at my skull. *Wolfe?* I asked. *Any chance we can stop a .45 Long Colt to the head?*

Not likely, the serial killer said; a little glumly, I thought.

"Harry," Phinneus said, shaking his head slightly as he chuckled, "you're making a bad bet on this one."

"I ain't betting, Phinneus," Harry said, swirling his water glass around, clearly wishing it were something else, "and she's not going to be the one that kills you. You're going to die the same way she is."

Phinneus looked like he was pondering that one over, poking his tongue at the inside of his cheek. "All right, Harry, I'll bite. How am I going to die?"

"At my hand," Veronika said, striding down the stairs behind Phinneus, her hands aglow. I heard movement up at the bar on the upper level; it sounded like the patrons were wisely leaving, probably without paying their tabs. What a bunch of sensible thieving assholes.

"Afraid not, Veronika," Harry said, looking at the water in his glass before tossing her a look. "You're going to die the same way."

Veronika was wearing another classy suit, and she deflated. "You screwing with me on this, Harry?"

"You know I wouldn't," Harry said then broke into a grin. "At least, not like—"

"Mind on the game, Harry," Veronika said, unamused.

"Here's the reason I summoned you all here," I said, pulling my Glock up and aiming it right at Veronika.

"You didn't summon us," Veronika said. "We got a message from—"

"Dr. Art Gustafson," Reed said.

Veronika kept a straight face, but Phinneus blew it. "Shit!" he said. "The doc's going to be pissed you figured it out. You were supposed to die before you caught up with him."

"Way to give away the farm, idiot," Veronika said, blowing

air out her red, red lips. She refocused on Harry. "So, how is it you think we die, Graves? Is it that moron Fannon?"

"No," Harry said, shaking his head. "He's about to have a personal tragedy that's going to put the kibosh on his killing plans." He drained the last of his water.

"I ain't buying this," Phinneus said, his grip still firm on his Colt Peacemaker. That barrel still loomed, pointed right at me.

"Just chill," I said. "Give me five minutes and I'll explain everything. If you don't like my explanation, then … well …"

"What if I don't want to wait?" Phinneus asked. He sniffed.

"Then I guess we'll turn this steakhouse into a slaughterhouse," I said coldly, staring right down Shadow's barrel at his skull. If he was going to open up on me, I was going to make sure my last act was to wipe him off the earth in return.

"Slaughterhouse five!" J.J. shouted. Everyone except me looked at him, and he pointed to Chang, then me, then Harry, then Reed, and finally, at himself. "Because there's five of us."

"Why do you need five minutes?" Veronika asked, her hands still aglow with that hellish plasma. It was coloring the restaurant, reflecting off the windows behind her.

I looked sidelong at Harry. I hadn't told him my plan for stopping Colin the Speedster, but he clearly had it figured out. "When is Colin going to—" I started to say.

"Right now," Harry said, and pointed his hand to the left.

A pitched scream came from the hallway to the kitchen, followed by the sound of a body colliding heavily with several walls. Colin Fannon came bursting out into the restaurant from behind J.J., and he smashed through the nearest table, shattering the glassware and sending the whole thing toppling over. He was bleeding all over the place, and it wasn't from his landing, either.

"Oh, yeah!" Augustus Coleman said, rolling up behind Fannon, his gun drawn and pointed at the speedster. "Didn't see that coming, did you?" He waved his free hand and suddenly Fannon was enshrouded in shards of broken glass, a barrier like the one Augustus had put up at the back entrance. Clearly, Fannon hadn't seen it and had charged right in, shredding himself without even realizing it until the deed was done. "How'd you like my little trap, Jay Garrick?" Augustus asked.

"I honestly thought you would have said Wally West," Reed said with a furrowed brow.

Augustus puckered his lips, looking at my brother in disdain. "Pfft. I bet you think I'd pick John Stewart over Hal Jordan, too? Don't be so one dimensional, Reed."

"This isn't a rave," Kat Forrest called as she descended the stairs from the bar area, the last guest to leave the party, her pistol pointed right at Veronika's head. "Put the glowy hands away, lady."

"Slaughterhouse seven!" J.J. shouted, drawing every eye back to him. He looked at Reed and bumped him with an elbow. "I totally knew Kat and Augustus were here because they were on the plane with me. I was just, y'know, playing, so I wouldn't spoil the surprise."

"Yeah, I got that," Reed said tightly.

"Sorry to drag you into this, Mr. Chang," I said. "But I appreciate you pushing our meeting back to accommodate my special requests."

"You calling me special?" Augustus cocked an eyebrow at me, clearly not taking it as a compliment.

"No," I assured him. "I was totally talking about Kat."

"Thank you," Kat said brightly.

"Not a problem, I hope." The lawyer looked more than a little discomfited. "I'm just going to sit here and hope not to get shot or … burned or … whatever you plan to do."

"You best get to explaining, girl," Phinneus said, looking impatient as Colin Fannon mewled in pain from the floor. "He says something's going to kill us—" He nodded at Harry. "Let's get some words flowing, because I got a bounty I would love to collect."

"Every meta in this room is going to die, at the same

moment, in the same screaming way," Harry said, letting his empty water glass clink onto the table in front of him. "It's less than twenty-four hours away, and it's not … well … it's not clear, exactly. Looks like … disease or something." He frowned then shuddered. "Oh, I need that scotch."

"So we're all going to catch a nasty cold and croak?" Veronika asked, hands at her sides, giving Kat a hostile look behind her. "Pretty farfetched, Graves."

"Not really," I said. "How about this? We all get killed by a bioweapon designed specifically to target metas and no one else."

"That's not any nearer-fetched than what Harry suggested," Veronika said.

"Is it more or less farfetched than a gas that takes our powers—" Reed started.

"Or a chemical that gives humans meta powers?" Augustus said, maintaining his vigil over Fannon, who'd gotten quiet and was listening, though his face was still contorted in pain.

The slightly smug look on Veronika's face faded and she looked sidelong at Phinneus, who showed his first waver of uncertainty. There was something there, something that hinted that they knew something they weren't saying. "Spill it," I commanded.

Phinneus raised the barrel of his pistol back slowly, away from my head, and then returned it slowly to its holster. "Shit," he said and looked like he was about to break into a cold sweat.

"Gustafson …" Veronika said, and now she looked rattled. "He … we all know him."

"'We all'?" Harry asked, surging ahead of me and stealing the exact words I was about to say. "Is there a club for assassins now?" He flashed a grin at me that told me he'd done that just to tease me, since he and I were the only ones that knew what I'd been about to say.

"Hah, that totally sounded like something Sienna would say!" J.J. was practically rolling with glee. It was like he didn't even realize how close to death we all were just by being in the same room.

"Gustafson contacted us all once before," Veronika said, putting her hands on her hips, which I interpreted as her version of disarming herself, a sign of peace. "We ... contributed to a project that he ran here at the early stages of NITU's startup. They were studying meta genes and powers when they first got the grant money, and the way they went about it was ..." Her voice trailed off.

"They found metas for hire and paid them money for gene samples," I said, and she nodded. "Did they pay you, too, Fannon?" The speedster gave me a hostile look, then looked away and nodded.

"Mmm," Harry said, stretching his neck to see if anyone was still at the bar. "Looks like this place has gone all-you-can-drink. Just as well, because I doubt we're going to get any of that bread we would have had to pay for." He pushed against Reed, then slipped his way over J.J. and my brother in the most bizarre set of movements I might have ever seen.

"So Jacobs and Gustafson were experimenting with some sort of meta plague," Reed said, shifting after Harry had climbed over him. "I guess based on Harry's prediction ... they found it."

"That wasn't what they were supposed to be working on," Veronika said, and she was starting to get angry for the first time. "We donated—"

"You took cash," I cut her off, causing her face to pinch in irritation, "technically, you whored yourself."

"—we gave DNA to them not just for money—" she went on.

"Oh, it was totally about the money for me," Phinneus said.

"—because they said they were working on something that would help slow the aging process in everyone—normal humans and metas alike," Veronika said, looking like there was a flint grinding against a rock in her soul as she said it. "They were supposed to roll back the clock on ... time." She flushed, looking abashed and maybe a little insulted. Part of me wanted me to know what deep personal motivation was driving Veronika, making her less coldly impartial about this turn of events.

The other part of me wanted to shoot her in the head while her hands were at her side and call it good. Needless to say, the new and improved me was keeping that impulse heavily under wraps, where no one could see it.

Harry came wandering back over with a tallboy full of scotch and slipped back in next to me. "That percentage on you shooting Veronika and Phinneus is wavering pretty heavy. Maybe you should stop going to war with yourself and get it over with one way or another, huh?"

Dammit.

"The thing I don't get, though," J.J. said before I could turn too red (Veronika totally shot me a look that told me she'd heard what Harry said), "is why would anyone be experimenting with trying to kill all the metas?"

"Because we're just so good for the world, obviously," Kat said, the gun in her hands still pointed at Veronika. "We do such amazingly awesome things, like that time my brother almost blew up Minneapolis, for example—"

"And that time Sienna almost blew up Minneapolis," Augustus said.

"Let's not forget Sovereign," Reed said stiffly.

"Or that time Western Kansas got burned," I said, trying to shift the focus to something I had absolutely nothing to do with.

"Then there's also Soldier Field and the Great Chicago Fire," Harry said, calmly, between sips of his drink. "One of them caused by this little lady," he nudged me in the ribs, "and the other by your old friends Winter and Sovereign." My eyes widened as I stared at him. I had no idea that those two had caused the Great Chicago Fire. "Yeah, we're kind of a plague on this world, but I might suggest, no more so than any other human. It's not like we invented the nuclear bomb, or war, or anything like that." He sipped. "We just ... maybe refined it a little from time to time."

Veronika looked ashen. "You're kinda making me not want to save us, Harry."

Harry looked around the room. "Well, why not? What, you think metas only do bad? We've all seen what our race can do in the bad times. Hades, Ares, Zeus, we've heard the legends." He raised his glass to Phinneus. "Hell, Chalke might even have seen some of those things personally—"

"Screw you, Harry," Chalke said, folding his arms in front of him.

"Death's a fact of life, kids," Harry said, holding his glass precariously between two fingers. "Humans killing humans is a fact of life." I suspected he caught the fact that he was sinking the room into a collectively deeper depression by the second, because he stopped, kind of took a breath, and started again, looking each of us in the eye in turn as he spoke. "Look … I kill when I can feel the pain of others. It's like a swallow of castor oil, sick and greasy, and it runs right through me." He brought his gaze over to look me in the eyes. "Like that guy on the beach. I could feel what he was going to do to those girls, and it was like someone jabbed a knife right into me. I couldn't—" He grimaced. "I've never been able to take that, not really. The drinking helps, but … I still feel it sometimes." He raised his glass and stared at the deep amber liquid within. "It's nice to numb the pain, to dial it down so I don't feel it always." He took a long drink. "Not to worry about tomorrow." He swallowed and made an *Ahhh!* sound. "Well … there's a lot of people about to not have a tomorrow. We all know about the worst of us." He tipped his glass toward Veronika, then Phinneus, then Fannon. "We hear the rumors, the stories. But we don't hear about the kid I passed on the street earlier, who had the same ticking clock as the rest of us, but none of the horrific baggage." He sniffed. "He's going to go his whole life without hurting a soul. He's innocent. Sweet. In a way none of us are anymore." He looked pained. "Doesn't he deserve a chance?"

"Shit, Harry," Phinneus said, frowning, "you didn't have to get all sappy. I would have partnered up with you clowns just to save my own ass in this."

"Same," Veronika said, sounding madly uncomfortable.

Fannon grunted from the floor. "The old dinosaur … makes a good point, though."

"Like I was talking to you cynics," Harry said, making a face at Phinneus and Veronika. "I was speaking to the younger and more idealistic crowd."

Fannon looked right at me, clutching at himself, skin wet with blood. "What do we do?"

I hesitated, lulled by Harry's speech, which had produced some very odd emotions in me. "Uhm …" I glanced at Harry.

Harry gave me a nod. "They're all in. I can read the probabilities. They're not going to stab you in the back later. Gustafson's the one paying them, and if he's dead …" He waved his drink, careful not to spill.

"Yeah, no contract," Veronika said, thoroughly irritated. "I came to town on my own dime so that I can do charity work. Whoopee."

"All right," I said, nodding. "We need to get to Gustafson and stop him before this clock ticks down." I looked at J.J. "This is your moment, J.J."

He nodded solemnly, a serious look falling over his face at the grim moment we found ourselves in. He opened his mouth, licked his lips, and said, "Does this make us the slaughterhouse ten, now?"

I just rolled my eyes and barely kept from slamming my head against the table. You can take the geek out of government service, but he's still a geek.

59.

"The cops are coming," Harry pronounced suddenly.

"Yeah, I won't be sticking around for that," Phinneus said, throwing a furtive glance behind him at the large windows onto the street.

"I'm … I'm just gonna get on a plane," Veronika said, seeming to gather herself together at last. "You don't need my help catching some pencilneck. Gustafson … he's the kind that carries a slide rule in his pocket, not a gun."

"Hmm," Harry said, staring at her carefully, "that doesn't change anything for you, survival probability-wise. Either you're already infected with whatever this is … or this thing's going global."

"Fine," Veronika said, looking rattled, "then I'm going to—"

"Won't help," Harry cut her off with a shake of the head. "The only probability change I'm seeing right now is if we go the 'fight' route." He downed the last of his drink. "I know. Wouldn't be my first choice, either."

"What do we do?" Reed asked as the first sound of sirens echoed through the steakhouse. The sound of a shattering plate in the back kitchen was like a warning that things were about to break all over if we didn't get moving.

"J.J.?" I asked, but he was pecking away on his keyboard.

"He won't give you anything before the cops get here," Harry said.

"Also," Reed said, under his breath, "Slaughterhouse Five was the name of the slaughterhouse, not a name for a group." J.J. didn't stir, but I saw Reed relax a hair, clearly relieved now that he'd corrected the incorrect geekery foisted upon those of us present, none of whom gave an actual damn.

"Fannon," I said, looking at the speedster still surrounded by Augustus's prison of shards, glittering the steakhouse's low light, "why don't you go up to Northern Illinois Technical University and grab Gustafson?"

"I'd love to," he said, voice wrought with pain, "but I'm kinda gonna be pushing glass shards out of my internal organs for the next couple hours, and moving fast would be … really detrimental to my health during that time." He glanced at Augustus. "Thanks for that, by the way."

"Hey, man, you were the one who took a contract to kill my friend offered by a genocidal mad scientist," Augustus said.

"Why not get your friends the cops after Gustafson?" Phinneus asked.

"Not a terrible idea," I said, looking back at the street.

"Whoa, no, that's a terrible idea," Harry said, pretty definitively. "That one kills the small chance of survival we all had."

"Damn, this is grim," Reed said, looking as grey as I'd ever seen him.

"We gotta go now," Harry said, standing up. "Otherwise, the cops are gonna try and detain us, and Phinneus and Veronika are going to kill eight of them."

"Yep," Phinneus said with a nod when we all looked at him.

"Fine, we leave," I said, matching Harry and standing up.

"Where do we go?" Reed asked. "Do we just … all pile in a bunch of cabs and head up to NITU to snag Gustafson?"

Everybody sort of looked around uneasily except Harry, who chortled. "Like a convoy." He seemed to sober up, his childish grin disappearing. "I guess I'm the only one who thought three cabs full of metahumans rolling through the streets of the Gold Coast was cause for amusement." He pushed at Reed, who started to move. "All right, let's go."

"I got a bike outside," Phinneus said, as we started to move ourselves toward the door, kinda slowly for a bunch of people with metahuman speed. "One of you can ride with me."

"Oh, man, I want to ride on the bike," J.J. said, looking up as he snapped his laptop shut just before he tripped over one of the stairs.

Phinneus looked at him in askance. "Not quite what I was hoping for." He looked straight at Kat, who was leading the way, her gun holstered beneath her aquamarine designer suit. "How about you, girl?"

"She's out of your league, Phinneus," Veronika said, brushing through the door. She looked straight at me with a smirk. "How about Sienna? I've seen her naked. She's your type."

"What the hell is that supposed to mean?" I asked a little hotly.

"I saw it, too," Harry said, breezing out, a whole bottle of scotch now clutched in his hand. He smacked his lips together idly, like he was thirsty. "It's good."

"I only saw it for a minute," Fannon said, his voice still low and grunting as he hobbled out with Augustus walking warily at his back, "when she was turning into a dragon, but before she got all scaly, it was all right."

Phinneus paused at the curb, one foot off, the very image of a rugged frontiersman … dressed like an old biker. "What, did you take your clothes off for everyone but me? Did you do it after you blinded me?"

I rolled my eyes. "Yeah, you've got me figured out. I'm leaving government service to become a stripper."

"Your ride is here," Mr. Chang said, and a steel grey Hummer limo came pulling up in front of the steakhouse.

"You know, I can get my bike later," Phinneus said, clearly admiring my new conveyance.

The sirens were drawing closer. "Okay, everyone in," I

said, and they started piling in like it was a clown car.

"I haven't seen her naked either, man," J.J. said, putting a hand on Phinneus's arm in sympathy. Phinneus gave him a look, and J.J. removed it and skittered into the limo.

"This is where I leave you, Ms. Nealon," Chang said, not exactly cool as a cucumber. He looked pretty relieved to get off the party bus. "I trust you'll give me a call when you've decided whether to take my client's employment offer?"

"I'll be in touch," I said, giving him a nod as Reed shot me an evil look before he climbed in the limo.

"I'll be waiting," Chang said and turned to stride off down the sidewalk. His hair was wet and streaked down the side, probably from getting caught in the most intense negotiation he'd ever been part of. He walked a little stiffly, but seemed to relax more with every step he took away from us.

The sirens blared in my consciousness. "Now would be a good time to leave," Reed called to me from the open door of the limo, throwing a little extra judgment into it.

With that, I sighed and got in, and the limo sped off toward the college and hopefully Gustafson, where we could put an end to this thing for good.

60.

I found myself on a leather seat between Phinneus Chalke and my brother. Harry was stinking up the limo with the smell of cigarette smoke on his clothes that he dragged everywhere with him like a cloud. Somehow, probably because of the tight quarters, it made me make a face.

"You know," Phinneus said, showing me just a hint of a smirk, "that was a hell of a chance you pulled in that restaurant, trying to turn us all around on Gustafson. It might not have worked out for you. That took guts. You got a big ol' brass pair."

Veronika sat up, and I could see that what Phinneus had said was chafing on her. "I told you I saw her naked, Chalke. The only thing she's got a pair of is tits. Which explains why she can take a kick to the groin without falling apart, unlike the rest of you helpless dicks in this car."

"Oof," Reed said next to me as all the guys in the limo but J.J. cringed at that. My brother looked at me. "So ... now we've recruited assassins and a hard-drinking, gambling murderer to help save the world." He looked at Harry, who was clutching his bottle of scotch in front of him like a shield as he frowned at Reed. "No offense."

"None taken," Harry said with a shrug.

"I really just wanted to get them off my back," I said. "I wasn't ... planning to recruit anybody. I'd just like to not have the metas of Chicago or the world die, though, and that's something we can all agree on."

"Uh huh," Reed said, jaded. "You know, when this over and we're unemployed, you could just go work as an assassin like them." He nodded toward Veronika. "I bet she'd give you some pointers."

Veronika turned her head toward us from where she sat next to Kat. "Being an assassin requires anonymity, lunkhead. Nealon fails on that basis alone. She couldn't go anywhere in the world without someone recognizing that face." She pointed right at me.

"Not all of us have to show our face to get the job done," Phinneus interjected with a smirk. He looked right at me. "I've seen you shoot on TV. Who taught you?"

"An old friend," I said, looking at Phinneus's grey hair and beard. "Actually ... you kinda remind me of him."

Phinneus's eyes twinkled. "You learned from Glen Parks, didn't you?"

I stared back at him. "You knew Parks?"

Phinneus cackled like it was some great joke. "I taught him and he went and taught you. Now that's what I call training your own competition." He quieted down and got serious, the wrinkles around his eyes subsiding. "He didn't make it through the war with Century, did he?"

"No," I said, feeling a sudden lump in my throat. "He didn't." I didn't bother to elaborate.

The limo hit a bump, and I looked out to see we were on Lake Shore Drive heading north. Again. I turned my gaze to J.J. down the row. "You got anything?"

He took a second to realize I was talking to him. "Uhmm ... I've got ... uh ... yeah, no, I got nothing more right now. I can't get through NITU's firewall without brute forcing it, which is probably a good thing, since it'd be disappointing if a school that emphasized science and technology had servers as easy to break into as an elementary school."

"Then I guess we wait until we get there," I said, and we settled back into an uneasy silence as the limo rolled on.

61.

When the limo pulled up to the Northern Illinois Technical University campus, the sun was already coming out from behind its clouds. Which was good, because I was starting to believe Illinois maybe didn't have a sun. We headed across campus at a quick walk, the whole damned cluster of us: me, Reed, Augustus, Kat, J.J., Veronika, Phinneus, a still-limping Fannon, and Harry, who looked surprisingly steady for a guy who'd downed as much booze as he had.

"Man, we got the full-on Justice League going here," Augustus said as we made our way through the campus. People moved out of the way, probably because I was at the lead. I saw a few cell phone cameras, and saw Veronika wince at them, trying to keep herself from just going over and destroying them in peoples' hands, probably.

"Avengers," my brother said, making that coughing noise under his breath.

"These geeks," J.J. said, elbowing me, like he wasn't dying to just join in with them. His inside-baseball expression melted as he realized I wasn't buying it.

We stormed the stairs of the science building where Gustafson had his office, and I nearly shoulder checked President Breedlowe as she came out of the entrance. She looked dazed, but her eyes snapped into clarity when she saw me and my scary-looking entourage. "Oh," she said, smoothing out the front of her suit as she came to an abrupt halt. "What are you doing here?"

I decided to just hit her with the truth. "Dr. Jacobs and Dr. Gustafson were working on creating a biological weapon for use against metahumans with funding from Edward Cavanagh," I said. "Tell me where he is." At that point I dropped any pretense of being nice.

She put up her shields, folding her arms, and her face darkened. "I'm—no, I'm not telling you that."

"Fine," I said, "then I'll arrest you for obstruction of justice. I have a feeling Gustafson isn't going to want to be taken alive, so the war crimes tribunal will just have to content itself with drawing and quartering you and your university."

"BOOM!" Augustus whispered, at meta-low volume, voice filled with quiet awe.

Breedlowe fell apart in a second. "He just left, in a big truck, and I don't know what he was doing because he was being really evasive and—"

"What kind of truck?" J.J. asked, sneaking forward to insert himself into the conversation.

"Big," Breedlowe said, looking like she was about two seconds from breaking into a sweat even on this chilly day. "Transfer—err—tractor trailer? Whatever they call them. The big shipping trucks. He was driving it."

"Not every day you see a fancy doctor relegate himself to truck driver," Veronika said from somewhere behind me. "Looks like Gustafson's moving down in the world."

J.J. had his laptop open. "I need your WiFi password," he said to Breedlowe, who looked like she was heading fast for catatonia. J.J. stared right at her. "Now, lady, before your employee of the month drops the bomb on Chicago and kills more people than you have enrolled in this dump!" My eyes widened a little as J.J. played his hand hard.

"It's, uh," Breedlowe stammered, "… number one uni in I-L-L." J.J. looked up at her. "It's spelled like it sounds," she said with a broken voice.

"I'm in," J.J. said, staring at his laptop, which was holding with one hand and pecking away at with the other. "Bypassing into the security ... okay, I've got surveillance cameras ... rolling back ..." He looked at Breedlowe. "Where did you see him in this truck?"

"Behind the building," Breedlowe said, pointing to the science building behind her.

"Got him and a timestamp," J.J. said, staring at the screen. "Switching to CPD camera network ..." He glanced at Breedlowe. "You should be proud of your IS department, I couldn't breach them. City of Chicago, on the other hand ..." He concentrated as we all held our breath. "Okay, got him. Let's get to the limo and give chase."

Everyone kind of stood there, stock still for a minute, J.J.'s sudden bout of hard-charging intimidation turned leadership taking a moment to settled in on us all, even the newbies who had just met him.

"You heard *the man*," I said, putting emphasis on that last part and causing J.J. to inflate with pride. "Let's go get Gustafson."

62.

"Take a left," J.J. told the driver, switching his attention between the computer sitting on his lap and the front windshield.

"Don't," Harry said with a shake of his head. "If you go that way, we'll never get him. Take Lake Shore south."

I blinked at Harry. "You can read that in the probabilities?"

"Yeah," Harry said, nodding. "Probably a wreck or something." The driver took his course as Harry looked at me. He'd finally put aside the bottle. "Our odds are improving somewhat."

"Good," I said, as Harry eased closer to me by a couple inches in what could have been an innocent readjustment to the way he was seated but didn't quite feel like it. "What?" he asked me.

"What are you doing?" I asked, eyeing him.

"Sitting next to you," he said, giving me a little bit of a smile. It was charming. "Is that a crime now?"

"It probably takes a back seat to the two self-confessed murder counts I've got you on," I said, as seriously as I could.

"Ooh," Harry said, making it seem like something uncomfortable. "You are the most serious young person I've met. What are you? Thirty? Forty already?"

"I just turned twenty-four last month," I said.

His brows shifted up in surprise. "Oh my. You are young."

"And *you're* hitting on me," I said, feeling like I'd caught him in dirty old man mode.

He shrugged it off without any guilt. "Look, when you get a couple centuries on you, it's not exactly easy to date in your age bracket. So … what's an older gent to do? Just give it up?" He chortled. "Not likely. I've still got the physiological needs of a thirtysomething."

Harry's whole persona was so laid back that I didn't feel uncomfortable with the way he was going about making his case to me. All the same, I wasn't buying into it, either. "Kat," I said, calling over Reed and Augustus, "I found you a new boyfriend."

Kat peered down at me, then at Harry, appraising. "Uck, not even."

"Thanks, Klementina," Harry said with a tight smile. "You just keep pretending that winter in Smolensk never happened."

"Whut?" I asked, my jaw suddenly loose.

"Huh?" Kat's eyes were like hubcaps.

"Did he just call her …?" Reed asked.

WHAT DID YOU DO TO MY SISTER?! Gavrikov shouted in my head, loud enough to make me blanch.

Dammit, Gavrikov, you didn't hit the ceiling like this when Scott or Janus or that nasty assclown Taggert had their way with her. I felt Aleksandr relax a little in my head, though he was still watching Harry suspiciously through my eyes.

"Besides," Harry said, glancing subtly at me, "I like a girl with a little meat on her bones."

Kat gave herself the once-over, self-consciously. "What am I, a vegan meal over here?"

"Not much of one," Harry said, "besides, you had more personality before you lost your memory."

"Take a right," J.J. said into the awkward silence that followed. "And then an immediate left."

"Don't do that," Harry said, shaking his head sagely. "Take the second left."

"Probabilities again?" I asked.

"No, this is just basic knowledge of Chicago traffic," Harry said. He pointed at the computer sitting on J.J.'s lap. "Plus, I'm watching his future, and correcting for the five times I've read him shouting, 'No, that was wrong, my bad'!"

J.J. looked up at Harry in awe. "Wow. Thank you."

"Yeah, I'm not exactly being a hero here," Harry said. "There's self-preservation involved."

"All right, I'm up to the live feed," J.J. said, glancing back down again. "Looks like Gustafson is on Lower Wacker."

I stifled a giggle. Harry didn't bother, guffawing loudly. "That kills me," he said then got serious. "I mean, uh … yeah, it still makes me laugh after all these years. 'Wacker.'"

"And here I thought you were too old for me," I said. "Really, you might be too young."

"You had a twelve percent probability of smiling when he said 'Wacker,'" Harry said nonchalantly. "Your control is good, but you found it funny. You don't even have to admit it, I just know." He smiled.

Dammit.

The limo turned and headed down a ramp, like it was descending into a parking garage. It wasn't a garage, though, it was like an understreet—a street running under the main one. I raised an eyebrow, because I couldn't quite recall seeing anything like this before. It was a steady, perpetual tunnel on three sides, with the fourth looking out over a river that I assumed was the Chicago.

"This makes things dicey," Reed said, tapping me lightly on the arm to get my attention. "Once we get eyes on him, you could fly …"

I looked up at the roof of the "tunnel." Yeah, I could fly in here, but not very high, that was for sure.

"He's five hundred yards away and moving fast," J.J. said. Our limo driver had his pedal to the metal, maneuvering his ride in between cars like it mattered. I could see him up there, a younger guy in a suit. Looked stiff, but it was probably just the tension.

"Screw your Uber, we should hire this guy full-time," I said to Reed.

He gave me a pained look. "Tell me you're not going to go with Chang's offer. Just tell me."

"Odds are against you on that one, sonny," Harry tossed right over me.

"There's the truck!" Phinneus shouted. He already had his pistol out and pointed, like he was going to shoot through the windshield.

Harry landed a hand on his arm, dragging it down, a serious expression on his face. "Whatever he's got in that truck, it's delicate. Survival probability of everyone in this car except the driver and the computer guy goes to zero if you shoot out the tires."

"Instant mission failure," J.J. said under his breath. "Ooh. The plot thickens."

"So we can't crash it," I said as the limo weaved hard to get around some ass in a BMW that thought he owned the whole road. "How about I fly up and yank Gustafson right out of the driver's seat?"

Harry cringed. "Odds do not look favorable if you do that. Not one hundred percent failure rate, but ... not good, either."

"Fannon?" I asked, and the speedster cringed. He was still being really quiet, his hooded sweatshirt pulled over his head.

"I can maybe do a sixty miles an hour right now," he said, and I realized his clothes were wet with blood, still. "And not for long."

"Can you fly me up to the top of the truck?" Veronika asked, leaning forward off the bench seat to talk to me.

I looked up at the bottom of the road above us, the supports racing by overhead. "Yeah. We should have enough clearance to do that."

"You get me up there," she said, turning around to look out, "I burn through and destroy whatever that plague thing is by superheating it." She had a hopeful, alive look in her eyes as she turned her head back to me. "Whatever disease he's carrying, I'm guessing it'll burn up under superheated plasma."

Harry stared out the window. "A lot better odds on that one."

"I can fly out, too," Reed said. "Provide support, maybe some covering fire—"

"Odds dropped at the covering fire part," Harry said, squinting at the truck.

"I can just fly out and make a nuisance of myself, maybe offer a second target," Reed said. Harry threw out a thumbs up.

"I'll see if I can open some barriers, maybe blow some conduits like in *Watch Dogs*," J.J. said. When everyone looked at him, he said, "Kidding! Totes kidding."

"That game was boss, yo," Augustus said.

"I know, right?" J.J. said, gushing. "I do not understand the haters."

"Our odds of success just dropped two percent while we endured that egg-headery," Harry said sourly.

"And out we go," I said as Veronika and Reed sprang into motion.

The truck had a long, grey trailer behind it, and it was driving at the speed limit. I wondered where Gustafson was taking this monstrosity, but I didn't have time to worry about it.

"I'm ready," Veronika said, and I stepped out of the limo with her clutched in my arms. We soared over two lanes of traffic and I dropped her with a thump on the roof of the tractor trailer before settling down myself.

"Whoa! Down!" she shouted and we both ducked a support beam. It was a few feet above us, but if we'd remained standing we both would have suffered a real headache. "It's every misogynist's dream," Veronika quipped. She must have caught my blank look. "We're both on our knees."

Reed came to a clumping landing behind us, way slower and more unwieldy than ours. He staggered and dropped just below the next beam, the concrete support nearly giving him a haircut. "Anything you can do ..." he said with a smirk.

"I bet the sibling rivalry is fierce in your family," Veronika said, her hand turning blue and hot in a second. The air lost all chill, the breeze of the moving truck the only thing keeping her plasma from overwhelming me even a few feet away.

"Look out!" Harry's voice shouted across the divide between lanes as someone honked.

There was another noise that followed his warning by a couple seconds—loud, terrifying—

Gunfire.

63.

Veronika

Bullets punched through the trailer around her, and Veronika instinctively threw herself to the side. They sounded heavy, and chunks of metal from the roof of the trailer blew away in inch-sized segments, instantly driving her into panic mode. Fistfights were fine, fire was her specialty, but guns?

Veronika didn't mess with guns. Not ever, if she could avoid it.

She maintained her balance when she dodged, but forgot that there was no edge to where she was standing. It wasn't her fault; it wasn't like she'd ever climbed onto the back of a trailer and stood there before. She just evaded the threat, like normal, and when she took a hard step back ...

... Her foot found not a damned thing there to catch her.

Nealon was dodging in her own way. Like a parachute had deployed on her back, she shot away from the gunfire. Her brother looked stricken, rolling backward just in time to catch a support beam on the shoulder. Veronika heard the crack just before she disappeared over the edge of the trailer, but she didn't see whether he landed on top of it or fell off the back.

And it didn't much matter to her at that point, either, because she tumbled right off the side into empty air, the concrete lanes below racing up to greet her like an old friend—

64.

Sienna

I instinctively sped back as soon as I saw the shots bursting hand-sized holes in the trailer. Whatever sort of cannon Gustafson was firing, it was coming from the cab and it was causing enough damage that any of us that took a hit from it would be out of commission for the rest of this fight.

I recovered my wits before I got too far away from the truck. Reed clobbered himself on one of the supports, clipping it with his shoulder and rolling off the back. He caught himself and came to a floating stop over the car behind him as traffic ground to a halt on Lower Wacker Drive. (I wasn't smiling about it now.)

Veronika tumbled off the side a second later, and I shot after her. She couldn't save herself like my brother could, and she was the linchpin of our current plan, so she was priority in my view. She threw out a glowing hand as she tumbled in a spin down the side of the trailer, her fingers burning and ripping through the metal in a vain and desperate attempt to slow her fall. It was instinctive, a grasp at straws, and it wasn't even slowing her down.

I soared in and caught her six inches from the ground, dodging over a Toyota pickup that screeched to a halt before veering into a wall to avoid the swerving tractor trailer. Gustafason must have either taken a hand off the wheel to fire at us or he was intentionally trying to smear me and Veronika. I shot back to the roof amid a hail of honking horns and screeching tires and dropped to a crouch, Veronika clutched in front of me doing the same.

"Well, that was a near thing," she said with a dryness that told me her talent for understatement was strong. Her hand was still glowing, and without hesitating she punched a finger into the trailer roof at a shallow angle and started to saw a circular hole. "What about the gunfire?" she said, concentrating as she dug into the metal.

"I'm guessing it was a big, fat revolver," I said. "Either .44 Mag or .357. A wheel gun like that'll take a few seconds to reload, assuming he has a box of ammo at hand."

"I don't respond well to lead," Veronika said, finishing making her entry into the trailer. "Be a dear and make sure he doesn't perforate me?" She looked back, firing me an encouraging smile before dodging a support beam.

"You got it," I said as she stood up and jumped into the dark trailer below like a SEAL toothpicking into water from a chopper.

I zoomed off the side of the trailer and went low, inches from the pavement low. The lane of traffic beside the tractor trailer was clear for the moment, and the truck wasn't weaving as hard as it had been when I was flying on the other side. I was going to try the stealth approach, sneaking up to the cab, where I could possibly wrestle with Gustafson for control of the gun.

I caught a glimpse of him in the cab, the back of his dark, curly haired head as he looked around, trying to see through the cab. The back window was all shot out, and he was alone. Apparently he hadn't trusted an accomplice for this particular genocide mission.

I eased in low while his back was turned, sliding up to the running board on my belly and then raising my altitude as we shot past an SUV like it was parked. He'd definitely hammered the accelerator, which was bad news for those of us worried that a crash might unleash the bioweapon. I let my feet rest on the running board and started to ease up. I caught sight of a flash of steel as he waved the gun around with one hand while trying to steer the truck.

"Hey, asshole!" Harry's voice crackled over the empty lane of traffic between us. The limo was a car length back from me and I turned, horrified. Harry had his head just barely out the window, the smoky, dark glass down just enough to let me see his eyes. He glanced down and winked at me, then disappeared inside the darkness of the limo.

A blast of blue fire shot out of the truck above me, inches above my head, as though Veronika herself were sitting in the cab. It arced over me and slammed into the Hummer limousine, consuming it from front bumper to rear in less than a second.

The gas tank exploded and the wreck rolled hard, lighting the darkness of Lower Wacker Drive as Augustus, Kat, J.J. and all the rest of them came to a fiery end.

65.

Veronika

It was dark in the trailer, and the dim flashes of light provided by the small opening she'd made in the roof and the slashed holes in the side allowed only a little of the tunnel light in. Veronika lit both hands and held them aloft, trying to get a sense of what she was dealing with, here.

"Oh," she said as the soft blue glow illuminated the truck's cargo. She swallowed hard. "So that's what it is." Her voice was at least a couple octaves higher now.

66.

Sienna

I couldn't be sure it wasn't Veronika in the cab, but I didn't want to believe that the assassin had betrayed me. She could have, though, easily, in spite of Harry's reassurances, just cutting her own path right into the cab and then destroying my backup, except for Reed.

And for all I knew, she'd torched him, too, after I'd flown off to deal with Gustafson.

I felt stiflingly hot on the running board, like I was going to burst out of my skin. The cold wind crackled around me as the truck accelerated away from the wreck of the limo, and my breaths came slower and sharper as the decision was made.

Gustafson had to be stopped, and if Veronika was in there with him, she had to be stopped, too.

I ripped the door off the truck and grabbed Gustafson's arm. His eyes widened at me and his arm burst into blue plasma light.

Crap. He was a meta.

I yanked him hard as he started to burn all over. The seatbelt vaporized instantly, along with my left hand, but I managed to set him in motion before it burned off. He moved like butter, like his flesh turning to plasma had greased him. It hadn't, but going superhot had freed him from all moorings and obstacles, and he tumbled over me, missing burning my face off by bare inches.

He hit the pavement hard and it sizzled as it melted around him. His skin was gone now, replaced by the blue plasma fire that Veronika wielded so easily. My lack-of-a-hand burned with the phantom pain of nerves now gone, and I fought against it, summoning Wolfe to the front of my mind to deal with this problem as I yanked myself into the sizzling seat that Gustafson had occupied only a moment before. My clothes started to burn from the residual heat, my skin boiling and blistering.

The steering wheel was a melted problem, now a half-circle of plastic secured by one fastening rather than three. If I pulled too hard on it, It'd break off and I'd lose total control of the truck. I looked down and noticed that Gustafson had also melted the accelerator into slag at the floor and completed burned the brake down to a tiny nub. Probably carried the pedal out with him when I'd yanked him.

"Shit," I said to no one in particular.

I kept one hand gently upon the weakened steering wheel and pressed my other to the nub of the brake. It burned through my shoe almost instantly, and started going through my foot and down to bone. My blood started boil, and it did not feel good. Cardiac arrest followed shortly thereafter, and maintaining muscle control became … well …

Gavrikov! I screamed in my head. I had to absorb this residual heat, and now, or Harry's much-talked-about probabilities were going to head down, and quickly. I stifled all thought of the people who'd been in the limo when Gustafson had taken it out. I needed distractions right now like I needed a big, flaming hole in my foot. And since I already had one of those, the other distractions were unwelcome.

The heat started to dissipate, absorbed through my skin. The burning wounds started to close, and new bones sprouted from my wrist where Gustafson had torched off the hand. The brake lodged in my foot and my skin started to heal around it. I didn't have time to pull it off to give the skin a chance to grow around it, I just kept it mashed, the pain of something jammed into my bone and tissue an agony that I had to grit my teeth against. I had the brake pushed all the way down and the truck was barely slowing.

I heard a grinding of gears and started to panic. Trucks didn't have automatic transmissions, did they? There was a smoking mess next to me where a center console might once have sat, but a metal shifting knob, good and melted, jutted out of the floorboard. Damn.

The engine stalled and suddenly the wheel got a lot harder to control. I looked into the rearview and saw the glowing blue figure of a man running after me, little smoke clouds of black burning off each time he put a foot down. "And here comes Doctor Manhattan," I muttered under my breath as the steering wheel tried hard to pull the truck to the right. I gently resisted it, afraid it was going to snap the last support holding the wheel to it. The speedometer still read sixty miles per hour.

And then the steering wheel support broke, and all that was left of the wheel was a circular nub around the center column.

"Dammit," I whispered as I tossed the wheel out the open door. My left hand wasn't anywhere close to healed yet, but I had plenty of grip in my right. I grabbed the center column hard, my fingers sinking into the plastic. I turned it slightly to the left and it responded sluggishly. The whole truck shuddered at the motion, but it didn't turn over or jacknife, and the speedometer now read 45 miles per hour.

The driver's side door clattered, still open, the latching mechanism not having caught the door lock yet. It moved open and the rearview mirror aligned to show me another glimpse of Gustafson. He was catching up damned fast, probably only thirty feet from the door.

"Crapola," I said, trying to grasp with my left hand to shut the door. It wouldn't buy me much time, but all I needed to stop this thing safely was a few more seconds …

Unfortunately, my left hand was only bone and sinew. The muscle hadn't quite shown up yet, so trying to articulate the digits to grab the door was kind of like getting a mannequin's hand to do anything.

"Crap." The speedometer was down to thirty, and Gustafson was almost there. I fired a light net blindly out the window as the muscles started to sprout along the bone, hoping it would at least distract him.

It didn't.

With twenty miles an hour left to go, I saw Gustafson make an abrupt, hard right turn behind the cab, and it struck me entirely too late that he wasn't even trying to get to me at all.

He was just trying to wreck the trailer.

He blasted right through the coupling that joined the tractor to the trailer, and I saw a flash of blue from behind me.

The trailer was now free of my control, and he'd set it up to crash perfectly.

I held on tight as the momentum from his attack swept through the cab and I was yanked sideways by the force. The truck tilted and then flipped, and I fell out and hit the pavement as the world spun into chaos around me.

67.

Veronika

Veronika hesitated when she saw what lined the walls of the trailer. Battened down with canvas straps, the glass containers were filled with liquid suspensions for their occupants, and blank, dead, human faces stared back at Veronika, lit by the blue glow of her hands within the belly of the dark trailer.

The nearest container didn't even have a body, just pieces of organic matter that looked like it had been mashed almost to a paste, floating in liquid. She could see bone fragments and she peered closer, momentarily lost in the wonder about what she was seeing.

"What the hell is this?" Reed said as he thumped down next to her, a gust of wind blowing through the trailer upon his entry.

"Test subjects?" Veronika asked, stunned into inaction by what she was seeing. She stared straight at the container of mashed remains. "I don't ... what is this one?"

Reed glanced at it then did a double take. "I ... I think that might be Sovereign. Or ... what's left of him."

"Gross," Veronika said, flaring her power and raising the temperature in the back of the trailer by ten degrees. "You might want to get out of here before—"

A muffled explosion rocked the trailer and the two of them were pushed into the glass nearest Reed. She doused her hands instantly, fearing she'd burn through him. She caught herself with a steaming hand, and it sizzled against the glass container she'd run into. Liquid inside bubbled as the heat transferred through at her touch.

"What was that?" Reed asked, looking in the direction of the explosion as if he could see through the wall of the trailer.

"I don't know," she said, "but I need to take this place up to five thousand degrees, and I doubt you'll survive that, so you might want to make your exit."

He cast a final look over the contents of the trailer. "All right," he said, hesitating. "I just …" he fixed on a face in the darkness and stared, peering. "Is that …?"

A hard shudder ran through the trailer as it started to decelerate. "Go!" she said, and brought her hands back up. She'd need to charge plasma in order to get this all in one good shot, with enough heat to make sure any biomatter was properly disintegrated through the glass …

68.

Sienna

I landed hard, but fortunately I was only going like twenty miles an hour when the cab of the truck flipped. It didn't do it because of my driving, either; it did it because of a side impact from Dr. Art Gustafson. The truck went tumbling, I fell and did some tumbling of my own, and I dodged getting crushed by the cab only because I activated Gavrikov's flight powers at the last second and slammed sideways into a minivan. They were doing sixty, I feel I should mention. I was doing considerably less than that.

I thumped to a hard stop on the pavement, feeling that Lower Wacker Drive was now well named, because I'd been both whacked and brought low. I lay still as Wolfe healed my wounds, and I floated back to my feet like I was being pulled upright. It was a landing that I'd walked away from, but I didn't feel like it was anything approaching a good one.

Gustafason was still all lit with blue plasma, burning in a roiling torrent from head to toe. He'd done the Gavrikov thing, covering himself in the blue fire, the surface of his skin rippling, almost looking like it was alive. I hadn't seen Veronika go all out on it, probably because like myself, she didn't see a need to burn off her clothing unless things got dire.

Gustafson was showing none of that restraint, though. His

eyes and mouth were nothing more than black sunspots on the surface of a blue star. "You think you can stop this?"

"The murder of all of our people?" I asked, cracking the vertebrae of my neck back into alignment. "Well, you can't seriously expect me to just sit back not even try."

He stood menacingly between me and the trailer, which was still upright. Apparently he'd hit the truck more than the trailer. It was tilting precipitously forward, but it was still intact. Hopefully, somewhere inside was Veronika, destroying the hell out of Gustafson's plan.

Please, oh, please, let Veronika be doing that, I hoped.

"So ..." I said to him, "either you were hiding who you were with the fancy glowy powers," I waved at his newfangled body, "or you did some juicing with the meta cocktail Cavanagh Tech invented."

He smiled faintly, a black gaping smile that looked like it was pulled off a poorly drawn comic book character. "Jacobs and I helped invent that serum. We were vital in the research process on both that and the suppressant gas. And as for this power," he looked down at his glowing hands, and though it was hard to tell, I felt like I saw ... disgust in his black eyes, "well, I extracted the last part of the breakthrough needed from Veronika's DNA, so it's ironic that when I used the serum, it unlocked her power in me."

"I don't know if you know this," I said, starting to circle toward him, wondering how much control he had over these powers, since they were probably new, "but Cavanagh Tech went out in a big way last year. I'm surprised you still have funding."

"It was a five-year grant," he said smugly. "But our work's done. Metahuman research is about to become a dead area of study." Now he was sneering. "Just like you and your kind."

Yeah, there was a definite hatred for all things meta in him, I thought. "What did we ever do to you to justify you rendering us extinct?" I asked softly. "And yourself in the process, it looks like." Honking horns down the tunnel told me that traffic had stopped in this direction, which was good. I had enough to worry about without playing Frogger while I stalled this ass.

"Yes, I'm going to die, too," he said, and he took a step toward me, his burning feet rendering the pavement liquid as a hiss of black smoke boiled off beneath him.

I caught a glimpse of motion in the supports holding Upper Wacker Drive above us, and realized it was Reed, hanging up there, waiting for an appropriate moment to make a pain in the ass of himself. I looked away quickly so as not to blow the surprise for Gustafson, who looked like he was seething as he formulated an answer for me.

"Before you showed up on the scene," Gustafson said, "before you people ... revealed yourselves to the world ..." his mouth opened like a tortured version of Munch's *The Scream*, "... I was happily married until one night, a guy approached my wife and I on the street and demanded all the money we had on us. When we finished emptying our wallets ..." he blazed brighter, "... he reached out with his hair ... and strangled my wife to death, wearing a smile the whole time."

I stared at him, not really sure what to say to that. "Uhm ..."

He burned brighter. "What's wrong? No witty repartee? No threats to throw in my face?"

"Now doesn't seem like the time for a nuanced conversation about your inappropriate response to a personal tragedy," I said with a shrug of the shoulders. "Though, for the record, most people don't immediately leap to wiping an entire race of people OFF THE FACE OF THE EARTH as a solution. Just FYI. A more measured response might make more sense. Because, I hate to tell you this ... but you can kill all metas, and people are still going to die in muggings. That's not an exclusively meta thing, or gun thing, or knife thing, or geographic thing ... it's pretty much a universally human thing."

"You don't see because you're part of the problem," he said, leering.

"And you don't see because your head's up your ass," I shot back. "Also, welcome to the problem, now that you're one of 'us.'"

Reed, apparently either sick of waiting or losing his grip, came diving down right in that instant. He jetted over the top of Gustafson's head and the force of his gust blew what looked like a tornado of heat up around the two of them. It also knocked Gustafson down on his face, and I figured I'd take this opportunity to do something.

My response came in the form of eighteen shots from Shadow, delivered in seconds all over Gustafson's body. I peppered his ass with 9 mil rounds without mercy, even though he was down on all fours. The rounds disappeared into him like I was shooting them into a pillow, jets of blue flame spurting out with each impact. I hoped it was his current version of blood, but when he got back to his feet, I realized it was his version of burning them up completely.

"Ah, shit," I said, executing a combat reload out of habit.

"To say the least," Reed agreed, coming down for a landing beside me, blasting out a soft gust of air to cushion his return to the earth. "And in terms of a plan?"

"Uh ..." I'd had trouble with Veronika when she hadn't even completely shrouded herself in this plasma. Now that he'd decided to give in to the dark side of the fire force, I was tapped on ideas.

Fortunately, a distraction appeared and saved me from my intellectual bankruptcy.

The trailer behind us started to glow brightly, the sides melting off as Veronika went superhot inside it. Metal started sloughing down and the interior was bright like an Aurora-type had just lit off within. (They're light-casting metas. It's like a sun going off in front of your eyes, burns your retinas, maybe gives you a light tan if you're standing too close.)

Gustafson looked back in horror, and his mouth dropped

open as the fire shrouding his body started to dissipate to show his geeky little face. "NO!"

"Yep," I said, and started to aim at him. He looked right at me, and the blue plasma crept back up before I could line up my shot. Damn, he was fast.

But not fast enough.

The shot rang out from my right and I saw a squirt of blood out of Gustafson's ear as a .45 Long Colt round blew his brains out. He faltered, his plasma guttering out immediately as he fell to his face, naked skin reappearing where the blue glow had been burning moments earlier.

"I think this concludes our business, Dr. Gustafson," Phinneus Chalke said from a hundred feet away, Augustus lingering next to him with a torn-up piece of pavement hovering at the ready and Kat at his other side, her own pistol drawn.

With a flash, the trailer dissolved into blue, the last of the slag melting down as Veronika leapt out, her flesh alive in the way that Gustafson's had been, and I wondered as she landed if we had made it out without catching Gustafson's plague.

69.

Veronika's plasma flames pulled back to about mid-calf and down to her shoulders, giving her the equivalent of a glowing blue halter top and yoga pants. I stared at her in disbelief as she strode over to us, looking weary enough to convince me what she'd done had taken a lot out of her.

"I never even thought of that," I said, looking at her. "I could totally do that with Gavrikov's power."

"Good, yeah, stop showing your ass everywhere you go," she said, sounding more than a little cranky. Honking horns still sounded all throughout Lower Wacker as Phinneus, Kat and Augustus made their way over. Phinneus headed straight over to Veronika's side while Kat and Augustus drifted toward me. I looked over and saw Harry helping a grimacing Fannon along at a normal walking pace, a half-empty bottle of scotch clutched in his free hand. We all stayed quiet until he walked Fannon over to stand with Phinneus and Veronika, who were watching us warily. The divide was obvious, the battle lines clearly drawn.

Us versus them.

"I'm not going to jail," Veronika said, and I caught nods from Fannon and Phinneus to match.

"The three of them killed a lot of people," Reed said under his breath. "Phinneus killed Dr. Stanley, Harry did in Jacobs and that guy on the beach—"

"You know we can hear you, right?" Harry called, shaking

his head like Reed was an idiot.

"I guess it's a brawl for all, then," Veronika said, almost sadly.

"You know," I said to Reed, "I think we're done."

He gave me a wide-eyed look. "Done with what?"

"Government service," I said, taking a deep breath of the stale, kind of polluted air on Lower Wacker Drive. I saw Veronika's suspicious look fade just a touch. "If the US government wants to track any of you down, they can do it themselves." I shrugged. "I quit, effective now."

Reed looked a little stiff. I could tell he had some moral issues that weren't quite satisfied. "Look, I get wanting to let them walk for good behavior or whatever, but … Phinneus killed an innocent woman, accident or not."

"That wasn't an accident," Phinneus said, smacking his lips, his Peacemaker still in hand. "Gustafson ordered it done. Seems they used to work together, but she'd decided to go in a different direction or something. Some kind of argument between them. I don't know, I didn't get the details. He told me to kill her, though, and I did—as you say, by accident, but there was a bullet coming for her regardless."

I stared at him. "You're not exactly reassuring me about my decision to let you walk."

"Hey, you're not the only one unhappy about it," he said, sounding a little miffed. "I hate when a contract goes unpaid. I did my service years ago."

"Cost of doing business," Veronika said, never peeling her eyes away from me. "Sometimes you do a hit, sometimes you take a hit."

"Let's just go home," I said to Reed, then looked to Kat and Augustus. "Maybe stop off at a bar on the way to the airport?"

"I like that plan," Harry called out, "and I also like that the chances of anyone here killing each other just dropped to three percent."

I froze at that and glanced at Reed, who just shrugged,

looking mildly disgusted. "Uhm … okay, I guess you're invited, Harry."

"Count me in, then," Colin Fannon said uneasily, still holding his stomach. Blood oozed out from between his fingers. "I could use a stiff drink."

"Thirded," Veronika said, still glowing from her makeshift plasma clothing. "Also, maybe a change of attire."

"Shall we?" I asked, taking one last look at the crater and smashed cab where we'd wrecked the truck on Lower Wacker Drive. (It was back to worth a chortle again.)

"A drink can't come soon enough," Harry agreed, leading us on. "I guess this time, it's a series of cabs, eh …?"

"Oh, damn," I said mildly. When Reed looked at me, I shared my thoughts. "Remind me to make sure Chang covers that limo driver's loss."

"As a condition of your employment?" he asked, but with less bitterness than he would have a few days earlier.

"That's right," I said and started walking with the others. With the traffic flow stopped at our backs, I thought I could see an exit ramp leading up to the surface ahead. It looked like daylight, and for my part, I couldn't get there soon enough.

70.

Somewhat to my surprise, we all actually did meet up at the airport bar at Midway—or almost all of us, anyway. And we did take a convoy of cabs, after catching up with J.J., who was hiding well out of the line of fire during the fight near the truck.

I'd started to ask them how they'd survived the destruction of the limo, but the answer occurred to me before I opened my mouth and removed all doubt that I was an idiot—Harry had read the destruction coming before he opened his stupid mouth and provoked Gustafson to fire, so naturally he'd have made sure everyone was out or being evacuated before he did it.

When I looked back once we made it to Upper Wacker, Phinneus was gone. I probably could have predicted that, if I'd tried. If he trained Parks, I had a feeling that the two of them shared that antisocial tendency. Myself, Parks, Phinneus—we were lone gunners by nature. I only worked with a team because I'd kind of realized how lonely it got having your ass out on the line without anyone to save you if things went south. As an assassin in the shadows, things probably went south a lot less than they did when you were perpetually brawling with the most powerful people on the planet.

"So … that was a thing that happened," Colin Fannon said, taking a drink of beer. We were sitting in a bar that had a brick facade layered all around it, just past the security checkpoint at

Midway Airport. It was part of a much larger food court, and we'd pulled a couple tables together in the midst of a somewhat buzzing crowd. Fannon went on, almost a note of mourning in his voice: "We just turned against our employer in favor of the target." He met eyes with Veronika and shook his head. I saw liquid go spreading out on his freshly changed shirt, which told me he'd either peed high or he still had a leak. I didn't know how to say it, though, so I just averted my eyes and took a sip of my own drink, which had a very festive umbrella in it.

"The thing you realize about life after you see all the possibilities for a while," Harry said, waxing rhapsodic, his words starting to slur just slightly, "is that really, almost nothing is impossible. I mean, right now, there's a half a percent chance that a segment of roof comes crashing down in the corner of the bar in about five minutes." He threw up his hands like that illustrated his point. "And you know that fighter plane they've got hanging up in the walkway to the terminal?" His eyes twinkled. "It's not likely, but I'd walk around it if I were you."

"Harry," I said, and he turned to look at me, eyes partially glazed. "You can't just go around doing whatever you want."

"Knew you were gonna say that," Harry muttered, then raised his voice for the benefit of the table. "In case you missed it, I just bypassed security without having so much as a plane ticket or subjecting myself to a body scan. So tell me, darling," his eyes flashed and he grinned at me in a very charming way, "why not?"

"*They'll* come after you," I said, feeling pretty certain about it, even if I didn't fully know who the *they* were going to be as of next week. "And when they do ... I can promise they're not going to be as flexible about the concept of justice as I am."

"It's funny you say that." He looked down at the table, composing his thoughts. "See ... if I'd been thinking ahead, I wouldn't have hit Dr. Jacobs as hard as I did. But if I hadn't—" He lifted a finger and pointed it at me, "You wouldn't have come to town, and I might not have realized all metahumanity was about to die." He looked amused at the twisting sequence of events he'd just laid out. "Now, I don't believe in destiny, because I've seen the most probable outcome get thwarted on any number of occasions in favor of one that had like a .0000001% chance of happening, but—"

"Wouldn't that kind of prove the destiny theory?" Kat murmured softly.

"—but that's pretty damned close to destiny in my book, our meeting here," Harry finished, looking at Kat and giving her a wink.

"I just wish my destiny hadn't included giving DNA to a man who tried to use it to kill all our kind," Veronika said with her head down. She'd stopped off at her hotel and picked up clothes before joining us, and was now properly coiffed and in a pantsuit again. It was flattering on her, but I had to admit, that flaming tank top and yoga pants idea was a style I was stealing the next time I lost my clothes in a 'splodey accident. Hell, given how many magazines already criticized my fashion sense, maybe I'd be better off being the girl on fire all the time.

"I can't believe I ran headlong into a barrier of ground glass," Fannon said, looking at Augustus uncomfortably. "No one's ever hurt me like you guys have hurt me." He cast a look my way.

"Way to show weakness," Veronika said in a disapproving fashion. "Rookie."

Reed looked at me, still unamused. "I can't believe your strategy with her was to pound her in the face with hard objects."

Veronika and I exchanged a look, that grudging respect again. "Honestly, that's my strategy with almost everyone." It wasn't, but I wasn't telling Veronika that in case she and I ever ended up on opposite sides of the battlefield again. I feared the day she came after me with her body full-plasma like Gustafson's, because no bullet was going to stop her and I had a feeling she wouldn't allow herself to flicker back to skin for any little emotional bump the way he had.

She stared back at me and brought her drink to her lips, leaving it there for a second while she spoke. "It almost worked."

"Whoa, I gotta go," Augustus said, first to leave. He shot me a look. "I'm heading to Atlanta for the week ... sounds like you need me back on Monday, though?"

"Don't you have class?" I teased.

"And work, right?" he fished again.

"And work," I agreed, and Reed made a sound of disapproval next to me. "I hope Chang allows me a big training budget. I want to put you guys through your paces in a way that Phillips hasn't allowed me to lately. Maybe some live artillery fire?"

"Well," Fannon said, standing up, looking perhaps uneasy at my suggestion of firing artillery at my own co-workers, or perhaps just because he realized he was sitting with a bunch of non-assassins, "this has been fun. I hope I never run into the wrong side of you people again." He looked down at his stained, seeping shirt. "What the ..." He looked up at us. "Why didn't anyone tell me?"

"You wet yourself," I said, prompting a round of cackling laughter around the table. Fannon looked at me sheepishly. "That's why," I said.

He nodded once. "Well ... thanks for not killing me," he said, a little lamely, and then raced off in a flash before I could respond.

"He'll figure things out," Veronika said quietly, and I was hard pressed to tell whether she was saying that for our sake or to reassure herself, professionally, that the next generation of assassins was going to be all right. Frankly, I was worried either way. She glanced at the stylish watch that she wore high on her wrist, pushing back her sleeve to see it. "I've got to catch a plane." She shot me a tight smile. "'Til we meet again," she said and started to roll her bag away.

"Veronika, wait," I said, standing up to go after her.

She paused to look back, a slight smile turning up the corners of her red lips. The thrum of the crowds around us weighed on me, almost like I could feel it pressing against my chest in a weird way, like the buzz of the crowd was the beat of my heart.

"Thanks for the help," I offered, not really sure what else there was to say. After all, "I never, ever want to fight you again, you total and utter badass," didn't really fit, did it? That was the sort of thing warriors kept to themselves.

"Thank you," she said, turning a little more serious. "Gustafson … he got my help last time on false pretense. He was supposed to …" Her eyes looked far away for a second, "… to help people with my DNA. That he was doing the opposite … it was a betrayal. A very personal one." She looked stiff then relaxed. "So I'm glad I could help." She paused then smiled again. "Though, if you're going to work for someone with deep enough pockets to let you train with live artillery, you should definitely call me if you ever need paid help. I have very reasonable contracting rates."

"And how would I get ahold of you to discuss these possible contracts?" I asked, viewing her through a veil of suspicion. Her help was probably not in the realm of what I would consider 'reasonable,' but I was kind of a tightwad with money.

She pulled out a card and handed it to me. It was cream-colored, with embossed black lettering.

Veronika Acheron

Consultant

And her contact information was right there at the bottom.

"I'll keep you in mind," I said, very guarded, as she nodded once and walked away.

"And now we're down to a slaughterhouse five once more!" J.J. declared. He wasn't even three sheets to the wind; he was easily like twelve.

"You've never actually read that book," Reed said, sitting in sullen silence at my side.

"Nope!" J.J. said. He did not even care.

Kat was watching Harry carefully while he nursed his scotch. He still had the bottle he'd liberated from the steakhouse, though it was down to a quarter of the bottle now. "Harry ..." she started.

He seemed to perk up. "Yes, we really did spend a winter in Smolensk together," he said, presumably reading her question before she could speak it aloud. He, too, was quite drunk by now.

"I just can't even," Kat said, and she stood up and walked out. I couldn't quite put a finger on where she was emotionally on that, she was so blocked and stoic and she hurried out so fast.

"We also spent a summer in Oslo, and a year in Prague," Harry said, his eyes very far away and showing the first hint of wistfulness since I'd met him, all his usual buoyancy gone. "A springtime in Paris ..." He was whispering now.

"Harry," I said, and he looked at me again like he was on the verge of dropping off to sleep. "Stay out of trouble."

"I'll keep my head down," he said, nodding once. He got up, zipping his old jacket as he did so, and started to turn away before stopping. "A piece of advice," he said, looking right back at me, and plunging ahead before I'd even had a chance to tell him whether or not I wanted it, "I know you feel it. The same pain I do, when I don't keep my head down. It's why you do ... all this." He waved around to encompass the bar, the world, something. "Trying to help people is your version of drinking and gambling."

I stared back at him, unblinking. "Some of us have to worry about tomorrow, Harry. Since ... you're not watching after it."

He broke into a grin and a low laugh. "It couldn't be in better hands." He straightened up. "Still and all ... live for today every now and again, Sienna. You'd have more fun." And with that, he wandered off, still carrying the bottle of scotch like a wino. He dodged a luggage cart and he was gone, off to wherever he had to go to make the world feel right for him again. A card table, probably.

"Are you going to take his advice and live for today, Ms. Nealon?" Reed asked from next to me. He sounded slightly less tense now that it was down to just me, him, and a stupefied J.J.

"Maybe tomorrow," I said with a slight smirk. I met my brother's eyes and saw his worry. "As for you ..."

He cocked an eyebrow. "Yes?"

"Are you with me on this or not?" I asked, as gently as I could. "This Chang thing. The NGO?" He still didn't answer, so I went on. "This gift horse, this—"

"I know what you're talking about," he said with mock impatience, then lapsed into silence again. "And yes, I'm with you. I wouldn't let you roll a massive wooden horse into your city without standing next to you in case a bunch of Trojans pop out."

"That really sounds dirty," J.J. said, his voice low and throaty. He was truly obliterated.

"I'm with you," Reed said, nodding at me, but not smiling. "Somebody's got to watch your back, after all."

I couldn't think of a thing to say, so I just smiled back. He had me worried for a while there.

Epilogue

"Call me Gerry," President Gerard Harmon said to his guest as they both sat down, the guest in front of the *Resolute* desk and Harmon behind it. The Oval Office had the perpetual aroma of a room that had just been cleaned even though it probably hadn't been touched since last night. That was Harmon's impression of it, anyway. It was a nice enough smell, faint for the most part, and would have been reassuring if he'd been the germophobic sort. He wasn't.

"Thanks for the invitation," his guest said, taking a seat in the chair opposite him when prompted. Harmon liked obedience to power; it reassured him that the manners and dictums of the world were still in place in some form.

"Have you been watching the news?" Harmon asked, sitting down in his custom-made, bulletproof chair. The lights were on in the Oval Office because it was late, night shrouding the lawn outside.

"Caught a little on the way. Sounds like there was a ruckus in Chicago."

"Indeed there was," Harmon agreed. "Sienna Nealon and her team just prevented the dispersal of a bioweapon specifically tailored to kill every metahuman on the planet." His guest shifted in discomfort. "A terrible thing, obviously, that never should have been invented, but then ..." he chuckled lightly, "... one could say that about any weapon of mass destruction." Feeling a little restless, he stood again, fully aware that he probably seemed antsy to his guest. "If anything, this proves that the agency—well, now it's a department of the FBI, but you get the point—it provides a vital service as a bulwark against all the hazards out there in the metahuman world." He came around the desk and leaned back against it. "I know you had ... other ... employment opportunities available, but I'm glad you put them aside to take over for Ms. Nealon now that she's left us."

His guest stared at him with dark eyes. "How could I not?"

Harmon pressed his lips together. "Of course." He looked away for just a second. "Let's not dance around it, then, shall we? One of the biggest threats you're probably going to run up against, at some point ... is the person who occupied your position last. You'll need a team, and we've got a list of people you can start talking to that might be a good fit." Harmon felt his face go stiff as he drove the point home. "Make no mistake, that confrontation will come. I guarantee it." He looked up again, positive he had the full measure of the man in the chair, but still eager to see the look in his eyes when asked the question. "Are you ready for that? Going head to head with Sienna Nealon?"

His guest didn't stir, didn't look away, just sat there in the chair. Harmon had an impression for a moment of an empty suit, even though the designer suit sitting before him wasn't empty at all, really. The man inside it was filled with emotion, specifically rage, from his impeccable shoes, up past the ruddy face colored with anger, all the way to the sandy blond hair at the top of his head.

"You're damned right I'm ready for that," Scott Byerly said, a rough, hateful smile twisting his lips. "In fact ... I can hardly wait."

Sienna Nealon will return in

MASKS

Out of the Box
Book Nine

Coming July 12, 2016!

Author's Note

If you want to know when future books become available, take sixty seconds and sign up for my NEW RELEASE EMAIL ALERTS by visiting my website at www.robertjcrane.com. Don't let the caps lock scare you; I don't sell your information and I only send out emails when I have a new book out. The reason you should sign up for this is because I don't like to set release dates (it's this whole thing, you can find an answer on my website in the FAQ section), and even if you're following me on Facebook (robertJcrane (Author)) or Twitter (@robertJcrane), it's easy to miss my book announcements because…well, because social media is an imprecise thing.

Come join the discussion on my website: http://www.robertjcrane.com !

Cheers,
Robert J. Crane

ACKNOWLEDGMENTS

Editorial/Literary Janitorial duties performed by Sarah Barbour and Jeffrey Bryan. Final proofing was handle by Jo Evans. Any errors you see in the text, however, are the result of me rejecting changes. Thanks also to Lauran Strait, whose changes I didn't have a chance to implement this time, but thanks to her for her extensive read.

The cover was masterfully designed (as always) by Karri Klawiter.

Alexa Medhus did the first read on this one, and my thanks to her for it!

Once more, thanks to my parents, my kids and my wife, for helping me keep things together.

Other Works by Robert J. Crane

The Sanctuary Series
Epic Fantasy

Defender: The Sanctuary Series, Volume One
Avenger: The Sanctuary Series, Volume Two
Champion: The Sanctuary Series, Volume Three
Crusader: The Sanctuary Series, Volume Four
Sanctuary Tales, Volume One - A Short Story Collection
Thy Father's Shadow: The Sanctuary Series, Volume 4.5
Master: The Sanctuary Series, Volume Five
Fated in Darkness: The Sanctuary Series, Volume 5.5
Warlord: The Sanctuary Series, Volume Six
Heretic: The Sanctuary Series, Volume Seven
Legend: The Sanctuary Series, Volume Eight* (Coming
    June 14, 2016!)

The Girl in the Box
and
Out of the Box
Contemporary Urban Fantasy

Alone: The Girl in the Box, Book 1
Untouched: The Girl in the Box, Book 2
Soulless: The Girl in the Box, Book 3
Family: The Girl in the Box, Book 4
Omega: The Girl in the Box, Book 5
Broken: The Girl in the Box, Book 6
Enemies: The Girl in the Box, Book 7
Legacy: The Girl in the Box, Book 8
Destiny: The Girl in the Box, Book 9
Power: The Girl in the Box, Book 10

Limitless: Out of the Box, Book 1
In the Wind: Out of the Box, Book 2
Ruthless: Out of the Box, Book 3
Grounded: Out of the Box, Book 4
Tormented: Out of the Box, Book 5
Vengeful: Out of the Box, Book 6
Sea Change: Out of the Box, Book 7
Painkiller: Out of the Box, Book 8
Masks: Out of the Box, Book 9* (Coming July 12, 2016!)
Prisoners: Out of the Box, Book 10* (Coming September 27, 2016!)

Southern Watch
Contemporary Urban Fantasy

Called: Southern Watch, Book 1
Depths: Southern Watch, Book 2
Corrupted: Southern Watch, Book 3
Unearthed: Southern Watch, Book 4
Legion: Southern Watch, Book 5* (Coming May 10, 2016!)

* Forthcoming and subject to change

CPSIA information can be obtained
at www.ICGtesting.com
Printed in the USA
LVOW13s1248230917
549813LV00009B/432/P